I0780908

MIDNIGHT'S QUEEN

HEATHER GREYE

Midnight's Queen

Copyright © 2025 Heather Greye

All rights reserved.

No part of this publication may be reproduced, distributed, or transmitted in any form or by any means, including photocopying, recording, or other electronic or mechanical methods, without the prior written permission of the publisher, except as permitted by U.S. copyright law.

If you would like to use material from the book (other than for review purposes), prior written permission must be obtained.

This book is a work of fiction. Names, characters, places, and incidents are products of the author's imagination or are used fictitiously. Any resemblance to the actual persons, living or dead, business establishments, events, or locales is entirely coincidental.

Published by Black Sheep Media LLC

Editor: Elizabeth MS Flynn, emsflynn.com

Cover Design: Deranged Doctor Design, www.derangeddoctordesign.com

BOOKS BY HEATHER GREYE

Stroke of Midnight Series

Midnight's Pawn

Midnight's Captive

Midnight's Queen

Fortune's Favor Series

Stolen Stars

(coming fall 2025)

*For my family and friends who supported my dreams,
especially this last year. Thank you!*

*For the readers who took a chance on a new author.
I appreciate you so much!*

*And for Thom, who gets to stop reading this series and start
reading the next one. Love you!*

CHAPTER 1

FILTERED sunlight hit Portia's face, slipping past her lashes and waking her up. Groaning, she pulled the pillow over her head and burrowed deeper under the covers. Colliding with a warm body, she hummed with pleasure and wiggled closer.

After a little shifting, her back was pressed against his chest and her knees bent around her companion's so their feet could tangle together. Crisp leg hair gently tickled her calves. His arm banded over her hips and he rested his chin, bristly with stubble, on her shoulder. With all the warm muscle curled around her, she felt safe and loved.

"Mmmm," she murmured sleepily as she snuggled in. "The only thing that would make this morning better, Tommy, is coffee waiting for me when I get out of this bed."

The body wrapped around her tensed. The arm withdrew, leaving her cold in its wake.

"What's the matter?" She rolled over and came face to face with a man—who wasn't Tommy.

Portia screamed and scrambled backward. The movement carried her over the side of the bed. She landed hard on the floor, barely registering the soft carpet under her butt. Her bare butt. Brain still fuzzy with sleep, she blinked up at the bed in surprise.

"Are you okay?" Her unexpected bed partner leaned over the edge, concern in his blue-green eyes.

She ignored him and grabbed the sheet. Her first tug met resistance, so she tugged harder. The sheet flowed over the side of the bed to puddle on her legs. Portia grabbed it with both hands and held it close, covering her breasts and her lap.

Wrapping the sheet around the rest of her body, without losing control of it, was difficult, especially butt ass naked on the floor. Tucking the sheet under her armpits, she rolled onto her shins, careful not to flash the man above her. Finally, she was able to whip the sheet around the rest of her body.

Definitely not high fashion, but at least she didn't feel as vulnerable. Slightly less freaked out, she took a minute to assess her situation. "You're not Tommy."

Way to state the obvious, Portia. She'd been in bed with not-Tommy. *Naked in bed.*

"No, I'm Aleksander." The man in the bed spoke slowly, his accented voice low. It was also familiar. "We met last night."

Given her nakedness, "met" was the understatement of the year. "What happened?"

From her vantage point on the floor, she watched his jaw tense. He didn't like her question.

He disappeared from view and the bed squeaked. Portia assumed he was getting up. She took the opportunity to look around.

They were obviously in a hotel room. A nice one. High

thread count sheets. Soft, luxurious carpet. Better than average art on the walls.

And a big king bed. With rumpled bedding.

They'd obviously used it well.

Now that the panic was receding, she remembered everything from the night before. The conversation that, despite occasional awkward pauses, had flowed freely. That single whiskey. Arriving at Aleksander's suite. She hadn't paid much attention to the room at that time because they'd been too busy tearing each other's clothes off once they'd made it inside.

Two well-formed legs appeared in front of her, bringing Portia back to the present. Her gaze traveled up to the blue boxer briefs that hugged his thighs. She blushed and dragged her eyes over his pelvis quickly.

Staring at his bare chest wasn't any less embarrassing. She remembered the coarse tickle of his chest hair against her . . . well, all of her.

She bit her lip and her face flamed hotter. Memories of the hours they'd spent tangled together were front and center now. The feel of his ripped abs and muscled chest under her hands and mouth.

His touch.

His taste.

Portia forced herself to meet his gaze. She didn't know what she'd expected to see on his face—amusement, maybe? desire?—but his expression was one of concern.

"Are you okay?" That soft, soothing voice again.

Was she?

"I . . . think so?"

He bent slightly and offered his hand.

Portia tucked the sheet tighter around her body and

placed her hand in his. Ignoring the tingles where their skin touched, she planted her feet on the ground.

He pulled her upright so effortlessly that she fell forward against his chest. His body was warm where they pressed together. It felt so good. She'd been cold for so long.

Ever since the bombing.

That unwelcome reminder of who she was snapped her out of the cozy feelings.

She pulled her hand free and took a careful step back. Gathering the excess sheet in one fist, she backed away further. Once she could breathe without his scent—his warmth—clouding her thoughts, Portia gathered the rigid control by which she lived her life and donned it like a familiar outfit. It was hard to radiate authority wrapped in a sheet, but she tried her damnedest.

"I should be going." Somehow, she managed to keep her voice steady when her whole world had been shaken by the fact that she'd slept with someone who wasn't Tommy.

Tommy's death had destroyed her. In the bright light of day, last night's impulsiveness threatened the fragile foundation she'd painstakingly rebuilt in the months since.

Aleks studied her intently. His look of concern lightened, but didn't ease completely. "Do you need a ride?"

"I can call for a car." They'd come to the hotel in a taxi. No one expected Portia Tremaine to leave a shadowy bar with a one-night stand, so she hadn't worried anyone would recognize her last night. This morning was a different story. She wanted—no, *needed*—to keep her identity under wraps. But who did she call to do that?

"Okay." He turned away to grab a robe.

She should have spent the time considering her options. Instead, her attention focused on the rippling of his back muscles. His taut glutes. Her fingers clenched as a memory of gripping them tightly as he'd rocked into her flared to life.

Heat pooled between her legs.

"Is there anything you need? Coffee? A shower?"

His question jerked her out of her reverie and she barely managed to keep from mentioning a cold shower. Even covered by the robe, he was distracting.

Embarrassed to be caught staring, she shook her head. "No, thank you. I'll get out of your hair."

He opened his mouth like he wanted to say something. Closed it again.

She looked around for her clothes.

"You remember what we did last night, right, Portia?"

Heat raced up her cheeks. "Yes. Ohmigod, yes. I remember." She hated that her pale skin blushed so damn easily. Usually, she could control it better than this.

His voice was gruff when he spoke. "I wasn't sure. You jumped out of bed like you didn't."

The fog of sleep and waking up in another man's arms had thrown her earlier. Even with the gorgeous evidence standing in front of her, she still couldn't quite wrap her head around that decision.

"I hadn't been with anyone since my husband." She'd never been with anyone but Tommy.

His gaze dropped to her left hand.

She held out her hand, more for her than for him, as she stared at her bare ring finger. "Widowed," she said quietly. They'd cut the ring off when they raced her to the hospital after the bombing. When they'd informed her that Tommy was dead, she hadn't bothered getting it repaired. The pieces were tucked away in her jewelry box, a tangible reminder of her broken heart.

"I'm sorry for your loss."

She dipped her head in acknowledgment. She'd run out of responses months ago.

"Can I do anything for you?" His lips pressed into a firm line and his eyes had lost their sparkle.

She had the completely irrational desire to make him smile again. But how? How did people navigate a morning after? She'd completely ruined this one and there wouldn't be another. Couldn't be. "I should go," she said abruptly.

He nodded, then disappeared into the suite's sitting room. When he returned a moment later, he held her clothes.

Cheeks flaming, Portia tucked the sheet tightly under her arm and reached for the pile of clothing. Then, as regally as she could, she swiveled on the tasteful hotel carpet and hastened into the bathroom.

CHAPTER 2

PORTIA ALMOST JUMPED when she saw her reflection. A flush of color in her cheeks. Blond hair tousled the way only sex could manage. Pale skin swathed in the wrinkled white sheet.

Who was the woman in the mirror? The one who'd slept with another man . . . and liked it?

That was the worst part. Or maybe the best part. Her heart still missed Tommy. Her body had apparently moved on.

Sure, she'd freaked out when she'd discovered that the man in her bed wasn't Tommy. But once the tumble to the floor had shaken the sleep out of her system, Portia had remembered Aleksander. Aleks, as he'd said he preferred. Had remembered every touch, every sigh, and every look since he'd spoken to her in the bar.

Not even tipsy, she'd said yes when he'd asked her if she'd like to come back to his room. They'd barely made inside. He'd pressed her up against the door and her clothes had practically fallen off.

Portia released her death grip on the sheet and let it fall

to the ground. Staring at the mirror, she studied the marks that passion had left on her skin.

Whisker burns freckled the slopes of her breasts. The faintest impression of fingers lingered on her hips.

Embarrassed, unable to process her conflicting emotions, she dropped her gaze to the haphazard pile of clothes. Dressing provided the distraction she needed from the stranger in the mirror. The one with the tangled well-fucked hair and the love bite just below her jaw.

The one with aches in her inner thigh muscles and more intimate places.

Trying to embody a calm she didn't feel, Portia pulled on her underwear and pants.

She could do this. She could make it out of the bathroom, then out of the hotel.

Her hands fumbled with her bra. Heat flooded her body again. Less embarrassment and more memory of the way Aleks had removed it with firm kisses and impatient hands.

"Fuck!"

She finally gave up, stuffing her bra into her pocket. Next, she pulled on her sweatshirt, fluffing the collar to hide her hickey. Her sensitive nipples brushed the soft, worn fabric. She shivered, the sensation as titillating as it was unwelcome.

Portia Tremaine didn't go braless. She didn't accompany strangers back to their hotel rooms, either. Who was this stranger in her body?

Wetting her hands in the sink, she finger-combed her hair until she could weave it into two loose braids. She grabbed the tiny bottle of mouthwash from the counter and took a big swig. After swishing and spitting—to rid herself of morning breath or Aleks's taste, she wasn't quite sure—she gripped the edge of the sink and leaned toward the mirror.

Her reflection startled her a second time. It was the braids. They made her look younger. Made her look a lot more like Dizzie—her newfound and unwanted sister.

Breaking eye contact with this unrecognizable, unwelcome version of herself, Portia took a deep breath and stepped back. She'd stalled as much as she could. Hiding in the bathroom all day wasn't an option. She wanted—needed—to be at home.

It was just as well that she didn't look like herself. She needed to make a low-profile exit; no one needed to catch the head of the Tremaine Corporation in a walk of shame.

Portia pulled out her phone and used the biometric scanners to unlock it. She called up her contacts list . . . and stared at it.

She didn't know who to call.

Her driver would be available. Quiet and kind, he'd been with her for years and wouldn't comment about picking her up at the hotel, but he'd know it was not the place he'd left her.

She shouldn't care what he thought, but she did.

Scrolling through the woefully short list of people she considered friends, she paused at a familiar name and number. Killian.

They'd been best friends for years. Her, Killian, and Tommy. Except she didn't know where they stood now.

A spurt of anger welled up, answering that question. Nope. Not back to being best friends yet. She still had a lot of anger against him that she needed to work out because of his relationship with Dizzie.

There was Ash. She and the talented hacker had been on the way to becoming friends, maybe, until he'd confessed his role in the events leading up to Tommy's death.

No. That didn't feel right, either.

She scrolled down again and stared at the entry for the Jack. Taryn, known to most as the mysterious Jack, wasn't a friend, but Portia admired the other woman's business savvy and discretion. Taryn would arrange a ride for her. For a fee.

Portia laughed. The Jack would do practically anything for a fee. That could work.

She nibbled on her thumbnail, studying all the angles.

Last night when she'd slipped out of the bar with Aleks, Taryn had checked to make sure she was okay to go. Before she could second-guess her decision, Portia messaged Taryn.

The response was nearly immediate, simply asking for her address. She sent her location, grateful for Taryn's lack of questions. *Ten minutes* was the last response.

With a sigh of relief, Portia shoved her phone back into her pocket. She didn't want to leave the sanctuary of the bathroom, but the sooner she faced Aleks, the sooner she could go home and forget this happened.

The bedroom was empty when she opened the door. A small rush of emotion speared through her. Relief, not disappointment. She was glad he wasn't waiting for her in the bedroom. Right?

Although she didn't see Aleks, she sensed his presence. He'd thoughtfully placed the rest of her belongings on a chair right outside the bathroom door. Portia slipped on her shoes and threaded her purse over her arm. She took a deep breath, summoning her Ice Queen armor, then left the bedroom.

He'd opened the curtains and hazy morning light filtered into the small sitting room through the privacy shade. It was a nice space, what you'd expect from a high-end hotel, but her gaze was drawn to the man in the middle of it all. Aleks sat on the small couch, an open laptop on the coffee table in front of him, and a cup of coffee cradled in one hand.

He'd taken advantage of her time in the bathroom to dress as well. The casual jeans and button-down shirt with the sleeves rolled up fit him perfectly. While it was a damn shame to cover his amazing body, she'd be a lot more uncomfortable if he were still in his robe, so close to naked.

In her don't-notice-me clothes from the night before, Portia felt dowdy in comparison. She shoved that thought away. Ten minutes. That was all she had to get through. Less, probably.

"Good morning, Mr., um, Aleks." It was impossible—and embarrassing—to greet someone formally when you didn't know their last name.

He looked up from his computer and smiled at her. "Good morning, Portia."

His attempt to match her gravity eased her discomfort.

"My ride will be here shortly." In the meantime, she had no idea what to do. Did she sit? Stand? Flee for the lobby?

That last thought settled it. She was a Tremaine. She would not run.

He closed his computer and stood. "Would you like me to wait with you?"

"No. Thank you." Her cheeks flushed. This whole morning-after thing was awkward as hell. How did people do this?

She didn't know what else to say, so she smiled, then moved toward the door.

He followed her and while his presence could have been creepy or intimidating, it felt almost comforting. What the hell did that mean?

Turning when she reached the door, they were face to face again. She shivered at the echo of last night's passion.

"Thank you." The words slipped out. Surprising, because she had no idea what she was thanking him for. For a satisfying sexual encounter? For being so easygoing? For being a safe place for her to regain her life and her sex drive?

"You're welcome," he said with a smile that lit up his eyes and warmed her blood. "Can I see you again?"

Pulse suddenly loud in her ears, her body urged her to say yes. But logic—and a sudden rush of guilt for enjoying herself, for thinking of doing anything other than cleaning up her father's messes and identifying any other secrets behind Tommy's death—stopped her.

She shook her head. The swish of her braids across her neck was disconcerting. "I don't think so."

He nodded. A part of her wished he would try to change her mind, while a part of her was glad he didn't. She didn't know which part she wanted to win.

"Be well." He brushed his thumb over her cheek. Just a whisper of pressure against her skin, then he stood in front of her again like it had never happened.

"You too," she said. She turned around and fumbled with the doorknob. *Pull it together, Portia!* Portia Tremaine did not get discombobulated. She always had a plan. Always knew what her next step was going to be.

Until her whole world had fallen part.

Aleks didn't try to help and eventually she got the door open. She didn't turn around, too embarrassed by her struggle—internal and external—to face him again. He held the door open for her, his hand braced against the metal several inches above her head.

Portia slipped through the opening and strode down the

hall, listening for the sound of the door closing. It didn't happen immediately and she was incredibly conscious of him watching her until the elevator opened.

She didn't allow herself to turn around. This was how it had to be. No regrets.

CHAPTER 3

ALEKS WAITED until the elevator doors slid shut behind Portia before he closed the door to his suite. He leaned his forehead against the cool metal and tried to corral the thoughts bouncing around his skull. Every scattered thought was a step closer to a raging headache or, worse, overload.

He pushed away from the door and stalked into the bathroom to grab his pain pills from his Dopp kit. They'd keep the headache away, or at least under control, so he could get through the day. He had a meeting today that he couldn't—and didn't want to—miss.

Shaking two tablets into his hand, he tossed them into his mouth. Swallowing them dry, he returned to the bedroom, grimacing at the bitter taste of the coating as it dissolved.

Light flickered behind his eyes. "Fuck." Stripping to his boxers, he dropped to the floor. He crossed his legs and tried to sink into the meditative state that calmed his brain.

Fucking neural augmentation. The brain implant had promised faster reflexes and increased strength, skills that would have served him well on the Solveig Consortium security team. What a joke.

Instead, the implant had increased his analytical skills exponentially. He picked up languages easier. Solved problems faster. Which would have been great, if the "improvements" hadn't come with debilitating side effects like the crippling headaches and overwhelming mental overload.

Settling into his body, not his brain, Aleks focused on his breath. In, hold, out, hold. That narrow focus gave his brain the anchor it needed to stop examining every possible angle of every possible decision. The rigid control was necessary to keep him from having a meltdown or doing permanent damage to his mind.

The hotel carpet was that weird combination of smooth and scratchy found in industrial carpets. The throbbing pressure increased as his brain automatically started comparing it to the carpet in other hotels he'd visited. With conscious effort, he recognized the thought and then envisioned letting it fly free. The pressure decreased a barely noticeable amount.

He'd washed out of the Solveig security program, but failed augmentation or not, the company had spent too much money on him to let him go. Instead, overlooking what they deemed his brokenness, they sent him out as a troubleshooter, using his skills but leaving him to manage the side effects alone.

Last night had tested his control. No, *Portia Tremaine* had tested his carefully crafted control. Fortunately, his brain *and* his body had been so focused on her that he'd maintained a delicate balance and hadn't worried about headaches all night. He'd focused on cataloguing every nuance that made up Portia Tremaine—her soft skin, the breathy sighs she had made when he discovered a particular sensitive spot.

His breath sped up and his pulse followed suit.

Dammit. He needed to rebuild his control, not shatter it again. But banishing her from his thoughts was proving to be nearly impossible.

Portia Tremaine had been nothing like he'd expected. Sure, the Ice Queen had come out to play when a drunk patron had approached her table. Aleks had observed with interest as she eviscerated the man with her cold smile and sharp words. And that was all it had taken to gain the attention of the highly curious aspect that lived in his brain.

At least, that was his excuse for approaching her table, for daring to invade her space with a pithy comment judging her dismissal technique. She'd been startled, then intrigued. And he'd worked hard—harder than he had since the surgery—to keep up with the sharp mind and biting wit that lived behind her gorgeous exterior and terrible choice in clothes.

She'd been intelligent and funny, making it increasingly difficult to remember that she represented the Tremaine Corporation, a truly reprehensible company that would best serve the world by no longer existing. It was his job to make that happen.

The contradictory information—Portia's positive traits and her company's terrible actions—sent the pressure in his head skyrocketing. Focusing on his breath again, Aleks wondered if he would make it out of this assignment without permanent damage.

Until then, he'd hold the demons back one inhale and exhale at a time.

CHAPTER 4

PORTIA'S PHONE vibrated and she glanced at the screen. *Here.*

The sudden rush of relief surprised her. The tension in her shoulders eased a little. A sleek red car with darkened windows pulled up in front of the hotel. While the valet hurried over to help and the doorman kept a watchful eye on the new arrival, Portia slipped out the door and hurried over to the car.

Chewing on her lip, she eyed the fancy car with concern. Was it Taryn? Would the Jack, a notorious underworld figure, really draw attention with a look-at-me car?

The passenger window rolled down. Taryn sat behind the wheel, but she leaned over the passenger seat to get Portia's attention. "You getting in or what?"

Ignoring the heat burning her cheeks, Portia hustled over to the car. So much for making a quick getaway.

Last night with Aleks had been great, but so far this morning, she was starting to regret her impulse to come back to his hotel room. All morning she'd tried to wrap herself in the Ice Queen's invulnerability, but it wouldn't stay in place. She felt exposed. Raw.

Head down, she reached for the passenger door. Her hand collided with the valet's and she jerked it back. "Sorry," she mumbled.

Never looking at him, never meeting his gaze, when he held the door open for her, Portia dropped into the seat with none of her usual grace. "Thanks," she murmured, long ingrained manners coming to the fore.

Taryn had the window up before the valet closed the door. Only once she was inside the vehicle did Portia take a breath.

"Are you okay?" Taryn asked, watching her closely.

"I don't know," Portia admitted. The events of the last hour had stressed her out.

"Did he hurt you?"

Portia jerked her head toward the woman who had practically growled the question. "What? No. I didn't realize he was going to open the door for me. I thought he was still on your side of the car."

Taryn's sigh echoed in the small space. "Not the valet, Portia. The man you left with last night. Is he the reason you practically sent me an SOS this morning?"

Portia studied Taryn. Had the Jack been worried about her? Come to think of it, Taryn had checked in with her when she and Aleks had ordered drinks. And again when Portia had gripped his hand when they left Razor Jack's.

"He didn't hurt me," she said firmly. "He was the perfect gentleman."

Except when they'd practically ravished each other. Heat crawled up her cheeks and Portia looked away. "I . . . hadn't anticipated the morning after."

And she probably should have. But she and Tommy had

been together since high school. They'd never *had* a morning after.

"Ah." Taryn finally put the car in drive and pulled out of the hotel's driveway.

"What's that supposed to mean?" Portia asked.

"Office or home?" Taryn asked, ignoring the question.

"Home." Definitely home. She needed time to regroup before facing her job as the chief executive officer of the Tremaine Corporation. Pulling out her phone, she fired off a message to her assistant, directing her to move or reschedule her morning meetings.

She and Tommy had purchased the penthouse condo right after they got married. It was a couple blocks from Tremaine headquarters, the location a hard-won compromise. Close enough for Portia to get to work easily, but far enough away that Tommy had hoped it would curb some of her workaholic tendencies. It hadn't worked.

Portia sighed. Since Tommy's death, their home felt empty and lonely and she spent a lot of time at the office to avoid going home. But today, she wasn't ready to face the one hundred and one things that demanded the CEO's attention.

The silence built until Portia couldn't stand it any longer. "What did you mean, 'Ah'?"

Taryn navigated the early morning Seattle traffic with ease. "I worried about how you would handle being with someone who wasn't Tommy," she finally answered.

"Why? What do you mean?" Portia blurted the question before she could consider if she really wanted the answer.

When they stopped at a light, Taryn looked at her. "I know you loved Tommy," she said softly. "I can't imagine that it's easy to move on."

"I'm not moving on!"

Taryn gave her a sad smile. "Yeah, that's what I figured when I got your text." Returning her attention to the road, she was quiet for another block. "Don't beat yourself up about it. As long as you had a good time, just let it go."

Portia turned the words over in her mind. *Just let it go.* She exhaled. "I can do that," she said with more confidence than she felt.

"Of course you can. You're Portia Tremaine." Taryn slipped into the alley behind Portia's building and parked near a nondescript door. "I thought you might want to go in the back way."

How in the world did Taryn know about the back way? Portia shook her head. A reminder that she should never underestimate the Jack. Speaking of which . . . "What do I owe you?" She kept her tone level, but inside, worry niggled at her.

Canting her head, Taryn studied her. "That's up to you."

"What do you mean?" Portia hadn't expected the ambiguity. Decided she didn't like it.

"I can charge you an outrageous sum for a very short ride or you can owe me a favor. It's up to you."

"A favor," Portia said before she could change her mind. That was how the Jack worked. She'd learned that much about the mysterious figure from all her time at Razor Jack's. Deviating from the norm would probably be very expensive. Although a favor from the Tremaine Corporation CEO— perhaps that was the more expensive option.

Cursing the lack of caffeine, Portia didn't try to backtrack. That wasn't her style. "Thank you for the ride," she said and exited the car.

"You're welcome," Taryn said, her tone once again soft.

"Take care of yourself, Portia. And don't forget to come in and clear your bar tab from last night," she added with a wink.

Color flaming her cheeks, Portia shut the car door. Taryn waited until Portia had opened the building with her keycard before pulling away with a rev of the engine.

CHAPTER 5

"YOUR APPOINTMENT IS HERE, MS. TREMAINE."

Portia frowned at the intercom on her desk. Physically and emotionally exhausted after waking up in Aleks's bed, she'd intended to spend the morning pulling herself back together. "I asked you to reschedule anything that wasn't urgent."

There was a pause, then her assistant replied with a faint snap to her voice, "This looked urgent."

Portia pinched the bridge of her nose. She'd wanted to replace Melanie for months. The woman had been a temporary hire shortly after Portia took command of her father's company. She'd selected the best option that HR had sent up, too overwhelmed to do her own search. Time was proving that might have been a mistake.

"Is it marked urgent?" Portia kept her tone calm and even, though it was a stretch. She'd been very good so far about not releasing the Ice Queen on Melanie.

"No, but it looked important. It's someone from the Solveig Consortium."

This time the long pause was on Portia's end. "Thank

you, Melanie. Please offer a beverage and escort them into my office in five minutes."

The fucking Solveig Consortium. The last people Portia wanted to deal with, especially not today.

She'd known this moment—this meeting—was coming. But the more time that had passed, the more she'd hoped she was wrong.

Why did this have to happen today? She was off her game, severely undercaffeinated, and not ready to face a representative from Dizzie's family.

Portia took a long drink of her mocha, then stood. While she waited for the caffeine to kick in, she stepped into her private bathroom and checked her appearance in the mirror. The circles under her eyes had been there since Tommy's death and she'd learned the coverage extent of nearly every concealer product on the market.

She smoothed her hair with first her right hand and then her left, making sure each and every hair was tucked into her bun. A final touch-up to her lipstick and a deep breath and she was as ready as she would ever be.

"Send my appointment in," she directed her assistant when she returned to her desk.

Although her desk—the whole office, really—was designed to emphasize the Tremaine power, she couldn't bear to sit and wait. Instead, she crossed to the floor-to-ceiling windows that were the showpiece of the office.

A blanket of mist covered downtown Seattle, hiding the skyscrapers and blocking her view of the water. Hand against the window, her finger traced an imaginary skyline on the glass. She didn't need to see the city to know it was there.

Her office door opened and Portia dropped her hand.

"Your appointment is here," her assistant announced. "Please have a seat, sir."

"Thank you, Melanie," Portia said. The door closed again, leaving her alone with the Solveig emissary.

Portia didn't turn around. Not just yet.

It wasn't just a power play. She cast a longing look at the window, wishing she could play hooky and go home. Tommy had always encouraged that kind of behavior. Every damn day now, she regretted how many times she'd said no.

"Thank you for seeing me, Ms. Tremaine."

The hairs on her neck stood straight up.

That voice. She knew that voice.

No. It couldn't be. Surely lots of men had that accent.

For all she wanted to drop her head against the cool glass and rage against the universe, Portia pulled herself together and faced her visitor.

It was him. Aleks.

She'd known. Her body's traitorous reaction to his voice had confirmed it.

Last night, Aleks had told her he was in town on business. She'd intentionally avoided asking about his employer, not wanting to disturb the fragile sense of peace she felt in his presence.

At Razor Jack's, he'd been irresistible in jeans and a long-sleeve pullover. Mouthwatering this morning in a robe and thigh-hugging boxers. She'd have bet money that nothing could top either of those looks.

She'd have lost.

The exquisite charcoal suit draped his body perfectly, emphasizing his height and his strength. His tie was an almost perfect match to his eyes. Although he could just as easily belong on the catwalk or in the boardroom, the air of danger around him said he didn't spend much time in either.

Pull yourself together, Portia!

She tucked her emotions inside. All of them—the embarrassment, the lingering desire, the growing rage. Pasting on a cool smile, she crossed the room and extended her hand. "I'm afraid you have me at a disadvantage, Mr.—"

His hand enveloped hers and when their fingers touched, she remembered how they'd felt on her body. *Not the time, Portia.* His grip was neither too strong nor too weak —he wasn't trying to intimidate her or ingratiate himself. She'd appreciated that if she weren't so mad at his deception.

"Aleksander Lind."

"And you're here on behalf of the Solveig Consortium. Is that correct, Mr. Lind?"

"Please, call me Aleksander." His gaze held hers. "Or Aleks, if you prefer."

Neither. She preferred neither. He'd obviously known who she was last night. Had he slept with her deliberately? Did he intend to use last night against her? Her stomach roiled at the thought.

Portia extracted her fingers as quickly as she could and gestured to the chair in front of her desk. "Please have a seat."

Grateful for all the years of hiding her emotions behind the Ice Queen's impenetrable exterior, she shoved her unruly emotions and questions about last night down deep. She would not show weakness in front of this man. Not again.

Spine straight, breath steady, she took her seat and folded her hands together on the desk's sleek surface. "What can I do for the Solveig Consortium?"

"Portia . . ."

"Ms. Tremaine," she corrected, her voice as icy as her nickname.

Her tone seemed to take him aback, although he recovered quickly. "Of course, Ms. Tremaine. The Solveig Consortium has sent me here to discuss reparations."

She raised a brow. "Reparations?"

Aleksander leaned forward in his chair. His gaze as focused on her as it had been last night when they'd flirted. This time she wouldn't be seduced by it.

"Yes, reparations. As I'm sure you are aware, the Solveig family recently learned that they were kept—intentionally—from their granddaughter."

Yes, you could say Portia was aware of the fact. "You're referring to Dizzie." Dizzie hadn't known her true identity until earlier this year.

"Your sister," he countered.

Those words were still a punch. The fact that she had a sister both thrilled and disappointed her. She'd always wanted a sibling, but the one she'd gotten had ruined Portia's life.

"If you'd like my sister," she almost choked on the word, "to meet her grandparents, you'll need to speak with her."

Jealousy was a tangled knot in Portia's stomach. Of course, Dizzie had grandparents who wanted to meet her. She had everything.

Killian.

The newsies' adoration.

A life without the back-breaking expectations of their father.

Everything was coming up roses for Dizzie.

"Her assistant should be able to make that appointment

for you." She swiped her hand over her desk, activating the computer screen. "If that's all?"

Aleks laughed, a rich deep laugh that sent shivers through her last night. But not now. She was immune now.

"I'll arrange visits later." He waved his hand as if he were dismissing the issue. "From what I understand, your sister doesn't have any financial power within the company."

"That's correct." Portia frowned. How had he learned that? It wasn't a secret, but it wasn't common knowledge either. Dizzie's Tremaine heritage had just been revealed. There was no way Portia—or any sane person—would give an unknown entity that kind of power.

"Then she really isn't in any position to negotiate on reparations."

So they were back to that. "And you are?" She raised a brow. All she had was his word that he was from Solveig.

He acknowledged the dig with a nod, then slid his sleeve back to reveal a communicator. He pressed his thumb against the screen and a holographic recording sprang to life.

Portia activated a receiver on her desk to verify the authenticity of the recording.

"Aleksander Lind," the computer voice said. An image of him swirled to life. "Authorized negotiator for Solveig Consortium." The soft computer voice continued speaking, relaying stats and other details intended to confirm his identity.

His image faded away, leaving them alone in the room. Portia glanced at the verification results on her screen. He was authentic.

Her stomach sank. He'd known who she was. He had to have known.

"Satisfied?" His voice was gravelly.

Satisfied? Not remotely. Not while she was waiting for him to throw last night in her face. Still, she couldn't let any of that show.

"It still doesn't explain what your bosses think my company owes them." She leaned back in her chair. "If anything, the Tremaine Corporation should be asking for payment given that we raised her for eighteen years."

His lip curled and he shot her a disbelieving look. "*Raised?* Is that what you call your father hiding her away in the corporate orphanage? Which I doubt was a loving home."

What did she know about a loving home? For all Portia knew, the orphanage had been nirvana compared to the Tremaine household. After Portia's mother died, their home had been a lot of things—quiet, sad, empty—but definitely not loving. Portia squelched her lingering grief and focused on her opponent.

"The Tremaine Corporation educated Dizzie, clothed her, and fed her. Trained her in a trade. What about that suggests that she was neglected?" Portia didn't know if she believed the words coming out of her mouth, but her job was to protect the company.

"Interesting," Aleks murmured. "If Dizzie had been raised by her mother's family, she would have attended the best schools, been accepted at the top of society. Possibly even been placed in a position of authority like yourself. The two of you might have developed a closer relationship between the two companies, rather than the tense relationship now."

"Is it tense?" It was an honest question, although Portia wasn't sure he would take it that way. The Tremaine Corporation did little business with the Solveig

Consortium. The smaller company had strong regional ties, but Tremaine had the global footprint. Prior to the bombing, Portia would have said she knew the business inside and out, but the last several months had emphasized how many secrets her father had kept.

"You don't know?"

"We don't do very much business with Solveig," Portia said. "And most of what we do is handled by our overseas office."

"It's a good thing, then, that the Consortium is exploring a Seattle expansion. The better for them to get to know Dizzie." A shark's smile accompanied his words.

The Solveig Consortium wanted to open an office in her city? Over her dead body. The two companies had never been friendly and whatever goodwill that might have existed between them had died when her father seduced Dizzie's mother, or whatever the hell had happened between them. Fortunately, the Consortium had never been big enough to truly challenge the Tremaine Corporation.

But if they wanted to set up in Seattle, they were definitely looking to cause trouble. And that she wouldn't allow.

"I'm confused about what exactly your role in all this is, Mr. Lind. Messenger boy? Advance guard?" Seducer?

A flicker of something she couldn't decipher passed over his face. "I'm what they need me to be."

"You're a fixer," she said, her voice flat as she considered the ramifications of his presence and of what had happened last night. Had their encounter been a setup? Was she a problem to be fixed? Her stomach churned at the thought.

He winced. "I don't like that term."

"Let me guess, you prefer 'problem solver.'" Her tone was mocking. It didn't matter what fixers called themselves, they existed in the shadows, usually at the beck and call of the CEO.

"Yes, I solve problems, but not like that." He clenched his fists and closed his eyes.

Had it been anyone else, she would have said he was in pain. But that was ridiculous. They were just having a conversation.

He opened his eyes and pierced her with that blue-green gaze that had enthralled her last night. Damn him for being so good-looking, so distracting.

"I heard you out, Mr. Lind, but as I said, I don't control Dizzie's calendar. I wish your employers the best of luck finding office space in Seattle."

The corner of his mouth crooked up in a there-and-gone smile. "Thank you for your time, Ms. Tremaine. I appreciate your candor and I'll pass on your message. I'm sure we'll see each other again."

Whether the words were a threat or a promise, Portia knew they were true. Next time she would be better prepared to face him and to deal with this new challenge.

"It was a pleasure seeing you again, Portia." The quiet words sent shivers through her.

With a dip of his head, he stood, buttoned his coat, and took his leave. She watched him go, torn between appreciating the view and worrying about what he—and his employers—planned next.

CHAPTER 6

PORTIA PACED the length of her office. She hadn't been able to concentrate since Aleks had left. After instructing her assistant that she was not to be disturbed, her focus had been on the threat posed by the Solveig Consortium.

There was no way the other company would meekly let the matter drop. They might not have the reach that the Tremaine Corporation did, but they had something more potent: a desire for vengeance. She'd understood the unspoken threat—they were coming for Portia's company. And she didn't know if she could stop them.

Although it had pained her, she'd called Dizzie and asked for a meeting. She'd been surprised when the other woman had agreed to meet her this afternoon. The easy acceptance felt like another trap to Portia and she could only fight so many battles at once.

Halfway through her back-and-forth circuit, the office door opened and her assistant announced Dizzie.

Keeping her back to the door, Portia pressed a hand to her uneasy stomach. Surely it was lingering resentment over Dizzie's role in the bombing, rather than nerves.

"Hello, Portia. You wanted to see me?" Dizzie's tone was cool, businesslike. And for some reason, it ratcheted up Portia's tension.

This was just a business meeting like any other. Pasting on her corporate smile and steeling her spine, Portia turned and faced her nemesis. Whenever she saw Dizzie, Portia experienced an entire range of emotions. Rage that Dizzie lived when Tommy had died. Wonder that she had a sister after so many years alone. Isolated when everyone around her was creating twosomes.

"Hello, Dizzie," she said, marveling that she didn't choke on the words. "Thank you for coming."

Dizzie stepped into the office slowly, followed by Killian St. John—Portia's best friend. Or maybe that was former best friend. Portia's feelings about Killian were just as conflicted as they were for Dizzie. For many of the same reasons.

"Killian." Part of her wanted to run to him and fling her arms around him and pretend everything was the way it used to be. Would they ever get back to that place?

"You're looking well, Portia."

She searched his words for hidden meanings, hating that they were so stilted with each other. "Thank you."

He looked happy. And while she was truly happy for him, a tiny part of her was jealous too.

Tamping down that irrational emotion, she returned her attention to Dizzie. She wore heeled black boots and leg-hugging leather pants with a blue silk blouse that highlighted her eyes. Somehow, she'd managed to merge the styles of her days as a courier with the high fashion of the corporate world. Portia had never been effortlessly stylish like that.

Bitch.

"Please have a seat." She gestured toward the corner of her office where a small cluster of more comfortable furniture provided a tiny oasis.

Dizzie eyed the space warily. She shook her head and her ponytail swung behind her. "I'll stand."

Portia felt a twinge of empathy. When she'd moved into her father's office, the place had been filled with memories. A few were good, some were neutral, but most of them were bad. How many times had she stood at attention in front of his desk while he berated her for not meeting his standards? How many times had he shut down her ideas for change?

Even their conversation on the day he'd disappeared had been contentious. Though she'd tried to put her own stamp on the office's decor, years' worth of memories remained. So Portia understood Dizzie's reluctance.

That didn't mean she had time to indulge it. "Please? I have a lot to discuss with you."

Dizzie's lips pressed together. Portia clenched her jaw for a moment and then added, "Both of you. Please."

That got Dizzie to sit, though she took the chair in front of Portia's desk. As soon as Portia was seated as well, Killian grabbed a chair and arranged it next to Dizzie.

Sitting side by side, Dizzie and Killian looked like the power couple they were. The newsies had heralded her as a real-life Cinderella story, the lowly courier who was actually a corporate princess. And now she had the chance to gain even more power in their world when she was embraced by the Solveigs.

Portia had no problem with Dizzie joining the Solveigs. But it seemed unlikely to stop whatever else they were planning.

"Am I here so you can yell at me again?"

Portia hid a smile. Dizzie's bluntness was refreshing

compared to some of the games played in the business world.

"No. Not today."

Dizzie snorted.

Portia ignored the interruption and continued. "I have a request for you. Actually, I've been asked to pass on a request."

"No," Dizzie said.

"Hear me out. Please," Portia added.

"No." Dizzie shook her head.

Killian leaned over and whispered in her ear. She rolled her eyes, then sighed. "Fine."

Dizzie smoothed out her expression. Suddenly, her face gave away nothing of her feelings. Portia was almost proud —she'd obviously been practicing. That skill would serve Dizzie well in their world.

"What can I do for you?" Dizzie asked in a voice just as smooth, just as expressionless.

"I met with a representative of the Solveig Consortium today." She paused. "Your mother's family would like to meet you."

Dizzie paled and jerked back in her chair. Her mouth opened but no words came out. In the next instant, she popped up and raced from the room, back into the reception area.

Portia blinked in surprise. That was unexpected.

Killian stood then stopped and looked at Portia. "Does this have anything to do with Tremaine?"

"It all has to do with the company," she answered honestly. "But the first thing the representative asked for was a meeting with Dizzie. I directed him to her assistant, but thought I should let her know in advance. I don't know anything more than that."

"Thank you," Killian said after a long pause. "We'll get back to you."

The "we" struck Portia in the heart and she sucked in a breath. She missed being part of a "we." After a careful exhale, she said, "I appreciate that."

Killian half-smiled and tipped his head. Then he followed Dizzie out of the office and left Portia all alone again.

She stared at the closed door. The meeting hadn't been as terrible as she'd expected. In fact, as far as meetings with her sister went, this one had been relatively painless. Still, it left her feeling edgy and out of sorts.

Everyone wanted Portia to embrace Dizzie as her sister, but no one was giving her time to get used to that unexpected development. She ran her thumb over her bare ring finger. There'd been so many changes over the last year.

Portia had barely gotten used to her new normal and now she worried that things were about to change again. She didn't like change. It never worked out for her.

Her spacious office suddenly felt small and airless. She had to get out of here before the walls closed in on her.

CHAPTER 7

SAFELY BEHIND HER FRONT DOOR, Portia shed her clothes as she strode across the penthouse apartment she and Tommy had purchased just before they got married. She paused to trail her fingers over the picture frame sitting beside the couch. It flickered to life, revealing images from their wedding. Images of their vows, their first dance, and them laughing at the cake cutting cycled across the screen. Happy moments, forever frozen in time.

"I miss you," she said as the loop started again.

Her voice echoed in the empty living room. The once-perfect home was too quiet now. Too big. Too Tommy-less.

She hated the emptiness, but she wasn't ready to leave yet. Wasn't ready to start over. And where would she go?

Once in her bedroom, Portia stripped off her remaining clothes and pulled on high-tech black running tights and a matching top. Breathable and lightweight, the fabric also provided the wearer with light protection. It wouldn't stop a bullet—initially, it had been developed to prevent scrapes and bruises—but it would stop a knife. She'd learned that the hard way.

Next, she pulled a special brush through her hair. Each stroke applied a thin layer of nanos and temporarily changed her from a blonde to a brunette. Then she ruthlessly scraped her newly dark hair into a braid. A pair of tinted glasses completed the look.

Portia studied her reflection. For the second time that day, the woman staring back didn't look like Portia Tremaine. Whoever the hell she was.

Her whole life, she'd been Portia Tremaine, Phillip Tremaine's daughter.

Portia Tremaine, Ice Queen.

Portia Tremaine, Tommy Gilmore's wife.

Who was she now? And what the hell was she supposed to do for the rest of her life?

Questions to ask herself while she ran.

She laced up her custom running shoes and slipped her phone into a hidden pocket in her pants. With some credits, ID, and her keycard tucked into another secret pocket, Portia left her lonely apartment.

Her high-security building was designed to keep people out, not in. She and Tommy had explored all the different ways to leave their building and avoid the newsies who occasionally camped outside, looking for a juicy story about any of the wealthy residents.

Portia used one of those exit routes now. Descending the stairs that led to the ground floor warmed her muscles and elevated her heart rate. At the bottom, the door opened into an alley at the back of the building. It wasn't as sketchy as some—the partial lighting discouraged lurkers and the security cameras captured everything that happened back here. Portia wasn't worried about the cameras. Her glasses were embedded with technology that prevented them from clearly capturing her image.

She stretched her hamstrings and her quads, breathing in the night air. The salty tang and hint of seaweed told her tonight's breeze was coming in from Puget Sound. Those were her favorite nights, when the air smelled like home instead of oil and people and decay.

Pulling up a high-energy playlist, Portia darted out of the alley and headed toward the city center. Her feet hit the sidewalk in time with her music. Speakers built into the glasses allowed her to listen while remaining aware of her surroundings.

Two blocks in, the tension in her shoulders started to melt away. The rhythmic in–out of her breathing, the slap of her feet, the pulse of her music, all those sounds drowned out the noise in her head.

She let the traffic lights decide her route. She took advantage of every green light, exploring the city she stared down at day and night. The ground-level perspective was completely different.

Tonight, the streets still teemed with people. No longer tiny ants on the ground, but full-size people. Seattle was almost, but not quite, a twenty-four-seven city. Not a New York or London or Hong Kong—not yet—but it was getting there. And as the head of Tremaine Corporation, she was a part of it.

Her body on as close to autopilot as it ever got, Portia studied the people she ran past and the buildings that towered over her. The rumble of a passing car sent a spike of adrenaline through her. She ignored the faces of the startled people she dodged on the sidewalk. Rounding the next corner, she stepped into the street to avoid a cluster of users.

Running was her drug. Why use synthetics like Vyne when the natural endorphins of running could fix you right up? It was like a miracle cure—it cleared her head, worked her body, soothed her soul. If only it hadn't taken Tommy's death for her to discover it.

Portia paused at a driveway that cut across the sidewalk, jogging in place as a motorcycle pulled out of the garage and slipped into traffic.

The slim figure bent over the handlebars reminded her of Dizzie. The other woman had spent her life racing around the city, running packages and whatever else wherever they needed to go. All for the benefit of people like Portia. The people who made the decisions and ran the companies.

Portia shuddered and took off again. It sounded awful. She couldn't imagine trading places with Dizzie.

She liked her life . . . mostly. At least she had, before the bombing.

Following her mother's death when Portia was in middle school, every day after school she'd made her way to Tremaine headquarters, hoping to spend time with her father. But it had never happened. By the time she was a teenager, she'd stopped trying and started working.

That had been the secret formula and the ticket to weekly meetings and progress reports with her father.

God, she'd been so naïve then. Believing that her father loved her.

Portia shook herself free from those thoughts and ran on.

New songs, green lights, red lights, pedestrians. Taking it all in, she wove through the city.

Then slowed as she neared a familiar building. She passed the ornate entrance and the uniformed valets, then stopped on the other side.

Hands on her hips, she paced in a small circle, sucking

in one deep breath, then another. *This was so stupid.* There was no reason to stop at Aleks's hotel.

She hadn't meant to come here.

Had she?

Of course not. Her route had been completely random, determined by traffic lights. This was pure coincidence. *Just keep running, Portia.*

But her feet didn't move. She stopped pacing and stared up at the building.

The sooner she sorted out the Solveig Consortium's demands and arranged a meeting with Dizzie, the sooner Aleksander Lind would be out of her hair.

She could get that ball rolling now. Let him know about her meeting with Dizzie this afternoon and be one step closer to resolving this. Despite her reaction today, Portia thought it was likely that Dizzie would want to meet her family.

Portia could tell him now . . . or go back home. To her lonely, empty apartment.

She shivered. Home would still be there when she was done.

Steeling her spine, Portia patted her braid to make sure it was still intact and approached the hotel entrance like she belonged there. Which she did. She may not look like Portia Tremaine at the moment, but she still *was* Portia Tremaine.

CHAPTER 8

ALEKS STARED at the email from his bosses, the one demanding to know how much progress he'd made with "the Tremaine situation."

"Progress? I've been here one damn day." After verifying the speech-to-text function was off, he dropped his phone onto the couch cushion next to him and rested his head against the back.

He closed his eyes and rubbed at the space between his brows. His pulse throbbed behind his eyes. A headache was threatening. Dammit. He didn't have time for this.

The Solveigs were riding his ass, demanding to see their granddaughter as soon as possible. They didn't care that the situation was out of his hands. If she didn't want to see them, there was nothing he could do about it.

Not that they would accept no as an answer. Not after all this time.

And short of kidnapping her, how was he supposed to make that happen?

Unbidden, his brain latched onto the question and started working on an answer. "Stop it," he muttered.

Reluctantly pushing off the couch, he headed for the bathroom and his meds. They would hopefully stop the headache before it fully emerged.

If he could focus past the pain, he might be able to rein in his brain and regain his focus. Otherwise, this whole night was going to be a waste.

Tapping the pills into his hand, his gaze shifted to the barely visible bed in the next room.

"Oh, Portia," he whispered. Meeting her was the best thing to come out of this entire visit to Seattle. And also the worst. His employers were gunning for Phillip Tremaine and the Tremaine Corporation and they wouldn't let anyone or anything stop them from bringing it all tumbling down.

"Focus, Aleks. You've got work to do." He swallowed the pills dry and returned to the couch. The throbbing had lessened and he was able to think a little clearer.

Trading his phone for his computer, he pondered his response.

A dozen possible replies whirled through his thoughts. Some were profane, but the rest were more measured. He chose one of the more professional responses and transformed it into a message. The email included a quick summary of his meeting with Portia— the one in her office, not the one in his bed—and what he perceived as the next steps. Which at this point involved more meetings.

He read it over quickly. When he was satisfied that none of his frustration or infatuation had seeped into his words, he hit send.

Now what?

Shutting the computer down, he stood slowly. The pain in his head had died down to a low simmer, but he knew if he didn't find something to quiet his thoughts, it would flare back up again.

It wasn't just the headache tonight, though. His body felt as out of sorts as his brain. Jittery, uncomfortable in his skin. Was that a result of meeting Portia or did this whole assignment have him off his game?

He shoved his hands through his hair and growled in frustration.

After the implant surgery, he would have said the swings from lack of focus to hyperfocus were the worst side effect. But after years of living with the implant, he knew that the headaches were the true killer. He could manage the rest. Fighting or fucking were how he'd coped the first couple years. Now he'd learned other, less destructive tricks to maintain his equilibrium.

Clubs were one. Loud music, flashing lights, writhing bodies. Too many options for his brain to keep track of caused it to just sort of . . . chill out.

Aleks grimaced. No. A room full of hot sweaty strangers was not what he needed tonight. The other option was the fully stocked hotel gym. A completely different version of hot sweaty strangers.

The throbbing between his brows worsened.

Fuck. He had to make a move soon.

The sudden knock on the door was a shock to his overstimulated senses.

He frowned and approached slowly. Who was it? The only people who knew his location were back home. And he hadn't ordered room service. Although now that he thought about it, he should probably eat.

At the second knock, Aleks stalked to the door, intending to direct whoever it was—probably some drunken business traveler—that they had the wrong room.

He pulled it open and his words dried up. "What—"

He'd never seen the woman standing outside his door and yet he still knew her immediately. Hot and sweaty, high-tech workout clothes, dark hair and all, even angled away like she was about to leave, he *knew* her.

"Portia? What are you doing here?"

CHAPTER 9

HIS HEAD SPUN as his brain conjured reasons for her to be back at his hotel. "Are you okay? Are you hurt?" Was she here for a repeat performance? His heart—and brain—almost stuttered to a stop with that thought. He slammed the door shut on the possible scenarios his wayward brain was cooking up.

She looked at him and their gazes met. "We should talk. Can I come in?"

"Yes. Of course." He stepped back into the room, holding the door open so she could enter.

Portia looked left and right down the hallway, then slipped inside. Aleks gripped the door and as he closed it, he checked the hall too. All clear.

When he turned around, it was to find Portia all the way across the room, staring out the privacy-shaded window. Her hands were tucked into her pockets.

He approached slowly, making sure she could hear him coming. He didn't want to startle her.

Questions bounced around his head and he clenched

his jaw to keep from blurting them out. The suspense might kill him, but he'd let her start.

"I love this city." She spoke without turning around.

Aleks took it as an invitation and joined her at the window, standing close enough to hear her, but not crowd her. "It seems to be a very nice city," he said carefully.

"Seattle will never be a New York or San Francisco, but we're still a world-class city. High technology nestled in a beautiful location." She turned to face him now.

He shifted sideways to watch her and waited to see where she was going with this.

"At least, that's what I've always been told. I'm used to seeing it from this high. More an abstract painting than a true city. Dizzie's the one who knows it inside out at the ground level."

"Your sister."

The words fell between them. There was no explosion, just a subtle tightening of her lips.

She sighed. "I spoke with her this afternoon. Told her that your employers wanted to meet her."

"What did she say?" He asked because it was expected, not because he cared at the moment. Portia fascinated him and he wanted to talk about her, not her sister. Wanted to get to know the real woman instead of the digital dossier.

She opened her mouth and his gaze dropped to her lips. Memories of kissing her, of the enticing blend of whiskey and her essence flooded him.

"She didn't say anything," Portia said.

That pulled him back to the present. "What? She won't meet them?"

Portia laughed. "She didn't say anything at all. Honestly, I think she was overwhelmed."

His brows furrowed. In light of that, Portia's presence made no sense. "If she didn't agree, then why are you here?"

"Idontknow." Her words ran together and she turned back to the window, pressing her palm against the glass.

His brain picked up the puzzle that was Portia Tremaine again. Was she here to see him? Needing a distraction, he fell back on the manners his grandparents had drilled into him. "Can I get you something to drink?"

She looked over her shoulder and smiled. "Water, please. I'm always thirsty after I run."

"You *ran* here?" he blurted. Her workout attire made sense now, but the thought of her running alone through the streets at dusk chilled him to the bone.

Not your problem, he tried to remind himself.

It didn't work.

Removing a bottle of sparkling water and one of still water from the small in-room refrigerator, he offered her the choice.

She took the bottle of still from him, their fingers brushing. Shivers ran up his arm. He'd had the same reaction last night every time they touched. He set the other bottle unopened on the coffee table, too distracted by her presence to drink.

Her attention back on the city, she opened the bottle and took a long sip, presenting the perfect opportunity to study her. Her long neck was emphasized by her movement and by the braid that hung past her shoulders. The dark color was fine, but he missed the sunny blond cascade he'd tangled his fingers in.

"Is that your disguise?" He cringed. *Way to make conversation, Aleks.*

Portia lowered the bottle and smiled at him.

His heart skipped a beat. Even as a brunette, she was

still so beautiful. And her smile—it was real, versus the tight, fake one she gave the newsies.

"Yeah, I guess you can call it that," she said. "It keeps people from bothering me when I run."

Questions tumbled out of him. "Are you safe? Do you have security? Does anyone know you're out alone?"

She raised a dark brow at him. The Ice Queen look didn't work as well that way. "Yes. No. No."

He quickly processed her answers and frowned. But was she really safe if she was out running without security? And why did he care so much? "What if something happened to you?"

"Is that a threat?" She lowered her bottle and stared at him.

"No!" Startled, he stepped backward and ran into the table. The other bottle of water fell over and rolled off the table, hitting the carpet with a thud.

"No," he repeated as he bent to pick up the bottle. He took the moment to pull himself back together. "Never a threat. It can be dangerous for women alone at night. That's all."

Sadness flashed over her face and he cursed internally. Of all the choices he could make around her, he always seemed to pick the wrong one. "I'm sorry."

Her lips curled up into a shadow of a smile and she shook her head. "It's okay. It's been a while since anyone has worried about me. In a positive way, I mean." She laughed self-depreciatingly.

"No one?" That couldn't be true. How could anyone leave this beautiful, dangerous, vibrant woman alone?

"No one who isn't paid to."

Fuck! There he went again, saying the wrong thing.

"Oh." His fingers wrapped around the bottle cap, twisting it off until it released with a soft pop.

The silence between them grew. It wasn't awkward, but he wouldn't call it comfortable. More like . . . waiting.

Because he couldn't trust himself not to say something stupid, Aleks sipped his water with an air of calm he didn't feel. When he neared the end of the bottle—and his breaking point—Portia finally spoke.

"Thank you."

Aleks tipped his head. "For what?"

"For letting me in when I showed up completely unannounced." She rolled her bottle between her palms. Her voice carried a hint of question in it.

Was she asking him why he let her in? Or asking herself why she was here? "You're welcome. Any time."

Her return smile was strained.

"Would you like to sit?" The suite's living room had a number of places to sit. He swept his hand out to indicate any of them.

"Thank you." The smile that accompanied her words was less sad.

He waited until she had taken a seat—she chose the sofa, with a view of the city—then sat far enough away that he hoped her presence wouldn't short-circuit his brain. He felt like an idiot, tripping over his words.

"I should have waited until morning, made an official appointment in my office," she said, gazing at the window.

"Why didn't you?" He'd turned her presence over in his mind, exploring all the angles for why she might be here, but nothing made sense. Before arriving in Seattle, he'd been given a dossier on Portia Tremaine, compiled by the Solveig Consortium's intelligence division. The woman in that report wouldn't have just shown up here.

In all honesty, she also wouldn't have come back to his hotel room last night. Either intelligence had gotten it wrong, or Portia Tremaine had hidden depths. Aleks was sure it was the latter.

Portia fiddled with her water bottle. "I was in the neighborhood."

He huffed out a disbelieving laugh.

She groaned and light pink tinged her cheeks. "That sounds so cliché, I know. But it's true."

He grinned at her. "Your run took you by my hotel?"

"Yes. I know it sounds crazy. I just . . . run. Wherever the mood takes me." She shot him a smile that lit up the room. "I like to see my city from the ground."

"Instead of from up high?" he asked to show that he listened to her. That he *liked* listening to her. Portia was . . . *soothing* wasn't the right word . . . but she settled his brain since it was completely, 100 percent focused on her.

"Exactly."

"At night?"

She frowned. He replayed his words and realized they sounded judgy. "I mean, there's not much to see in the dark, is there?"

"Are you kidding? It's—pardon another cliché—night and day. During the day, it's all business. But at night, when the buildings are illuminated, it's a beautiful nighttime rainbow. Energetic and pulsing with life. Didn't you notice it last night?"

Aleks canted his head and thought back over the previous evening. He'd been so focused on getting his glimpse of Portia Tremaine, he hadn't paid much attention to the city. "No, sorry." He meant it—he was sorry that he hadn't seen Seattle the way she did.

She shook her head. "You should pay more attention,"

she admonished gently. "Seattle has different faces in the sun and the rain, too."

"And that's important?"

She tilted her head to study him. Aleks fought the urge to fidget under her gaze. Which was ridiculous. The woman had seen—touched—his naked body. But now she studied him as though she would strip him bare.

"You've never studied your city? Stockholm?"

He shook his head, reluctant to interrupt this decidedly romantic perspective from the woman that the newsies—and everyone else—called the Ice Queen.

"In the sun, Seattle shows off her finery, the sparkling blue jewels of Puget Sound. In the rain and fog, she's moody and mysterious."

"That's beautiful." Aleks hadn't expected that level of poetry from her.

Portia flushed and for a moment it reminded him of when she'd been wrapped in his arms, their bodies entwined.

He crossed his legs to hide the sudden redirection of blood and changed the subject. "Tell me more about your meeting with your sister."

As soon as the words left his mouth, he knew it was too abrupt a change. The room's energy changed. Their friendly, flirty camaraderie was buried under the new business-like atmosphere.

Dammit, Aleks.

Portia's lips pinched together. "She and Killian St. John came to my office this afternoon."

Left unspoken was the timing: the same day as their meeting. He hadn't expected that.

"What did she say about our offer?"

"*Our* offer?" Her arch tone wasn't the turnoff she likely

intended. Instead, that prissy, pissy voice heated his blood, just the way it had last night at the bar.

But if she wanted to spar, he'd spar. Aleks nodded. "The Consortium's offer, then."

Her lips curved into a small smile. Was she enjoying this as much as he was? Before his brain could go wild exploring that thought, he reined it back and refocused on their conversation.

"Nothing," she said. "Dizzie ran out of the room when I mentioned it." Now her smile reached her eyes.

"She ran out of the room?" Aleks blinked and tried to process Dizzie's unexpected reaction.

"Like it was on fire." Portia laughed.

Aleks smiled, but he was still confused. "That's . . . not a good thing, right?"

Her shoulders rose and fell in a shrug. "I have no idea. We're not close."

That made him sad. He'd always believed family should be treasured. "Perhaps you should be."

She snorted. "Why?"

Wasn't it obvious? "Because you're both Tremaines. The last two, if I'm not mistaken."

Her eyes glimmered softly, then she turned away. "And my father."

Fucking Phillip Tremaine. Aleks refrained from saying that out loud. From what he knew, the man was a monster, both in business and in his personal life. But Portia appeared to have loved him and Aleks didn't want to upset her.

"Right, your father. What happened to him? No one has seen him for months." Keeping his tone flat was a struggle.

When Portia turned back to him, the sheen of tears was

gone and her face was composed. "I have no idea," she said stiffly.

Aleks gazed at her, soaking in her beauty, her spirit, the peace her presence brought him. And he hated himself, but he was about to destroy the moment. "That's too bad."

She wrinkled her brow and studied him. "Why is that?" Hints of the Ice Queen colored her words.

"My employers have some . . ." he paused and considered his words ". . . strong feelings about your father. If you knew his whereabouts, they could deal with him directly, rather than put you in the line of fire."

Portia's gaze turned to ice. "Is that a threat?"

Tension flared between them, a volatile mix of anger and passion. He held her stare, not threatened by her icy demeanor. "It's not a threat, Portia. It's a warning. One I shouldn't be giving you."

His hands clenched at the thought of anyone threatening her. "The Solveigs want to destroy the Tremaine Corporation."

She scoffed. "They've tried before. Several times." One slender finger tapped against her lip. "The last attempt was industrial espionage, if I'm remembering correctly. We stopped them. Hard."

His jaw tightened. "Yes, so I've heard. But this time . . . " He tried to find the right words. "This time they know about Dizzie. And they're pissed." Aleks wasn't entirely sure they were even rational about the subject. "They want no trace left of the company."

The color drained from Portia's face, but she didn't flinch. "That's ridiculous," she said. "I'm in charge of the company now. And there are no more secret projects like my . . . like my sister." She bit off the last two words.

How could she not understand what a precious gift family was? He'd give anything to see his brother again.

Not the time, Aleks. He was here to do a job, not facilitate her reunion with a sister she obviously didn't want.

He stood and stalked toward the window, staring down at the city she loved so much. Colorful lights decorated the buildings and the traffic on the roads below painted lines of red and white. But he was too agitated to see the beauty she described.

After several deep breaths, he turned to face her. "I don't want to be the bad guy, Portia. But I'm not going to sugarcoat it. They want Tremaine destroyed. And they won't care if you're caught in the destruction."

She stared at him a long moment before she stood too. "Thank you for the water," she said primly. "I should go. I'm sure I'll be seeing you." Her lips pinched with her final words.

"Yeah, you will," he said.

With a haughty lift of her chin, she left his hotel suite for the second time that day.

Air whooshed out of his lungs when the door closed behind her.

He'd known this job would be messy when he had been assigned it. But now . . . it was going to be a clusterfuck.

CHAPTER 10

ALEKS FOLLOWED THE MAÎTRE D' to a table tucked back in the corner of the restaurant. Located on the top floor of one of Seattle's skyscrapers, the high-end eatery was known for both fine dining and the spectacular views of Puget Sound and the Olympic Mountains. Unfortunately, given the location of the table, he wouldn't have the chance to enjoy the vistas.

"Your dining companion, Mr. St. John." The maître d' gave a short bow, then smoothly stepped away, leaving Aleks alone with Killian St. John.

"Thank you for meeting me, Mr. St. John. I'm Aleksander Lind." Aleks extended his hand.

St. John took it with a firm grip. "Your request intrigued me, Mr. Lind. And that was before I started receiving calls from other investors." He released the handshake and gestured to the seat near Aleks's hip.

Aleks hid a grimace—he hadn't expected discretion from the people he'd met with yesterday and today—but he'd hoped for it, nonetheless. He took his seat, studying Killian St. John while he did so.

The other man was a key investor in the Tremaine Corporation. His family had invested when the company was just starting out and their wealth had grown exponentially in the decades since. Although he was dressed in a deceptively simple suit, Aleks knew that it probably cost more than he made in a month.

The moment they were both seated, a waiter appeared as if out of nowhere, offering them menus. Aleks took his with a nod of thanks.

"Your usual, Mr. St. John?"

"Yes, thank you."

"And for you, sir?"

"Coffee, please. With cream and sugar," Aleks added.

St. John leaned back in his chair, one arm draped casually over the back. He embodied the image of a wealthy, bored dilettante, but Aleks recognized the intelligence in his gaze. This was not a man to underestimate. His next words proved that true.

"I understand the Solveig Consortium is interested in acquiring shares of the Tremaine Corporation."

Yes, St. John had definitely spoken with the other investors.

"My employers are always on the lookout for investment opportunities," Aleks replied. This wasn't the first such "negotiation" he'd completed for the company.

St. John's lips curled in a hint of a smile. "And I'm sure this has nothing to do with Dizzie's sudden appearance on the scene."

Aleks studied the other man, contemplating the best way to answer. The intelligence dossier on him had primarily identified him as an investor who preferred a hands-off approach. But St. John was a longtime friend of Portia Tremaine and her late husband. And he was now the serious boyfriend of Dizzie, the missing Solveig granddaughter. Which Killian St. John was he talking to right now?

Taking a chance that he was talking to the boyfriend, Aleks said, "Yes, she's definitely a consideration. The Solveigs would like to ensure that she's taken care of in the future." Aleks put just enough emphasis on those last words to convey their dismay about how she had been treated in the past.

St. John opened his mouth, then closed it, when the waiter reappeared by their table with their drinks. "Thank you, Michael."

"You're welcome, Mr. St. John." The waiter beamed at the recognition. "Are you ready to order?"

Aleks hadn't even thought to look at the menu yet—hell, he hadn't even been sure he'd get lunch—but the other man beat him to the punch. "Bring us two of the chef's specials." He glanced at Aleks. "Any allergies, Lind?"

When Aleks shook his head, St. John confirmed the order. As the waiter disappeared, he said, "You really can't come to Si'ahl and not have the salmon."

"I appreciate the tip." While St. John wasn't treating him as an enemy, there was no sense in antagonizing the other man.

Aleks took advantage of the lull in service to present his case. "As I mentioned in my initial call, I represent the Solveig Consortium. The consortium is looking to expand their presence in the North American market and believes that acquiring the Tremaine Corporation is a good first start." Aleks knew the plan sounded ridiculous—Tremaine was at least twice the size of the consortium—but he had his orders.

St. John studied Aleks over the rim of his glass, but said nothing.

Aleks plowed on with his sales pitch. This wasn't his strength, but he turned up his charm. "With the two companies combined, the Solveig Consortium will become the preeminent player in the medical–industrial complex."

Lowering his glass to the table, St. John asked, "How many investors have taken your offer?"

Aleks kept his gaze steady. "That's confidential."

St. John laughed. "Bullshit. No one has accepted your offer."

He was right, but Aleks had no intention of confirming his guess. If it was a guess.

St. John continued. "The smaller investors are too afraid of Portia—really, Portia's father—to be willing to sell to a competitor. You need one of the major investors—basically me or Portia—to accept first. Then the others will fall in line." He studied Aleks. "Am I right?"

"My understanding was that Portia's father is . . . out of the picture." The news stories from the day of Dizzie's appearance and Tremaine's disappearance were confusing. One or two had mentioned that blood had been found in Tremaine's office. Phillip Tremaine's blood.

St. John, acting in Portia's stead, had announced her father's disappearance, but in the days and months that followed, no other statements had been made. Everyone assumed he was dead.

Aleks wasn't sure what to think, but without a body, Mrs. Solveig refused to believe his disappearance was so . . . permanent.

St. John laughed. "Phillip Tremaine was a mean bastard and until I see a body, I'm not writing him off just yet."

Aleks was shocked to hear St. John echo his thoughts. "So, is it Phillip Tremaine you're afraid of? Or Portia?"

St. John laughed again but his mirth wasn't reflected in his eyes. "I'm not afraid of Portia. We've been friends for years. But the others? Damn right they're scared. They don't call her the Ice Queen for nothing."

Aleks thought back to the time he'd spent with Portia. The Ice Queen had been on display with the man who'd hit on her at the bar and in her office when Aleks had surprised her for their meeting. But every other time they'd met, he'd enjoyed the company of a flesh and blood woman. Not a block of ice in a crown.

Aleks wasn't stupid enough to verbalize any of this. As a longtime friend of Portia's, St. John would probably feel duty bound to defend her, and Aleks would hate to kick his ass. Portia probably wouldn't appreciate it either. Except he'd heard Portia and St. John were on the outs because of Dizzie, so maybe she'd be okay with it.

What the hell was he thinking, worrying about how Portia would feel about his actions?

Fuck! That wasn't a good sign. Aleks refocused on this meeting. Despite the turmoil in his head, he kept it out of his voice. "Then how would you suggest I proceed?"

"If you were smart, you'd stop making these calls and let your employers know it isn't happening." St. John's words hung in the air between them.

Aleks already knew that wasn't going to happen. He had his orders and, as dumb as he thought they were, he would obey them. "Or you could agree to sell your shares and the others would follow suit."

St. John sat back with a huff of laughter. "I get that you've got a job to do here, but don't you see how ridiculous it is? If anything, Tremaine should be the one purchasing the Solveig Consortium."

Aleks clenched his jaw. "I believe that was tried previously. It's why we're in the current mess we're in." He spoke without thought and regretted it immediately. How much did St. John know about the merger negotiations where Phillip Tremaine had met Anna Solveig, Dizzie's mother?

"Ah, yes. Dizzie's origin story." St. John shook his head and sipped his drink again. "Past relations between the two companies were a mess to say the least, but that has nothing to do with any of us. The two companies have kept their distance—mostly—for more than two decades. Let's just keep it that way."

"My employers won't agree to that." Nothing short of wiping Tremaine from the planet would stop them.

"Then they're idiots," St. John said. "And it won't end well for them."

"Is that a threat?" Aleks asked. He wasn't concerned, more curious than anything.

"No, I'm a realist. Coming after the Tremaines in their own city is foolish. Coming after the Tremaine Corporation at all isn't the smart play." He stopped abruptly, his gaze focused behind Aleks.

Aleks turned to see the waiter bringing their meals.

With practice ease, the waiter slid the plates in front of them. "Anything else I can get you gentlemen?"

"No, thank you, Michael," St. John said.

"Enjoy." The waiter departed after another short bow.

Aleks studied the plate before him. The salmon looked perfectly cooked. He waited for St. John to take a bite before sampling his own.

Flavors burst in his mouth. The moist, flaky fish stood

up well to the citrus glaze. This was the best meal he'd had in this city so far.

"So how would you do it?" Aleks asked.

"Do what?"

"Take over Tremaine Corporation."

Another bark of laughter. "You don't give up, do you?"

Aleks forked up another bite of fish while he waited for St. John's response.

"I wouldn't, of course. Don't get me wrong. Phillip Tremaine was a bastard and I hope the man rots in hell, but the company itself isn't a reflection of the man. I trust Portia to lead it out of the shadows."

Shadows was such an interesting word. Aleks was sure it was doing the heavy lifting in that sentence. "What about Dizzie? Could she lead the company out of the shadows?"

The change in the other man was instantaneous. Aleks's easygoing, laughing lunch companion had been replaced with a steely-eyed, tight-jawed man.

"Watch yourself, Lind. Dizzie isn't a pawn to be moved around a board. When—and if—she wants to be involved in running the Tremaine Corporation or any other company, that will be her choice. She doesn't factor into your schemes —or those of your employers. Stay away from her."

Convincing Dizzie to meet her grandparents was his primary mission, so staying away was going to be impossible. He'd prefer not to go up against Killian St. John, but he would if he had to.

"You'd think she would be glad to see the company that held her captive go down."

"You have no idea what she wants or doesn't want." St. John's tone was pure ice.

"Does she want to meet her grandparents?" Aleks changed the subject deliberately.

This time St. John's response was more measured. "She hasn't decided yet."

That wasn't a no. Which was more information than Aleks had before the lunch. "I need to meet with her," he said.

"I won't push her," St. John said. "She'll make up her mind in her own time. Dizzie doesn't owe you—or them—a damn thing."

Aleks took another bite of his meal, pondering the best way to deliver the next message. Ultimately, he realized that there wasn't one. "They won't stop," he said quietly, repeating the same message he'd given Portia. "It would be better for her to meet them on her terms."

St. John dropped all pretense of civility and glowered at Aleks. "Are they a threat to her?"

Aleks leaned back and spread his hands. "I believe that they truly want to meet her and they don't wish her any harm. But I'm afraid that they've never been rational about their daughter's death or anything to do with the Tremaines. Dizzie is their last tie to her. I can't predict what they'll do."

"Fuck!" St. John stood. "Damn Phillip Tremaine for his schemes and games and complete lack of morals."

He strode away from the table before Aleks had a chance to stand. He shifted to watch Killian leave and contemplated his options.

The waiter hurried over. "Mr. St. John said to enjoy lunch with his compliments." He gathered up St. John's unfinished meal and glass as he spoke.

Well, that solved that problem.

"Thank you, Michael." When the waiter disappeared, Aleks took St. John's seat.

Now that he had a wall to his back, his shoulders finally relaxed. Aleks returned to his lunch.

He honestly hadn't believed that St. John would sell any of his shares, but it would have made Aleks's life much easier. The Solveigs wouldn't take being thwarted well.

They were determined to end the Tremaine Corporation and take care of their granddaughter, no matter what.

CHAPTER 11

"AS FAR AS we are able to determine, the Solveig Consortium will not be able to infiltrate our computer systems. They've tried before—numerous times—and they've always failed," Tremaine's head of cybersecurity said, then glanced at the man standing next to him, as if waiting for confirmation.

The other man jerked his head in a nod. He'd been introduced as Mendez, one of the cybersecurity team. Portia knew that meant hackers. Ash Cutter, a freelance hacker who worked for her on occasion, probably knew him, had likely worked with him. Maybe she'd ask. And maybe—most likely—she wouldn't. She was still pissed about his role, however unintentional, in Tommy's death.

"Are you willing to bet the company on that?" she asked.

The department head swallowed hard but nodded. "Yes, ma'am, we are." His voice wavered. From the corner of her eye, Portia saw Mendez smirk.

"Something you want to share, Mr. Mendez?"

He started at the question and Portia barely hid her smile.

Mendez paused to consider his words. "No system is 100 percent secure." When his boss opened his mouth, Portia waved her hand to stop him. She wanted to hear what the hacker had to say.

"They did manage to gain access to Tremaine systems, but that was over ten years ago. They haven't come close since. Unless they're investing in better tech and a better team, they are unlikely to be successful." He paused then added, "I can look into that for you."

Portia studied him. If Ash had taught her anything about the hackers who worked for the company, it was that they were usually smart and were always working an angle. What was Mendez's? And did she care enough to worry about it right now?

"What would you need?"

He blinked, but responded quickly. "Access to external systems and no handler."

Ballsy. Very ballsy. She was willing to give him some leeway but not that much. "Access to external systems is granted." His boss sputtered and she turned her attention to him. He quieted immediately. "Make it happen. No handler is a no-go. As a compromise, I'll let an external party shadow you, with the understanding that I'll get a full report of your activities. Ash Cutter. I believe you know him."

"Yeah, we used to be on a team together. Until he worked for you." Mendez studied her. "That's fine."

As if she cared about his preferences. "Anything else?"

"No, ma'am," the cybersecurity head assured her.

"Good. Now what do you have for me?" Portia turned

her attention to the duo standing patiently next to the cybersecurity team.

"My competitive intelligence team reviewed and updated our profile on the Solveig Consortium last night. It's usually updated every six months as they aren't viewed as a high-threat competitor." The woman spoke in a firm, steady voice, never once indicating that she was thrown by either Portia's request or her presence.

"And?"

"I'd like my analyst to review the report for you if that's acceptable." When Portia nodded, the other woman took a step back while her colleague stepped forward.

Portia smiled, glad to see a team that worked well together, especially in contrast to the cybersecurity team.

"The Solveig Consortium has an active presence primarily in Europe and especially the Scandinavian countries. Their sales, their footprint, and their market share have remained steady in all the years we've been tracking them. At least until recently."

"What changed?" Portia asked, although she had a very good idea.

"The appearance of, uh, Ms. T—, I mean, Dizzie's appearance," the analyst finally confirmed.

"What have they done?"

Portia listened intently as the analyst outlined acquisitions, divestitures, and other sneaky moves the company had been making.

"What's your interpretation of their actions?"

The analyst took a deep breath and straightened. "They're gearing up for something big. They have a lot of cash on hand and I think they either plan on making a very big purchase or they're going to war."

Dammit.

That was Portia's take as well. She had no doubts about who they were coming after.

Phillip Tremaine had spent his life being a total asshole and now she was stuck with the consequences.

"What kind of timeline are we looking at?"

Aleks's presence in the city indicated that it could be sooner rather than later. But what if a visit from Dizzie would slow them down? Would she agree for the sake of the company? If she were in Dizzie's shoes, Portia might just say fuck the whole lot of them.

"There's really no way to know for sure," the analyst hedged. "But based on other takeovers, some hostile, some not, that we've tracked, we're talking weeks, not months."

Sonofabitch. The news just got better and better.

Portia wanted to ask if they could win but stopped herself. That was a question she was supposed to know the answer to.

Could they though? She had no fucking clue. She'd spent the last few months dragging the company out of the mess her father had made. When she wasn't doing that, she'd been clawing her way out of grief.

Add in the number of senior management she'd had to cut loose because they were as corrupt as her father and the company was facing a potential corporate showdown with untrained staff and a dearth of trustworthy people.

This sucked. A lot.

If the Solveig Consortium wanted a fight, she'd give them one. She just wished she knew what that looked like.

"What does our—" Portia's question was cut off by the opening of her office door.

"We need to talk, Portia."

She stared as Killian strode into her office, more formally dressed than she had seen him recently.

Her assistant followed him into the room. "I'm sorry, Ms. Tremaine. I told him you were in a meeting, but he walked right by me."

Portia stood, determined to control the chaos in her office. "Killian, we can talk after this meeting."

He shook his head. "This can't wait."

She drew herself up to her full height. How dare he presume to determine what could or couldn't wait.

He met her gaze. "Please. We have a problem."

The sincerity in his eyes and the gravity of his tone won her over. "Very well. You can stay."

She shifted her attention back to her employees. "Thank you for your time. Send me your reports and analysis and be prepared for more questions." She dismissed them with a nod.

They filed out of her office without another word, but her assistant lingered.

"You can go, Melanie. Thank you." It was a struggle not to let her exasperation show. She really needed to get a new assistant. That hadn't been a priority before. Maybe it should be now.

Portia wasn't sure if she imagined a sneer cross her assistant's face before she turned and left the office.

After the door clicked shut, Portia offered Killian a seat.

"This better be good, Killian."

"It isn't, Portia. It's potentially very bad."

CHAPTER 12

PORTIA STARED at the man who'd been her best friend from childhood. They hadn't been as close since the bombing—and maybe they never would be again—but she trusted him when it came to the business.

"What's bad?" She sat behind her desk and waited.

Killian took the visitor's chair. "Aleksander Lind from the Solveig Consortium called me last night asking for a meeting today." He tilted his head and looked at her. "You've met, right?"

Portia caught her breath. That was a very mild word for her encounters with Aleks. She got her mind out of the bedroom and back on the company.

Truth be told, she hadn't expected the end run, but maybe she should have. Ridiculously, it hurt that he was talking to other people about the Tremaine Corporation. "Yes, we've met. He's the one who requested the meeting with Dizzie. Is that why he contacted you?"

Killian shook his head. He leaned forward, elbows braced on his knees. "He was surprisingly circumspect about Dizzie. His goal was something else." He looked her straight in the eye. "He wanted my shares."

Portia gasped. "Your shares?"

"Yes. And he offered a pretty penny for them. A few times more than their worth."

She swallowed hard. This couldn't be happening. "You told him no, didn't you?"

Her hands clenched. What would she do if Killian had agreed to sell? His family was one of the original backers of the company. Their stock ownership was second only to hers. Losing that much control to Solveig . . . Her stomach turned.

"I told him no," Killian assured her, "but I wasn't the first investor that he'd approached."

"What?" Portia stared at him in horror. "How do you know?"

Killian sat up, looking a bit abashed. "A few of them called me after their meetings with Lind. Apparently, the offers he's making are very tempting. Especially when he let slip to a few that the company would be worth significantly less in the future."

"What the fuck is that supposed to mean?" But she knew. Just as the analyst had predicted, the Solveig Consortium was either buying something big or going to war. Why not both?

"This is a disaster." Unable to sit still, Portia lunged to her feet. She paced a few feet away, then whirled to face Killian. "Why did they contact you after the meetings and not me?"

"We've worked together on the board. And I was the point of contact for information about the company while you were in mourning."

In mourning. What a nice way to say that she'd been

wrecked by grief. The only thing getting her out of bed those first days had been her driving need for revenge. After, when Dizzie had suddenly become untouchable, running the company and cleaning up the mess her father had left had kept her focused and halfway sane. Yet no one had come to her with their problems.

"It's because I'm a woman, isn't it?" Despite the fact that she'd worked at the company since she was a teenager and worked her way up, the amount of sexism and pushback she'd encountered since she'd taken over the company had been insane and infuriating.

Killian stood and ambled over to the window. He tucked his hands in his pockets and studied the view for a moment. He turned back to Portia and leaned against the glass, arms crossed over his chest.

"No," he said after a long pause. "It's the Ice Queen thing. The way you lean into it." She opened her mouth to argue, to defend herself, but he continued. "I know why you started it. And I know that you think it protects you. But I think it's doing more harm than good right now, Portia. It scares people off."

Not all people, she wanted to argue. It hadn't scared off Tommy. Or Aleks, she had to admit. He'd approached her at the bar after she'd delivered a particularly bruising setdown to unwanted company.

"What do you suggest I do, Killian? Get all touchy-feely with the investors? My employees? I've got a company to run. I don't have time for that." She rubbed her eyes. Why was the answer always to tone herself down?

"You need to make time, Portia, or you're going to lose the company. The consortium is gunning for you because your father was an asshole. If you turn into him, you might as well give up the Tremaine Corporation now."

His words stung. She was nothing like her father. "Is that a threat? Do as you say or you sell your shares? You'll help them dismantle the company?"

She regretted her words as soon as they left her mouth. Her fear had gotten the best of her and she'd lashed out at her best friend. Again. If he decided he'd had enough, she wouldn't blame him. But she'd fight him tooth and nail if he tried to sell his shares to anyone but her.

"I'll be honest, Portia. If Dizzie wanted me to dismantle this company brick by brick, I'd do it for her. This company has ruined too many lives. Hers, yours, Tommy's. But she doesn't, so I'll help you fight for it. What I won't do is stand by and watch you turn into a monster like your father. I can't. So please, *please*, don't ask that of me."

Portia stared at him, speechless. Is that really what he thought of her? That she was a monster like her father?

When she didn't respond, he sighed. "I'll run interference with the other investors and keep them from selling. But you need to solve this Solveig problem before they make a move that sticks."

With that, he left his post by the window and crossed swiftly to the front door. He turned to look back at her. "Take care of yourself, Portia." He gave her a sad smile and left her office.

"Fuck you, Killian," she whispered to the empty room. "I'm not a goddamned monster. I'm not."

CHAPTER 13

PORTIA'S FEET hit the pavement with angry strikes. Her entire afternoon had gone to shit. After Killian's bombshell, she'd thrown herself into the business of running the Tremaine Corporation. That had lasted all of thirty minutes. That was when she'd received the analysts' reports.

The Solveig Consortium was shaping up to be a much bigger problem than anyone had expected. They'd flown under the radar because no one had considered them a threat. Their hacks had failed. Their corporate espionage had been a joke.

Yet here they were, becoming the latest threat to her control of the company.

Fuck that. She'd fight them every step of the way. Starting with their representative in *her* city. Aleksander Lind.

Portia slowed to a quick walk as she entered the hotel and crossed the lobby. She knew exactly where she was going this time.

Knowing the elevator would be interminably slow, she took the stairs, running up them with ease.

Minutes later she stood in front of Alek's hotel room. She pounded on the door.

No response. Raising her hand to knock again, it suddenly—finally—opened.

"Portia?" The surprise and pleasure in Aleks's voice warmed her, but she ruthlessly forced the soft feelings down. That wasn't what she was here for.

She pushed past him into the suite, ignoring the tingle of electricity that raced through her where they touched.

"Please, come in." She caught the humor in his voice as he closed the door. "I didn't expect to see you tonight."

Her laugh was harsh. "I'm sure you didn't. You've been too busy trying to steal my company out from under me."

Aleks shrugged and she reminded herself not to be distracted by his shifting muscles under the t-shirt he wore. "I told you I was in town on business."

"You *said* your employers wanted to meet Dizzie," she reminded him.

His lips curled into a faint smile. "I believe I also mentioned that they were looking to expand into the city."

"But you didn't say that they planned on buying *my* company for that expansion." She knew her argument was ridiculous, but it felt so good to get it out. To have someone to yell at, someone to fight with.

Even Tommy hadn't fought with her. He'd teased and cajoled and charmed her out of her anger, but he'd never fought with her.

Aleks, though. She was sure he'd fight back, not that she understood why that should matter.

She couldn't yell at her employees, even when they brought her bad news or annoyed her.

She didn't have friends she could vent to. Besides, complaining made her sound like a spoiled little rich girl.

"You can't be that naive," he drawled in that accent of his. "I tried to warn you. My employers hate everything about the Tremaine Corporation. If they could, they'd burn it to the ground in a heartbeat."

"They sound like Killian," she muttered.

His brow rose. "Oh? I was under the impression that he wouldn't sell."

Sure he was laughing at her, she turned and wandered deeper into the suite. It really was a nice hotel. Beautifully decorated in blues and greens and more neutral colors that evoked the natural beauty of Puget Sound. Art—tastefully abstract but with a hint of the avant-garde that encouraged you to look closer—dotted the walls.

"Please sit." Aleks had come alongside her and gestured to the sitting room.

Too agitated to sit, she continued to prowl around the room. She whirled around to face him. "You won't get my company. There is no way the Solveigs will get their grubby hands on my business. You should tell your employers that and go back to where you came from."

The smile that blossomed on his lips took her breath away. She could only describe his expression as delighted.

And it was directed at *her*.

Warmth pooled in her belly. No one had ever looked at her like that. Not even Tommy. He'd looked at her with love and kindness and friendship and passion. But never as if she just delighted him.

In that moment, she understood that Aleks was dangerous to more than just the Tremaine Corporation.

"Did you fuck me as part of the job?" The words

slipped out. Her stomach roiled at the thought, but she had to know. *Had to.*

"No." His response was steady and strong.

Was that relief or disbelief that she felt? Still not satisfied, she lashed out. "Then you must be really bad at your job, because there was no way you didn't know who I was."

He took a step closer, his smile sad. "Oh, I knew who you were. I knew everything about you. But until that moment, you were just a name, a face, in a dossier."

Her laugh was harsh. "Bullshit. You knew nothing about me. It was all some scheme to get closer to me for your employers."

"Oh, Portia." The way he said her name made her shiver. "How wrong you are. That night at Razor Jack's? Almost everything I told you was true. I am in town for business. I had just arrived. I was restless from my flight and I was curious about the bar that you'd become a regular at."

She sucked in a breath. Did her own people even know she was a regular at Razor Jack's?

"My curiosity got the best of me. I wanted a drink, so I decided to check it out. I never imagined that you would be there. Our analysts hadn't figured out your schedule yet."

Okay, that was both reassuring and creepy.

He stepped closer. "Then I watched you shoot that guy down." Real amusement colored his words. "That's when I knew you were more than just a dossier—and that we didn't know a damn thing about you."

His words sent shivers coursing through her. Why? Why did this man of all people affect her like this?

Unnerved by the feelings he stirred up, she countered, "You still know nothing about me." That was the truth.

Wasn't it?

"That's not true." His smile was soft, kind. He closed the distance between them, stopping just within arm's reach. "I know that if I trace my finger just up your jaw here, you'll give a breathy little sigh."

He suited action to words, his touch a whisper along her jaw and behind her ear.

Her breath caught.

See, he was wrong, she hadn't sighed.

His chuckle was deep and warm and she fought the sensations it aroused.

"When I cup the back of your head and thread my fingers into your hair, you relax into my touch."

He was wrong, dammit. He had to be. But when his hand cupped her head gently, she wanted to sink against him.

"And when I kiss you right here," he whispered, his breath feathering over the sensitive skin by her ear, "you'll melt into me."

His lips were soft and warm against her skin. She shivered and leaned into him, seeking his warmth, his touch, his—

"No." She put her hands against his chest and pushed away. If her knees wobbled a little, well, that was to be expected. She'd recently run up several flights of stairs.

He released her immediately, his smile fading.

"It's just physical," she argued. Was she trying to convince him or herself?

"It's more than physical, Portia. You felt it too. I've never clicked with someone that quickly. That deeply. Tell me you have."

"I was married!" She and Tommy had been compatible. Had been happy.

"To your childhood sweetheart. Your compatibility had years and years to grow. This isn't the same," he growled.

"It's just physical," she repeated.

The light in his eyes faded and his expression smoothed out. Watching him withdraw tore at something deep inside her.

"If that's what you need to believe." He stepped back.

Her arm shot out to grab his shirt. He stiffened and glanced down at her hold. "What are you doing, Portia?"

"I don't know." Running on pure instinct, she tightened her grip and tugged him closer.

He resisted for a moment, but when momentum brought their bodies together, his strength kept them from tumbling to the floor.

Her arms snaked around his neck. One hand cupped his head as he had hers. His hair was short and soft against her fingers. She remembered weaving her fingers through it that night when he'd kissed his way down her body.

Heat flooded her cheeks and pooled between her legs. Embarrassed and aroused, she tugged his head down to kiss him.

"Are you sure?" he whispered against her lips. "Don't toy with me. Please."

"I'm sure," she murmured back. "I don't know what this is, but I'm not toying with you." The last bit of distance between them disappeared as she pressed her lips to his.

She nibbled at his lips. His resulting groan sent shivers through her body.

When she nipped at his lower lip, his mouth opened and she took full advantage. Her lips slanted over his and her tongue darted inside to tangle with his.

His hands were warm against her back. One inched

under the hem of her running shirt. His fingertips teased along the sensitive skin of her lower back.

One particularly delicate caress tickled and she gasped and arched into him. The move pressed her breasts into his chest.

His hands slid down her back to cup her butt and she practically purred. His fingers curled into the taut muscle compressed by her pants and he lifted her.

"Wow," she murmured. Her legs curled around his hips and her arms tightened around his neck. Then they were moving.

Portia didn't care where he was taking her. She only wanted more. More kisses. More of his strength pressed against her.

She didn't know how they made it to the couch without him running into anything, but they did. His hands shifted to the backs of her thighs and she released her legs from behind his back. He lowered them down to the sofa.

Her knees bracketed his and sank into the soft cushions. The position aligned her center with his hard length.

Remembering how he had felt inside her, she rocked against him. Her running tights were skintight, a barely-there barrier between them.

His hands cupped her ass again, presser her closer to his erection. Aleks tore his mouth from hers. She moaned in frustration.

His responding chuckle was sin personified. He nibbled along her jawline, then dragged his tongue over the tendons in her neck.

Her fingers curled into his shoulders and she arched back, giving him access to the sensitive skin of her neck.

He pressed kisses along her clavicle and then to the bare

skin above her top. Her head dropped back in pleasure and her brain short-circuited.

He raised one hand and gently cupped her right breast. His thumb brushed over her nipple again and again, stimulating it to a stiff peak. Her breasts pressed against—strained against—the compression of her sports bra and she whimpered.

"You okay?" His words fluttered over damp skin, pebbling her skin with goosebumps.

"Uh-huh." How was she supposed to answer when he wasn't kissing her any longer?

Trusting him to hold her in place, she released her grip on his shoulders and instead tightened her grip on his shirt. Gathering up the fabric by the handful, she bared his whole back.

He lifted his head from her chest and reached one hand behind his neck to grab the material. In one smooth move, he pulled his shirt up and over his head. Her body quivered when he removed it completely.

The man was built. Firm chest muscles dusted lightly with hair that narrowed to a thin trail over rock-hard abs.

Portia hummed in approval and leaned into him again. Her lips met the curve of his neck and she inhaled. He smelled good. Like man and sweat and a hint of cologne or deodorant. Whatever it was, he smelled so good. She buried her face against his neck.

His hands skimmed up her sides, lifting her shirt as they moved. Echoing his earlier move, she sat up and let him free her from the fabric.

Aleks's gaze dropped to her newly revealed flesh. Heat flared in his eyes. "You're so fucking beautiful," he growled. His hands cupped and molded her breasts.

His mouth dropped to her cleavage, made more

plentiful by her bra. He pressed open-mouthed kisses against her skin while his thumbs teased over her nipples.

She wanted him closer. Skin to skin. But there was no sexy way out of her sports bra. Dammit!

Frustrated and turned on, she was trying to figure out how to get out of her damn bra when his phone rang.

"Ignore it," she whispered, then nipped his earlobe.

The phone trilled again. And again.

"I can't," he finally gasped. "It's work."

Work. For the Solveigs.

His words were as effective at dousing her ardor as cold water.

"I've got to go." She wiggled off his lap, suddenly grateful for the tight spandex that still covered her breasts.

She ducked to grab her shirt, cursing his hotel room—cursing him—for his ability to steal her common sense and make her clothes fall off.

"Portia." He reached for her hand but she stepped back.

His gaze bounced between her and his phone, which had stopped ringing for a moment, then started right back up again.

"Duty calls." She pulled on her shirt, grateful it hid her face for a moment. She didn't want him to see her disappointment.

The interruption served as a reminder that she couldn't—shouldn't—repeat the mistake of their earlier night. She had too much to focus on—the never-ending problems her father left behind, keeping the company moving forward, and now the threat posed by the Solveig Consortium—to get involved with anyone. Especially not someone from enemy number one.

Ignoring the fact that she had appeared unannounced at his hotel room, Portia said, "Please set up an appointment with my assistant the next time you want to meet." She looked past Aleks's shoulder as she spoke. She needed distance and she needed it now.

"Portia," he said again, just loud enough to hear over the phone. "Please stay. We can talk about this."

As much as she would like to know what he and his employers spoke about, there was no way she was rehashing this with him.

All she wanted was to get home and go to bed. And hope that tomorrow was a better day.

"Good night, Mr. Lind." She turned and walked to the door like a queen.

CHAPTER 14

ALEKS STARED AT THE DOOR, his spinning thoughts nearly drowning out the ringing phone.

Dammit! He just needed a minute to focus. Why couldn't they leave a message and let him call back?

He grimaced. He knew why. The Solveigs were used to getting their way—as the owners of the company, no one ever told them no. Given that everyone here in Seattle had turned down their offers, this conversation was going to be fucking delightful. He wished, not for the first time, that he could just quit this job. But where would he go? When his implant had been classified as a failure, the Solveigs had kept him employed. They could have easily sent him to work in the factories instead.

The ringing stopped for one blessed moment of silence before starting up again.

Aleks grabbed his shirt and pulled it on. It was time to man up and deal with his employers. He counted to ten, focusing his thoughts as best he could, before picking up the phone. "Yes?"

The expected tirade started immediately. "Where have

you been? Why didn't you answer immediately? You're expected to report in regularly." Mr. and Mrs. Solveig spoke over each other, nothing new.

He dropped onto the sofa as the words washed over him. "My apologies. I was . . . indisposed." The Solveigs' heads would explode if he admitted to having been making out with Portia Tremaine.

"Hmmph" was Mrs. Solveig's only response. Aleks's employers didn't do sympathy. At least, not for the hired help.

"How were the meetings? How many investors have agreed to sell their shares?" Mr. Solveig asked eagerly.

This was the part he'd been dreading. "No one is willing to sell." He spoke cautiously, then held the phone away from his ear while they threw question after question at him.

"Turn on the camera," Mrs. Solveig demanded.

Smoothing his hand over his hair, he prayed that Portia hadn't left any marks. No, that wasn't right. He'd love it if she marked him. But for this call, he had to hope that they weren't visible. Aleks shoved all thoughts of Portia away. He'd need all his wits about him to navigate this conversation.

Aleks turned on the camera feature and his employers filled the screen. In their late sixties, both had gone gray. Mrs. Solveig kept her hair in a short, sleek style that might have made her look younger if not for her perpetually sour expression. In contrast, Mr. Solveig was rounder, with rosy cheeks and a salt-and-pepper beard, but his expression was grave.

"What do you mean, they won't sell their shares? Did you point out how much over market value we're offering?"

"Yes, ma'am. I made that point several times. I think one

or two may have been intrigued, but no one took me up on the offer."

"Then you must have made a mistake," Mrs. Solveig said.

Aleks bit back his response. Arguing with them never went well. "I met with Killian St. John today. He informed me that the other shareholders wouldn't sell because they fear the Tremaine family."

"This man, this coward—he's the one who is squiring our granddaughter around?" Mr. Solveig asked.

Aleks nodded.

"He's afraid of the Tremaine family?"

Aleks paused, considering everything St. John had told him. "No, he's not afraid of the Tremaines. I believe he's loyal to them. To Portia, at least."

"Portia?" Mrs. Solveig asked.

Fuck. He'd slipped up. "Loyal to Portia Tremaine, not Phillip Tremaine," he corrected quickly.

"Phillip Tremaine is dead."

It would solve a great many problems if that was true, but no one had been able to prove it. "Presumed dead, according to the people I've spoken to."

Mr. Solveig waved his caution away. "That bastard must be dead. His daughter is the only thing standing between Dizzie and her rightful place at the head of the company."

He and his wife shared a long look, communicating without words the way some longtime couples could. There was a gleam in their eyes that made the hackles on Aleks's neck stand up.

"All we have to do," they said in unison, "is eliminate Portia Tremaine."

His blood froze. They couldn't have just . . . Aleks stared at the Solveigs. "What?"

"Removing Portia Tremaine from the picture will destabilize the Tremaine Corporation. No company can survive the loss of two CEOs in such quick succession. With her out of the way, our granddaughter will be able to step into the CEO position."

There were so many layers to their plan that he could barely process them all. His brain latched onto the most obvious question. "Have you heard something to indicate that Dizzie wants to be CEO?"

Mrs. Solveig pinned him with a sharp gaze. "Does it matter?"

Aleks shook his head. "When you say eliminate P—, Ms. Tremaine, what do you mean?"

"Remove her from the CEO position by whatever means necessary."

His gut churned. Sure, he solved problems for them, but they usually didn't outright ask him to murder people.

Snuffing out the light that was Portia Tremaine? He didn't think he could do it, but there was no way he could admit that.

His brain started to buzz. *Fuck. Not now.* He raised his hand to his head.

"Is there a problem, Aleks?"

He winced and rubbed his temple. "No, no problem. My head is spinning with options." All of them bad.

They both stared at him for a long moment. "We trust you'll choose the right one."

"Of course." Surely among all the options, there was one that didn't involve killing Portia.

"Excellent. Once that is accomplished and Dizzie is at the head the company, we'll begin the process of assimilating Tremaine into Solveig Consortium. Within the year, there should be no trace of the Tremaine Corporation —or family—left."

Holy. Shit.

The Solveigs could hold their own in the backstabbing world of the multinational corporations, something they'd managed for decades, but this was unexpected. Honestly, he hadn't thought they had it in them.

If only he'd been right.

Aleks swallowed hard. He couldn't show any doubt. If he did, they could easily pull him off this task and replace him with someone who would have no compunctions about taking care of Portia.

"Timeline?" he asked.

Mr. Solveig looked at his wife. Whatever unspoken conversation they had ended with her pinched smile and sharp nod. "Sooner is better than later," he said.

Well, that was no help. Aleks considered his words carefully. "It will take time if you don't want this traced back to you."

"I don't care," Mrs. Solveig snarled. "They must pay for taking our daughter from us."

Mr. Solveig placed his hand over hers, a loving gesture Aleks had witnessed countless times before. Tonight was the first time it chilled his blood.

Who were these people? Was the loss of their daughter driving them to these new depths? Or had he just been blinded by gratitude when they gave him a purpose after his dreams had been ripped away?

"I've been seen with Portia Tremaine and would be the obvious suspect. St. John and the other investors could link any action to the consortium." Aleks tried to thread the needle, without outright countering their orders.

Another one of those silent, married-people conversations. "An accident would be better. Our granddaughter will be able to take over more easily," Mrs. Solveig said.

"But don't make us wait too long, Aleks. Justice has been egregiously delayed," her husband added.

"Of course." Aleks nodded.

"We're counting on you, Aleks. Don't let us down." With that, the screen went dark.

He dropped his phone next to him on the couch and grabbed his head with both hands. Once those words would have filled him with pride. Tonight, they sounded like a threat.

He'd known that his employers had unresolved issues with Phillip Tremaine. Anyone who worked for the Solveig Consortium knew that they held him responsible for their daughter's death. Aleks knew they wanted revenge—he'd even hinted at it with Portia and St. John. But he'd never suspected that they would want an-eye-for-an-eye revenge.

Aleks had his instructions. His brain had already started working on the problem of eliminating Portia. Imagining the vibrant woman who was slowly coming back to life dead turned his stomach.

There had to be a way to subvert his orders. To find it, he would need to study every possible option. His head already hurt from using that much processing power . . . and it was only going to get worse.

Aleks lay on his back and closed his eyes, praying that he could find another way.

CHAPTER 15

WHEN HER INTERCOM BUZZED, Portia was grateful for the interruption. She'd been staring blankly at her computer screen for—she glanced at her watch and blanched when she saw it was almost lunch time. She'd been staring at the screen for almost three hours and she hadn't gotten a thing done.

She blamed Aleks. No, that wasn't quite fair. She blamed the Solveig Consortium. They'd sent Aleks to Seattle to cause problems and he'd certainly done his job. She'd left his hotel suite angry and turned on. Running an additional hour hadn't settled her nerves any and she'd tossed and turned all night. Here she was the next morning, not getting a thing done. At this rate, she'd be handing the company over to them.

She laughed. No, hell would freeze over before that happened.

"Yes?"

"Ms. Tremaine, your, um, your sss—" There was a crackle of sound and her assistant's voice broke off.

Portia caught the faint murmur of voices on the other

end. Lips pursed, she glared at the intercom. "Yes?" she repeated, annoyance coloring her voice.

"Um, Ms. Dizzie is here to see you, Ms. Tremaine."

Of course she was. Portia dropped her head to her desk. What she wouldn't give for a day without problems.

"Um, Ms. Tremaine?" Her assistant sounded flustered.

Portia straightened and smiled. It was nice to at least have someone fear her like they used to. God, she was such a bitch.

She swiveled to stare out the windows. It had been cold this morning when she arrived, but at least the sun was shining now. Portia took a moment to center herself. Dealing with Dizzie dredged up a lot of intense emotions. Grief. Anger. A driving need for revenge.

A bitter laugh escaped. That one she had at least mostly dealt with.

Pulling her armor into place, she spoke to her assistant. "Send her in."

Her office door whispered open and Portia's shoulders tensed.

"You were mean to your assistant," Dizzie greeted her.

"She's practically incompetent." Portia released her tense shoulders with a subtle shrug. "To what do I owe this visit?"

Rather than waiting by Portia's desk, Dizzie crossed to the small sitting area in the corner of the two walls of windows. Portia gritted her teeth. She'd created that alcove as a sanctuary, where she could take a break. Now Dizzie just waltzed in like she had a right to be there.

If this was what having a sister was like, Portia wanted none of it.

"Please have a seat." Her voice oozed sarcasm. "Can I get you anything?"

Dizzie met her gaze with a wide grin and took a seat on the loveseat, leaving Portia the wingback chair. Obviously, she intended to get under Portia's skin. "Coffee would be great, thank you."

As tempting as it was to send Dizzie away, she obviously wanted something. The last thing Portia needed was another surprise, so she'd wait the other woman out.

Gritting her teeth, Portia accepted her request. "Coffee for two, Melanie. Please." The last thing she needed was Dizzie to take another dig.

Awkward silence filled the office while they waited for the requested coffee. Portia barely hid her sigh of relief when, a few minutes later, Melanie entered the room with a tray. "Over there." Portia pointed toward the seating area.

Though her assistant did as directed, the tray and its contents rattled furiously as she crossed the room. The racket only stopped when she set the tray on the low table between the seats.

"Thank you. That will be all."

Melanie practically raced out the office. Portia shook her head. She *really* needed a new assistant.

"You wanted coffee. Help yourself." She crossed the room and waved at the tray. Dizzie looked at the cups and her with suspicion, then took one.

Sunlight filtered through the windows and warmed Portia's little corner of sanctuary. Perching on the edge of the chair, she took her time fixing her coffee and let the silence between them grow. Dizzie obviously wanted something. Portia intended to make her work for it.

Once she was satisfied with her concoction, she settled back in her seat. Portia brought her cup close to her nose, closed her eyes, and inhaled the rich nutty scent.

Tommy had tried to teach her to savor the moment, but

the lesson hadn't stuck very well. There was always too much work to be done. But this little moment, this ritual, it had been theirs. Now that he was gone, it made her feel close to him.

A lump formed in her throat. She swallowed hard to clear it, then took another deep breath. She followed that with her first sip, letting the flavors roll over her tongue. Caramel. Sugar. Spice. Hot, with just a hint of bitter. Perfect.

She opened her eyes to find Dizzie staring at her with an expression that was a cross between confused and freaked out.

"What were you doing just now?"

Portia smiled on the inside. Dizzie definitely sounded disconcerted. "Enjoying my coffee." Another sip while Portia gazed out the window over Dizzie's head.

The silence between them stretched awkwardly until Dizzie said, "You're probably wondering why I'm here."

"Yes, that had crossed my mind. Especially since you raced out of here the other day."

A flush tinged Dizzie's cheeks, but she didn't look away. Portia respected that.

"I was overwhelmed." Now it was her turn to sip her coffee. "Going from no family to grandparents was a lot."

Did she even understand how that sounded? Portia raised her cup to her lips to hide her expression. Dizzie had gained family, while Portia had lost hers. "Are you going to meet them?" She forced the question out.

"I . . . think so." Dizzie tapped her nails against the cup. "Will you meet them with me?"

"What?" That was the last thing she'd expected. Portia didn't—couldn't—get past her shock to answer. "What about Killian?"

There was a long pause. "He'd be there if I asked. He *wants* to be there. I need to do this by myself."

Portia lowered her cup to the table. "If you want to do this alone, why are you asking me to go with you?"

Dizzie blew out an exasperated breath, then flopped gracelessly against the back of the couch. Portia bit her tongue not to say something snarky about Dizzie's upbringing.

"Why do you need me, exactly?" Portia prompted her.

"Killian would protect me." Dizzie's expression was pensive. "It's his first reaction, even when he isn't aware of it."

Having experienced Killian's protective instincts for Dizzie firsthand, Portia rolled her eyes. "That's a bad thing?"

Dizzie shook her head and smiled. "Not usually. I'm trying to temper that habit." Her blue-eyed gaze was so like what Portia saw in the mirror every day it almost made her squirm. Almost. "I know *you* won't protect me."

"True." Portia laughed.

"But," Dizzie continued, "you also won't let the Solveig Consortium take advantage of me in any way that would affect the company."

Dizzie's insight surprised Portia. "Also true. But why would you care? My understanding is that you were hellbent on buying your freedom not that long ago."

"Do you not see what's wrong with that sentence? The *buying* my freedom part?"

A flash of guilt rolled over Portia. Yes, that was a problem. One of many on the running list in her head called *Too Many Problems, Not Enough Time.* "Well, you have your freedom now." And then some. "Why wouldn't you want the Solveig Consortium to screw us?"

"Just because one side of my DNA sucks doesn't mean I'm going to automatically side with the other."

Portia could only stare at her. "Why not? You hate the Tremaines."

Dizzie's gaze was locked on a spot over Portia's head. "I don't. Not really."

"Riiiight."

Dizzie huffed out a breath. "Okay, fine. I hate your dad. My dad? Our dad?" She paused and pursed her lips. "Whatever I should call him, yes, I hate him. I hate that he kept me around for spare parts like you would my motorcycle. But the rest of the company . . . it's fine, I guess. I had a hell of a good time running wild in the basement of this building. Something that I don't think I would have had if I'd grown up with you."

She looked Portia in the eye. "If I grew up with you, I hope I would've turned out to be more like me than you, but we'll never know."

Her words cut in ways that Portia had never imagined. "What's wrong with being me?" *Shit.* She hadn't meant to say that out loud.

Dizzie's earthy laugh was another reminder of how different they were. "Nothing. You're exactly what you were raised to be, a pretty, corporate elite."

Her comment poked at insecurities Portia had believed were long buried and she lashed out with a cold smile and cruel words. "Aw, is baby sister jealous that I was the wanted daughter and you weren't?"

Dizzie blanched, but she didn't fold. Though she'd never admit it, Portia admired that about her.

"I know why you do that," Dizzie said. "Killian has told me stories about your childhood."

The blood drained from Portia's face and her stomach

churned. She'd thought Killian was her friend. Once again, he'd chosen Dizzie over her. "What stories?"

Dizzie leaned forward and Portia was sure she was going to twist the knife. Instead, she reached out and placed her hand over Portia's.

Portia jerked it back and stared at Dizzie. There was no viciousness there, only understanding, which was much, *much* worse.

"He didn't betray any confidences," Dizzie said quietly. "I swear. He only said you had a tough time after your mom died. That's it."

Tears welled in Portia's eyes at the reminder. She held them back through years of practice and sheer force of will. Picking up her coffee, she took a sip to moisten her throat. Otherwise, she might not be able to speak. And she would *not* show weakness in front of Dizzie, no matter what.

"I'll attend the meeting with you." It wasn't because Dizzie had been nice to her. There was no question of Portia's attendance; she had a company to protect.

"Thank you." Dizzie leaned back.

Iron will was the only way Portia met the other woman's gaze. "Shall I set up the meeting or do you want to?" Her voice was steady and tear-free when she spoke.

"I'd like you to. I don't want to deal with them until I have to," Dizzie admitted.

"I'll set it up with their representative and let you know." The thought of talking to Aleks again had a surprising and soothing effect on her ragged emotions.

Had Dizzie noticed? There was a gleam in her eye. "Thank you. My calendar is current and my assistant can answer any questions."

Portia's lips quirked into a smile. Dizzie sounded so corporate, although Portia knew it was mostly for show.

Dizzie could fit into this world now—being with Killian had given her confidence and practice—but Portia was sure she'd rather be anywhere else.

"Perfect. Was there anything else?" Portia hoped there wasn't. She needed time to rebuild her walls.

"No. Thank you for the coffee and for seeing me without an appointment."

Portia inclined her head. "You're welcome." She wouldn't—couldn't—say it was a pleasure. But it also wasn't the worst interaction they'd had.

Taking her cue from Dizzie's body language, Portia stood at the same time her sister did. It was a move she used to disconcert people and she needed Dizzie a little off-balance. She needed that little win.

Neither woman said another word as Portia escorted her to the office door. It wasn't until she was back at her desk and had asked her assistant to hold her calls that Portia allowed herself to slump into her chair.

CHAPTER 16

ALEKS HUNG up the phone and sat back in the desk chair in his suite. He'd done it. He'd set up a meeting for the Solveigs with their long-lost granddaughter. Yet, instead of the elation of a job well done, he felt . . . unmoored.

Portia's call had sent a rush of adrenaline through his system, revving up his body while at the same time focusing his usually overactive brain. He wouldn't say that she calmed him, but she definitely challenged him.

That right there was the problem.

He didn't know what to do about his burgeoning relationship with Portia. To feel anything beyond satisfaction for doing his job was a clear conflict of interest. He should report it to his employers, but they'd surely reassign him. Probably somewhere far, far away.

So he couldn't. Wouldn't. He would be here through the bitter end. If that meant he offered comfort to Portia when the Consortium brought the Tremaine Corporation to its knees . . .

His brain took that moment to unhelpfully remind him that the Solveigs wanted Portia to be part of that downfall. He surged up from the chair and began to pace. He'd considered the Solveigs' plan from all angles last night. He couldn't see a way this all ended without the Tremaine Corporation gone, even if he managed to protect Portia.

When they destroyed the company, the last person she would turn to for solace would be the man responsible for its destruction. She wouldn't forget—and probably wouldn't forgive—his role. "You're a fucking idiot, Aleks."

Clenching and unclenching his hands, he focused on his breath, calming his brain, stopping the spiral into a future he could never have. He had a job to do and it wasn't to moon over Portia Tremaine. His employers harbored very clear—and valid—ill feelings toward the Tremaine Corporation.

When the first news reports about Dizzie's identity had aired, Mrs. Solveig had burst into tears. Mr. Solveig, who was much less emotional than his wife, had dispatched an operative to Seattle to verify the reports.

Anna Solveig had died more than twenty years ago. Her story was whispered in the halls of the Solveig Consortium. Barely twenty-one, she'd left her family home and had followed Phillip Tremaine back to Seattle. The Solveigs had begged and pleaded with their daughter to return, but she'd claimed it was "true love" and had stopped taking their calls.

After months and months of silence, they'd received her ashes accompanied by a sterile note from a morgue technician, citing the DNA match and expressing rote condolences.

They'd blamed Phillip Tremaine for her death but had been unable to gather proof. Over the next two decades, their desire for revenge had grown. They'd tried, unsuccessfully, to bring the company down several times over the years.

The news that Anna had borne a child before her death had been welcome news. Terrible, wondrous, welcome news.

And in the eyes of Mr. and Mrs. Solveig, it had sealed Phillip Tremaine's fate. In the face of his disappearance, their focus had shifted to Portia. If Phillip Tremaine wasn't available, they would gladly take their revenge on his daughter.

That was why they'd sent him to Seattle. To start the timer on the last days of the Tremaine Corporation.

Aleks hissed out a long breath. He had his own reason to hold a grudge against the company, and it had seemed like an easy assignment at the start. But nothing was going according to plan.

He hadn't expected Dizzie to drag her feet about meeting her grandparents. What orphan would turn down the appearance of rich grandparents?

Nothing about this job made sense. Especially not his sudden and intense reaction to Portia. His employers would be horrified if they knew the pull she had on him. They'd chalk it up to the failed experiment that left his brain a mess and he'd need to prove—again—that his new thought patterns didn't affect his job.

So . . . he'd keep them from finding out. Aleks held that thought in the forefront of his mind and focused on it. It was a solvable problem—most easily by not mentioning it— but it gave his unruly neurons something to do while he made the phone call that could change a lot of lives.

Glancing at the clock, he saw it was late in Sweden, likely past the bedtime of his elderly employees, but they wouldn't thank him if he delayed this call.

"Hello?" The voice that picked up the call was female, sleepy, and annoyed.

"Mrs. Solveig, it's Aleksander Lind. My apologies for calling this late."

"Yes, and?"

He kept a smile pasted on his face through sheer will and forced an upbeat note into his voice. "The meeting with your granddaughter has been arranged."

His statement was met with a sharp inhalation. "Really?"

He nodded although she couldn't see him. "Yes, I just got off the phone—"

"You spoke to my granddaughter?" Her hope and excitement traveled across their connection.

"No, I spoke to her sister."

"That woman isn't her sister," Mrs. Solveig snapped.

Aleks contained his sigh. Expressing his frustration would only anger her further. That Dizzie's living relatives denied her closest relationship struck him as unbearably sad. Family should be cherished. Celebrated.

He'd learned early never to argue with Mrs. Solveig. She had very set ideas on how the world should work and didn't respond well when that worldview was challenged. "Portia Tremaine is acting in h— in your granddaughter's stead in this matter."

"I don't believe you!"

It was going to be one of those days. Mrs. Solveig required kid-glove treatment when she was like this. Which was difficult since he had to be laser-focused on their conversation. "Would you like me to conference her in?"

"Dizzie?" There was a world of emotion in that single word.

Aleks cursed his lack of clarity. It would only make this

more difficult. "No, ma'am. I only have contact information for Ms. Tremaine."

"That's what I get for sending someone with only half a brain to do such important work."

He ignored the sting of her words. Defending himself never ended well. Instead, he waited her out, mostly sure that she would relent.

"Fine." She huffed out on a sigh. "Add the bitch to our conversation."

"I'll need to put you on hold. One moment, please." He put the call on hold without receiving her permission. She'd be mad, but he needed a moment to think.

He called Portia and willed her to pick up.

"Aleks, I didn't expect to hear from you again."

She sounded happy to hear from him. That wouldn't last. "Hello, Portia. I have a request and it isn't a pleasant one."

"That sounds ominous." Her tone changed and he swore he could hear her frown.

He grimaced. "It is." He didn't want to lie to her. "I called the Solveigs to apprise them of the meeting and Mrs. Solveig does not believe that you're working on Dizzie's behalf."

"Of course she doesn't."

If the sound from the other end of the line had come from anyone else, he would have called it a snort. But he couldn't quite wrap his mind around Portia Tremaine snorting. Even the sexy, mussed-up Portia from the other morning.

"I have Mrs. Solveig on the other line. I offered to conference you in to confirm your role. Will you?"

A strangled laugh met his request. "You want *me* to

help *you* convince the Solveigs that I'm on *their side* with regards to their granddaughter?"

Shit. Was that what he was asking? "Put like that, it does sound a little . . . " He hesitated. "Suspect."

"Just a little." She paused and he was sure that she was going to refuse his request. "Sure. Fine. I'll do it."

"Thanks. I owe you." The words slipped out before he could fully process the ramifications. The silence on the other end told him Portia was doing her own processing.

"I'll hold you to that."

"Thank you." He managed to keep his voice level, because his mind had already started imagining all the different ways that he could pay Portia back. Many of them involved her naked body wrapped around his. Which wasn't only inappropriate, but also incredibly distracting when he needed to be on the top of his game. "I'm bringing you into the call now."

He pressed a button to start the conference call and cleared his throat. This was going to be an absolute disaster and he had no one to blame but himself.

"Mrs. Solveig, I have Portia Tremaine on the call with us to discuss the meeting with Dizzie."

"Took you long enough," Mrs. Solveig groused.

Aleks closed his eyes and counted to three before responding. But Portia beat him to it.

"Don't blame Mr. Lind," she said with such sharpness that he felt the bite of her words. "I'm an incredibly busy woman and you should be thankful that I took his call. He's already taken up significant amounts of my time with your demands."

The silence on the Solveigs' end surprised him. Either Mrs. Solveig was still half asleep or she hadn't expected

Portia to push back. Very few people did because it never ended well.

Finally, she responded. "You're just as lacking in pleasantries as your father. Very well. Aleks said you are negotiating on behalf of my granddaughter. I don't believe you. You must want something before you let her talk to me. You probably have her locked up in that basement again."

Aleks rubbed his eyes and bit back a groan. He prayed this conversation didn't blow up all the inroads he'd made with Portia over the last few days, both personally and professionally.

If the aggression bothered Portia, she didn't let it show. Her voice was as cold as ice when she replied. "As far as I know, Dizzie is at her boyfriend's home. Feel free to call and check." Her pause was carefully timed, allowing for the older woman's sharp inhale on the other line. "Oh, right. You *can't* contact my sister. Which is why you sent your emissary."

If this were a video call, he could watch Portia's expressions. This woman—the Portia Tremaine of the newsies and tabloids—was so very different from the Portia who'd lost herself in his arms. It was almost like she was two different people. Which one was the real Portia?

"I met with Mr. Lind, as you requested," Portia continued. "Dizzie has asked that the meeting be on Monday."

Mrs. Solveig squawked in protest. "It's already Saturday here. We can't possibly be ready in time."

"That's not my problem. You can attend the meeting or not, but until Dizzie requests any changes, the arrangements I made stand." Her tone was ice cold and he could practically hear her bared teeth when she spoke again. "Now, I'm going back to my other concerns. Good day."

Portia dropped off the call, leaving Aleks impressed in her wake. She was a formidable woman. Her strength and that hidden soft side drew him like a moth to a flame.

"That was distasteful."

Aleks struggled to tear his thoughts from Portia. "Pardon?"

"Dealing with that woman. Distasteful."

Despite the lack of video, Aleks easily pictured Mrs. Solveig's lips curled up in the sour expression she wore when she was displeased. And this entire situation displeased her.

"Dealing with Ms. Tremaine is my job." One he didn't find distasteful at all. "Would you like me to make your travel arrangements?"

He held his breath. Would she lash out at his overstep?

"No. My assistant will handle that. We'll arrive on Sunday. You'll need to ensure the proper clearances for the jet are in order." She paused. "Make sure that my granddaughter has the required paperwork—passports, whatever—for international travel."

"What if she doesn't decide to come with you?" It was a daring question, but he wanted the information for Portia.

That thought brought him up short. It was an indication of the effect she was having on his loyalties. They should belong to the Solveigs, to the people who'd given him a job and a purpose after the surgery had gone so wrong.

"Of course she'll come with us. Silly questions like that are why you can't be trusted with more complicated duties. Honestly, that implant was a disaster."

Unclenching his jaw required physical effort. "Of course, Mrs. Solveig. My apologies."

She sniffed. "Send the details to my assistant. I don't expect to hear from you again until we land in Seattle."

"Thank you, Mrs. Solveig. Good night."

Dead air greeted him. Another reminder that she didn't consider him worthy of her time.

Her words echoed in his head and his giddy mood evaporated. Yeah, his fucking implant had been a failure from the get-go. He laughed bitterly.

Aleks wasn't an idiot. IQ tests both before and after the surgery had proved that the implant had actually bumped him up a few points. Not enough to be noticeably different, but his problem-solving skills had changed. Drastically.

That was the problem. The consortium's security arm had no way to measure those changes. Their view of the augmentation surgery had been pretty damn black and white: did Aleks have super-soldier skills? No? Then they had no use for him.

So here he was, unappreciated by his employer, far from home, and hopelessly intrigued by the one woman he shouldn't be.

Yeah, that should be plenty for his brain to chew on right now.

CHAPTER 17

FRUSTRATED with his lack of results, Aleks set the computer down hard on the coffee table. He'd been studying the Consortium's dossier on the Tremaine Corporation—and Phillip and Portia—for hours. Ever since the call with the Solveigs.

He'd been sure that there was a way to end the company without endangering Portia. He was determined to save her life, though she probably wouldn't see it that way if his employers succeeded in destroying her company. He could practically recite the dossier from memory at this point and still no magical solutions jumped out at him.

Darkness had fallen across the city, but the flicker of colors from the buildings lit up the sky. It'd be pretty if he had time to enjoy it. He stared out the window. There *had* to be something!

"One more time." It wasn't the first time he'd said that tonight. Probably wouldn't be the last if he listened to that little niggle that told him he was missing something.

He stood, then grabbed his computer. Reopening the company dossier, he started to read it out loud. "Founded by the Tremaine Family. Headquartered in Seattle." He paced the room as he continued to read. It was just as boring listening to his own voice as it was reading it.

"With Phillip Tremaine declared missing, Portia Tremaine has stepped in as CEO. At this time, there is no indication that illegitimate daughter Dizzie is involved in the day-to-day operations of the company."

"Yeah, real helpful, intelligence team," he muttered. "Anyone listening to the newsies could have told you that."

He scrolled to the footnotes. Aleks had read them before. They were mostly links and citations for the report. He dutifully read them out loud. "A new drug, Vyne, has recently been growing in popularity in Seattle, one intelligence officer noted. When he asked about the source of the drug, no one could provide any information. However, one informant said they heard from a friend of a friend that it was created by the Tremaine Corporation. We were unable to substantiate this rumor."

What the hell? Had the answer been staring him in the face all along?

Aleks didn't know much about Vyne. Not surprising. And he certainly wasn't going to sample the stuff. His brain was already messed up enough; he didn't need random chemical reactions making it worse.

Settling into his desk, he pulled up a search screen. "Vyne" was an easy search term and his screen filled with news stories, party videos, and user images.

His lip curled in disgust as he read about the designer drug. No one knew where it came from, but, thanks to the dossier, he had that rumor. Tremaine was more biomedical than pharmaceutical, so he assumed it had to do with another project or it was a failed attempt to expand their market. Their legitimate market, at least. Did Portia know about this?

According to the news reports and disturbing videos of users, the extremely addictive drug provided euphoric highs. As a user's veins calcified and hardened, the chemical cocktail turned them green. The decorative—and deadly—patterns gave the drug its name.

He shuddered. Nasty stuff.

Focusing more on the news reports, he learned that the drug was nearly 100 percent fatal. Long-term use was measured in weeks or months and, by all accounts, breaking the habit was impossible. Vyne use only ended in death. There hadn't been any successful attempts to ween someone off it. Or, if there had been, no one was announcing the results.

This was it. The Solveigs could use this in their quest to destroy the Tremaines. Bring down the company, but leave Portia unscathed.

He sighed. That wasn't true. After losing her husband and father, Portia only had the company left. Aleks had to believe that she wasn't involved in the production and distribution of Vyne. That project had Phillip Tremaine's fingerprints all over it. While Portia was his heir, it appeared that her father had kept the seedier aspects of the business from her.

Her "Ice Queen" nickname was well earned, but every once in a while, she revealed a glimpse of something softer. That woman wouldn't touch a project like this.

Aleks started drafting a report on what he'd found. He'd weigh his options in the morning. Releasing the origin of Vyne may not bring the company down, but it would start the process.

CHAPTER 18

THE TRILL of an incoming message woke Portia from a restless sleep. She hadn't had a good night's sleep since . . . Scrunching her nose, she tried to remember. Since waking up in Aleks's bed. Before that, it had been months.

Now some asshole was messing with what little sleep she got.

Rolling over, she reached for her phone. If it was an emergency at the office, she wasn't sure she cared enough to fix it right now. Her father had left a hell of a mess in her lap when he disappeared. First, Dizzie. Then all the other kids he'd grown for organs.

Her stomach churned. That horror show had nearly done her in. What kind of monster created a plan like that?

Her father, that was who. So, what did that make her?

Portia pulled up the message. If it was really bad, maybe she'd pretend she hadn't received it and go back to sleep.

Need to see you.

Aleks's message sent her heart fluttering like a schoolgirl with a crush. Portia tamped that feeling down immediately. He'd chosen work over her.

Was this how Tommy had felt all those years? Her heart broke for him. All those times she'd put the company first. He must have really loved her to have stayed.

Steeling her spine, she set aside the grieving widow and stepped into the CEO role. No one, especially not the man working for the enemy, could demand her presence like that. No matter how much she enjoyed his company.

Why?

His response was immediate. *Meet me for breakfast?*

Looking at the time, she ignored that stupid little flutter again. It wasn't even seven yet. Ugh.

She'd planned to catch up on work. And, as much as she didn't want to, she needed to prepare for the meeting with the Solveig Consortium. She needed to be armed with as much information as she could be.

So really, spending time with Aleks could count as gathering intel against the Solveig Consortium, right?

I can fit you in. Where do you want to meet?

No response popped up. The sinking sensation in her stomach was *not* disappointment. She had plenty to do today. Plus, she wasn't a big fan of breakfast anyway.

She dropped her phone on the bedside table. It trilled with another message and practically bounced back into her hand.

Outside your place, 10 minutes?

Ten minutes? This obviously wasn't a date, so she wouldn't put date-level effort into it.

OK

She sprang out of bed and into her closet. So many clothes, but none of them projected the this-isn't-a-date-I-woke-up-this-way-vibe that she wanted. Except . . .

The slim-fit jeans were a few years old, but the trouser

cut was classic and the denim was butter soft and expensive. The fact that they made her ass look amazing was a bonus.

She paired them with a black tailored shirt in high-tech fabric that breathed like linen but never wrinkled. Something else to thank the space program for.

A brown leather jacket and heeled ankle boots finished the look. The outfit said she had dressed for the office rather than Aleks. Sixty–forty, maybe, but she'd never admit it.

Swirling her hair into a French twist, she donned understated but expensive jewelry, and grabbed her purse.

Portia slipped out of her apartment to the private elevator for her floor. She'd missed the ten-minute mark, but only by a minute. Alone in the elevator, she pulled a lipstick from her purse. Leaning close to the reflective interior wall, she slicked the color over her lips.

Pursing her lips, she studied her reflection. Almost there, but she still needed . . . something. Her gaze flicked to the counter marking the floors they passed. Just a few seconds until the doors opened. She swiped the lipstick over her lips again, this time with a heavier hand.

Another glance at her reflection showed her that the pink popped and provided the little something extra that she'd sought. "Perfect," she told the Portia in the mirror.

The elevator stopped on the ground floor with barely a bump. She pressed a hand to her nervous stomach, then dropped it, smiling as the doors opened.

The doorman greeted her as she crossed to the front doors. "Good morning, Ms. Tremaine." He glanced out the door, then looked back to her with a frown. "Your driver isn't out front. Shall I call a car for you?"

"No need, Sam. I'm meeting someone outside."

His rapid blinking was the only sign that she'd surprised him. "I see. Have a lovely day, Ms. Tremaine."

"You too, Sam." Portia smiled at the older man as he held the door for her. Sam had taken care of her and Tommy for years. What had started as treating the building's employees well to keep Portia and Tommy's business out of the tabloids had grown into a deep appreciation of the staff. Especially over the past year when they had taken extra care to ensure her privacy and protection. It was more than her father had ever done for her.

Portia shook off those thoughts. There was no time for sadness or bitterness. She was meeting Aleks for breakfast, and while it was likely to be a boring business meeting, she'd let herself enjoy his company.

She stepped out into the misty Seattle morning. Loose fog blanketed the city, though it didn't obscure the buildings today, the way it did some mornings. Instead, the fog gave everything a hazy overlay.

"Good morning, Portia." Aleks's deep voice came from her left.

She spun around to greet him and the words caught in her throat. He was dressed for the unpredictable Seattle weather, where autumn could bring anything from rain and sleet to unseasonably warm sunny days. Black jeans hugged firm thighs that she'd gripped with her own. An old-timey bomber-style leather jacket over a white shirt covered his broad chest. He held two cups and a small bag. But it was the grin on his face that made her heart skip a beat.

"Good morning." The greeting came out huskier than she intended and heat tinged her cheeks.

"Thank you for meeting me, especially on such short notice." His sincerity flustered her. He handed her one of the cups.

"I was surprised to get your message this morning. Especially after the call last night." The words came out a little sharper than she intended and she hid a wince.

He exhaled sharply. "I'm sorry about that. Ignoring my employers isn't something I can do lightly. They expect immediate and absolute loyalty." A shadow passed over his face.

"Dealing with my father was frequently like that." Crap. She had definitely not intended to say that. She needed caffeine immediately.

Taking a tentative sip of the drink he'd handed her, she let the contents roll over her tongue. Coffee, slightly sweet and balanced with steamed milk. "It's perfect." She looked up at him in surprise.

"Flat white, two sugars," he said smugly. "I used your dossier for something other than its intended purpose."

She should be concerned that the Solveigs' dossier on her was that detailed but decided to be amused instead. It was the kind of thing Tommy would have done. The thought made her smile. "Is that breakfast?" She nodded at the bag.

"Yes. There's a little European coffee shop near Pike Place Market." His smile brightened the morning.

"There is?" Coffee was still big business in Seattle. The reigning corporation had gotten its claws deep into the city years and years ago. Sure, rivals cropped up from time to time, but the odds of survival were low. The other coffee companies either faded away quietly or they were made to disappear . . . violently.

Aleks looked at Portia, laughter in his deep-sea eyes. "Yes. Tucked in a corner, only a few tables, known for delicious pastries?"

She shook her head. "It doesn't sound familiar." Admitting that felt like failure. How could she not know about a hidden gem of a coffee shop in her city, only a few blocks from where she lived? And it *was* her city.

Portia glanced from him to the bag of pastries. It was a sweet gesture, one that touched her a little too much, since it would have been so much easier to eat at a restaurant. At least then she wouldn't have to wonder where he intended them to eat. "Did you want to eat at your hotel suite? Or did you want to come up?" Panic nipped at the words. It felt too —soon? Too much? Too personal?—to invite him into the home she'd shared with Tommy. The apartment had been their place. Her escape from the pressures of work. The only person they'd ever had over was Killian.

"I thought we'd just walk, if that's okay with you." He was watching her closely and she worried about what her expression may have given away.

"Yes, that's great," she said, her relief obvious in her tone.

Aleks discombobulated her. He worked for the enemy and yet he made her feel things she hadn't expected to feel again. It was as infuriating as it was special. He made her want to lower her defenses, but that had proven to be a mistake two nights ago.

Yet here she was, meeting him for breakfast in broad daylight. Or at least fog.

"We can play tourist in your city."

Be a tourist in her own city? Portia had never even considered that. She was actually surprised that Tommy had never suggested it either. Then again, maybe she wasn't. He'd probably done everything there was to do in the city while she was working.

"I'd like that," she admitted. "But not today. I do have time for coffee and pastries, though."

Maybe Tommy had been right. Maybe she did need to spend less time in the office.

CHAPTER 19

"THIS DOSSIER OF YOURS. Does it say what kind of pastries I like?" Portia's smile was shy, her tone a little bit flirtatious.

Aleks's brain raced to catch up with this unexpected turn of events. He'd been up too late researching the Vyne situation and studying his options. After too few hours of sleep, he'd left the hotel in search of coffee. The coffee shop had been recommended online and he was desperate for a reminder of home.

Messaging Portia this morning had been an impulse move, born of insufficient sleep and caffeine deprivation. Her agreement had brought a burst of happiness; suddenly he'd been awake and his mind clear. Every neuron was focused on seeing her and his synapses danced with pleasure at the thought.

Which had to be another unexpected malfunction in the brain chip. Instead of overthinking it, he decided to enjoy this unexpected moment.

"You'll have to wait and see."

She opened her mouth to argue, then closed it. He was actually surprised that she agreed.

"Now put your phone away. Please."

She raised a brow, but complied.

"Ready?"

When she nodded, Aleks pulled a napkin from the bag and carefully grabbed one of the treats he'd picked up at the bakery. He handed her the spiced bun. Golden brown, still warm from the bakery, it smelled like home to him.

She took it with her free hand and studied it. "What is it?"

"Breakfast," he said with a laugh.

She rolled her eyes at him. "It looks kind of like a cinnamon roll." Lifting it to her nose, she delicately sniffed it. Her eyes flew wide. "It smells . . . floral?"

He nodded. "Try it first."

"Fine," she huffed. She raised the pastry to her lips and took a delicate bite. "Oh my god, it's so good. It's kind of . . . peppery?"

"Cardamom," he informed her.

Her next bite wasn't delicate at all. She moaned in appreciation and the sound traveled straight to his heart. *Oh, that was bad.*

"It's a cardamom bun," he told her. "They're very similar to a traditional Swedish pastry."

"It's delicious," she said. She shoved the last piece into her mouth. When she finished chewing, she asked, "Do you have another?"

He held the bag open for her as she grabbed another pastry. Then he took the last treat in the bag.

"What's that?" she asked around bites.

"Cinnamon roll. I wasn't sure whether you'd like the cardamom buns or not, so I got something more traditional."

"Not like, *love*," she said.

His heart went boom. "Shall we?" He gestured toward the sidewalk, desperate to ignore whatever that feeling had been.

They walked in silence several minutes. He could get used to this. Early morning walks with this beautiful woman. Exploring the city as it woke up.

He shook his head. It was an impossible dream.

"I always assumed you'd have newsies camped outside your door." He hadn't seen any as he'd approached her building. If the paparazzi caught them together and identified him, it could be catastrophic for both of them. The newsies would have a field day with the speculation about the Tremaine CEO and a Solveig Consortium employee.

The best of all the bad options would be if he simply lost his job. The worst option would be everything, including his mission, blowing up. So he just wouldn't let that happen.

Her smile was more of a grimace. "Is that what it's like in Sweden?"

His overactive brain conjured up armies of newsies camped outside the Solveigs' city apartment. He laughed at the image. "Uh, no."

"They're more polite?" Portia asked.

"Not exactly." Aleks tilted his head, considering everything he knew about them, which wasn't a lot. He wasn't really allowed to deal with the press, legitimate or not. "I think it's more that the Solv—" He caught himself and corrected quickly, "The corporations in Sweden are more boring."

Portia laughed. The full-bodied throaty sound was so at odds with the woman he'd expected to meet on this trip.

"Of course, I expect that the number of newsies will change drastically when Dizzie goes back with me." Aleks spoke without thinking.

"Did you have to bring her up?" Frost tinged Portia's voice.

This was one barrier that he couldn't understand. Both women were practically orphans and yet they resisted becoming family. Imagine how strong their bond would be if they put that energy into their relationship. They'd be unstoppable.

"You can't avoid her forever."

"I can try," she retorted smartly.

He met that comment with silence, wondering if she would fill it. Portia didn't seem like a woman who would fall for that. He guessed she was the one who used the silence to get others to talk.

Once again, she surprised him.

"Fine. Yes, I imagine that the Solveigs and your city will be overrun with newsies demanding the story of the long-lost heir."

"Maybe that will get them to leave you alone." He couldn't imagine living under the constant scrutiny she faced.

This time her laugh was a bit bitter. "Not once she tells the story of how the terrible Tremaine Corporation ruined her life and kept her locked away from her rightful family for years and years. The newsies will be camped out on my steps just like they were after the accident. And if Dizzie adds in how her own sister tried to kill her? Well, I'll never see the end of them."

"What?" He couldn't have heard that right. Aleks looked over at Portia, but she was looking away from him. "Did you just say you tried to kill Dizzie?" He tried to temper the horror in his voice, but his mind was too busy scrambling to make sense of her words to control his tone as well.

"Yes." Her answer was clipped. "It was just a few days after she killed Tommy." She paused, grief contorting her features. She took a sip of coffee, then rephrased her answer. "It was a few days after Tommy's death in the bombing and everything pointed to her being the killer. So, when I saw her with Killian, all I could see was a way to get justice for Tommy. I gunned the engine and hit her with my car."

She stopped walking, her body radiating tension. She was waiting for him to judge her.

He knew what it was like to be judged. He'd arrived with some preconceived notions about Portia already. She'd proven those wrong, so he wouldn't judge her now. "She, uh, obviously survived." Smooth, Aleks. Totally non-judgy.

Portia nodded but kept her gaze far off, never once looking at him. "Killian got her to the hospital in time. That's how they discovered that she was my father's daughter."

He noted her careful wording but challenged it. "Your sister."

Her gaze, tinged with sadness and a little heat, swung back to him. "Fine. My sister. Why do you keep doing that?"

"Doing what?"

"Pushing me to acknowledge her?"

"You're isolated from everyone, sitting up there in your cold office, looking out over the city, but not interacting with it. You need someone to connect you to the outside world. To remind you that there's more to life than work." He swallowed a laugh as the words tumbled out. He really should take his own advice.

"That's what Tommy did," she said quietly.

Aleks reached for her hand but stopped just before taking it. He tilted his head, silently asking for permission.

She hesitated, then shoved her empty napkin into a pocket. When she tentatively offered her hand, he took it, no hesitation.

"I'm sorry for your loss." He held her gaze, willing her to read his sincerity. Had he come to town while her husband was still alive, he'd have never known her on this personal level. "I'm sorry that you lost that key person, but you have a chance to build a new relationship. Maybe it won't work. Maybe she'll want nothing to do with you. Maybe she'll want to move to Sweden, but you'll never know until you ask."

"Is that the plan?"

His brain whirred, working to understand her question. "To build your relationship with Dizzie?"

She shook her head. "To get Dizzie to move to Sweden."

Aleks paused and considered his answer. Telling her the truth would be considered a betrayal by his employers, but keeping her in the dark would forever ruin any chance he had with her. Not that he thought a chance existed, but he could dream, right?

"It will be up to Dizzie." He chose his words carefully. "I think Mrs. Solveig believes that your sister will choose to come back to Sweden and join the family business there."

"After an angry repudiation of the Tremaine family, of course." Her tone was light, but her gaze was heavy.

He smiled, despite the seriousness—and accuracy—of her statement.

"Yes, that would be ideal." He added a touch of humor to his voice, so she wouldn't think that he believed it.

Portia didn't reply immediately. Instead, she studied their linked hands and started walking. He kept pace with her, confident that she would speak when she was ready.

"I don't think it will be that easy," she said finally.

"Getting Dizzie to Sweden?"

"Sure, that's part of it. But getting Mrs. Solveig to believe anything other than the pretty picture she's painted in her head." She paused, her forehead creasing in concentration. "Would she try to force Dizzie to go?"

Dammit. This was exactly what he'd been trying to avoid. Apparently, he'd been too busy mooning over Portia and hadn't focused enough of his attention on keeping control of the conversation.

If she'd already figured it out, he wasn't obligated to keep it from her, right? Balancing his loyalty to his employer and his infatuation with Portia was harder than he'd expected. "Do I believe that the Solveigs will try to force your sister to go to Sweden?" He sighed. "I wouldn't put it past them."

The smile completely disappeared from Portia's face. "Will you be the one to do it?" Her tone was dead serious.

Would he? He thought of the many distasteful things the Solveigs had required of him over the years. Yet, whenever it was a truly dirty job—murder or kidnapping or torture—they had called in those they deemed more trustworthy than him. "No, I don't believe that's something they would trust me with."

"I'm both glad that it won't be your job—not that I'd let it get that far—and angry on your behalf." Her expression was a mix of horror and curiosity and something that he really hoped wasn't pity. "Why wouldn't they trust you to kidnap my sister?"

CHAPTER 20

THIS WASN'T the strangest conversation he'd ever had, but it was close. That didn't negate the little rush of pleasure that came from her indignation on his behalf. No one ever stood up for him. His appreciation of her deepened.

"They think I'm defective." Now it was his turn to look away from a difficult conversation. He didn't want to watch her indignation turn to pity. "I joined the Solveig Consortium's security services right after graduation. During my training, they offered a super soldier program and I signed up."

"Super soldier? Like faster and stronger?" She squeezed his hand, drawing his attention back to her. Her grip was warm, compared to the cool air around them and the even colder memories.

He nodded. "They implanted chips in our brains that were supposed to create new connections, ones that would give us faster reflexes, that kind of thing." Aleks swallowed hard and ignored his racing pulse. He hated talking about this. "My chip failed."

"They can't possibly blame you for that!" Her voice rose.

Aleks surveyed the street around them, thankful it was still deserted and that they hadn't drawn any attention.

He continued walking. "They didn't blame me for the chip failure," he said. "The chip rewired my brain, all right, just not in the way that they expected. Because I didn't get the super-soldier attributes they wanted, it's considered a failure."

Portia gasped. "That's not fair!"

A bitter laugh escaped him. "You of all people should know that *fair* doesn't exist in the corporate world. There are the people who call the shots and there are the people like me who take their orders." It was the way of their world.

She opened her mouth to speak, but he continued because he really wanted this conversation over with. "Whatever the new wiring did, my brain isn't the same. It's like my brain can't stop gathering information and when it overloads, I make bad decisions or I get terrible headaches.

"The security team still gave me a chance after the tests showed I didn't get the physical improvements. They thought that maybe I could harness the rewiring to make on-the-spot mission decisions." That had been a debacle. "Not long after the surgery, I fucked up a simple test mission, because my brain basically short-circuited. It's broken. I'm broken." Except he didn't feel that way, not when he was with her.

"They're wrong," Portia said. "That wasn't a fair test."

He pulled his hand away and started walking. There was more. So much more that she wouldn't want to hear.

Portia kept pace with him, her presence both soothing and abrasive. His brain poked at the dichotomy, intrigued with her many facets.

Aleks slowed his pace and studied the unfamiliar architecture around them. Maybe it would distract his brain from its current dangerous path.

The buildings they passed were a mix of tall brick structures and mammoth towers of glass and steel. The tallest ones disappeared into the fog that hung over the city. Aleks preferred the smaller, older brick buildings tucked here and there amongst the skyscrapers. They reminded him of home.

"What happened after the test mission?" Portia asked.

He sighed. She wasn't going to let this go. "They booted me from the security program. I should've ended up at one of the company's factories, but the Solveigs found my new skills useful enough to keep me around."

He'd been given a second chance that day, but sometimes he wondered whether it had been worth the constant insults and indignities.

"And now you do whatever they tell you to."

Aleks couldn't read her tone, but it didn't sound complimentary.

"They're using you," Portia said after a long pause. She took his hand again.

"No, they're not." His defense was automatic.

She snorted.

Portia Tremaine, Seattle's Ice Queen, snorted. His head almost exploded.

"My family excels at using people. I know it when I see it."

"They gave me a job. What am I supposed to do, say no? All that would do is get me assigned to the factory. Game over. At least this way, I get to go interesting places. Meet interesting people."

And Portia Tremaine was the most interesting of all.

She stopped suddenly, her grip on his hand stopping him as well. She waited until he looked at her, then said, "They treat you like you're broken because they want you to feel indebted to them." He flinched when she said *broken* and tried to pull away, but she didn't let him. "The man I've spent the last few days with is anything but. Maybe the chip changed you, but it didn't break you."

He wanted to believe her. Wanted to take comfort in her words, but . . . "How can you say that? Your thoughts on augmentation are well known. You don't believe in it, despite how your family made its fortune." The last words came out bitter.

Portia sighed. "Yes, I have said that. More than once, because I've honestly never seen the appeal. And yet . . . if there had been a way to save Tommy by using augmentation, would have I have done it? Yes. A thousand times yes." She released his hand to wipe away a tear.

"Would you have done it to save yourself?" He was curious.

Her blue eyes shimmered with tears as she looked up at him. "I don't know. And that was before I knew the lengths my father had gone to preserve his own life."

Her honesty surprised him. The Portia Tremaine in his dossier was as cold as her nickname implied. But this woman . . .

Her words provided a deeper look into a woman who was already too interesting and dangerous to his mental health.

"I appreciate you trying to help," he said, "but I think you're wrong."

Portia reached up and laid her hand on his cheek. Her skin was soft, but her touch burned. He leaned in and closed his eyes. "You're worth more than you think you are, Aleks," she whispered.

He should move, break this connection. If he stood here much longer, soaking in her warmth, her belief in him, he'd do something stupid like kiss her. And this wasn't the time or the place.

A soft buzz distracted him from the moment. Eyes still closed, he pinpointed the sound. In one smooth move he whirled around, placing his body in front of Portia's while tracking the low hum.

His brain leaped into action, pulling in information, sorting through data, making and rejecting plan after plan.

"Aleks, what is it?" Portia's voice was thick with tension.

"Give me just a moment, Portia."

Finally arriving at a reasonable plan, he waited for the right moment to execute it. Five . . . four . . . three . . . two . . . *now!*

He launched his coffee cup into the air. The lid popped off and the remaining coffee flew upward.

The liquid hit the drone first, spraying the delicate electronics with fluid. Then the cup hit it, knocking it out of the air. Off balance, with its electronics impaired, the drone buzzed sadly and plummeted to the ground.

It hit the sidewalk with a clatter.

Portia gasped. She tried to step around him, but he kept one arm extended behind him to keep her back while he studied the area around them.

Pressing against his back, she peered over his shoulder. "Newsies." Disdain dripped from the word.

"Are you sure?" It was a logical explanation, but someone had tried to kill her only a few months ago. Not to mention his own employers had mentioned getting her out of the way. He wasn't taking any chances.

"Yes." She edged out to the side. Aleks didn't stop her this time, but he kept his body between her and the drone. She pointed to one of the small cameras on the ground. "See the logo on the side."

Aleks studied the crumpled black metal and the tiny cameras. One looked like it was still trying to focus. He took two steps forward and stomped on the drone, grinding it into the pavement until all the lenses were crushed glass.

"That won't stop them," Portia said. "The footage was likely transmitted to the studio before it even hit the ground."

CHAPTER 21

"WE SHOULD GET UNDER COVER," Aleks said. "Do you think there will be more?"

Portia stared down at the drone and shrugged. "Probably. They're all over the place." Everywhere. All the time.

She was so damn tired of being in the newsies' crosshairs. They'd ruined what had been a perfectly nice morning, the first one in a very long time. She'd forgotten what it was like to just *be*. Or maybe she'd never even known.

"Thank you," she said.

"For what? Saving you from a drone?"

Portia pursed her lips. He was frowning again and she wanted to make it go away. "Well, yes. No one has ever done that for me."

He blinked at her. Like he wasn't quite sure what to say. Was that because he was still processing it? Or because she had stymied him? She really wanted to know how his brain worked. He seemed to think that it was some kind of terrible curse, but the whole time they had spent together, it had never appeared to be a problem.

"Uh, you're welcome."

"I've always wanted to do that," Portia admitted. Not doing anything to turn the newsies against them had been drilled into her since she was a child. With Tommy at her side, she'd been able to resign herself to their presence. With Aleks at her side . . . Well, that opened up a world of new possibilities.

"My father expected me to just deal with them. 'You're a goddamn Tremaine,' he'd say." She dropped her voice to emulate him. "He'd say, 'If you want them to stop, make them.'"

Aleks shifted closer to her side. She soaked in the warmth that his proximity brought. "How were you supposed to do that?" he asked.

"No idea. I used to dream about buying them and making them stop."

His laugh made her smile. "And your husband?"

Oh, Tommy. She'd loved every reckless, charming, wild inch of him with all her heart. But every once in a while, she'd wished he was the steady, serious one and she . . . wasn't. "He loved the attention and could never understand why I didn't," she admitted, although it almost felt like a betrayal to say the words out loud.

The words hung between them and Portia held her breath. When he didn't respond, she said, "We should get out of here. If the drone got any clear shots of us, more newsies will swarm the area."

Aleks grabbed her hand and let her to the nearest alley. She wrinkled her nose—hiding in an alley wasn't her first choice—but the dark, narrow spaces were probably more difficult for the drones to maneuver.

"How did you do that?" She wanted to keep the conversation going. This place was creepy. Her hand tightened around Aleks's.

"Basic training." He didn't add anything more. That must have been when he was still intended to work for security.

Something skittered in the darkness and she leaned closer to Aleks. Dark places had never bothered her until she'd been trapped after the bombing. Thankfully, Killian had been with her. She would have lost her mind if she'd been all alone, but the fear and pain of that night had imprinted on her soul.

"You okay?" Aleks asked.

She pondered whether to answer honestly. He'd been open with her, so she decided to respond in kind. "No. I developed a . . . dislike . . . of dark closed spaces after the bombing."

"Dammit! I didn't think about that and I should have." He looked back the direction that they'd had come. "Do you want to go back?"

She shook her head vigorously. "No. Who knows whether they've sent another drone—or worse, an actual newsie—to that location. We should keep moving."

Staying close to Aleks's side, Portia drained the last of her coffee and dropped the empty cup into the nearest dumpster. She shuddered and snatched her hand back.

Aleks didn't say much as they traversed the length of the alley. Glass crackled and crunched under their feet.

Portia stepped on something small and round and almost turned her ankle. She grabbed onto Aleks for balance. When she set her foot more firmly, whatever it was she'd stepped on broke with a small crunch.

She paused and peered into the weakly lit space.

"Where is all this glass from?" She looked up. "It doesn't look like broken windows." Then looked back down. "It doesn't look like broken bottles either."

Keeping one hand on Aleks, she bent slightly for a closer look. No way was she getting too close to the ground. She pulled her phone out and aimed the flashlight at the ground.

All around them, the ground sparkled like little gems. "What the—"

She snapped a couple pictures then straightened. Aleks hadn't said a word. She looked up at him curiously, unable to read his expression. "What's wrong?"

"Nothing."

"That didn't sound like nothing." Why was she picking a fight in this nasty, glass-filled alley? Something told her this was important.

"Portia . . . " He sighed her name.

"Aleks," she echoed.

"You really don't know?"

That sounded ominous. "Really don't know what?" His words and the seriousness of his tone had her taking a second look around them. And a third.

Broken glass everywhere. An alley. Aleks sounded like he thought it should be obvious, but it really wasn't.

Hating what she was about to do, Portia took a deep breath and squatted low to the ground. It didn't look all that different from this angle, but it smelled worse, if that was even possible.

Aleks put his hand under her shoulder. "Stand up. You could cut yourself."

"Just a minute." She didn't brush his hand away, but used him as a steadying force as she panned her flashlight over the ground again.

Tiny bits of broken glass sparkled back at her, just like before. Except . . . what was that?

She dug into her jacket pocket and pulled out the napkin that had held her breakfast. She shook the last few crumbs loose and prayed they didn't draw any critters. Then she used Aleks's grip as a counterbalance and leaned forward.

"Portia! Don't—you might cut yourself."

"I'll be fine," she said absently as she focused on the little curve of glass that had caught her attention. She folded the napkin in half and carefully, so carefully, reached for the fragment. Mindful of the sharp edges, she cautiously picked it up with the napkin.

"Can you help me up?" She really didn't want to wobble and fall onto all this glass.

With a curse it was probably best she didn't understand, Aleks grabbed her under both arms and hauled her to her feet.

She kept her focus on the napkin and her open palm the whole time.

"Steady?" Aleks asked, his breath a warm tickle by her ear. Even as his hands dropped away, she leaned into his warmth.

"It looks almost like a piece of a little bottle, don't you think?" The fragment was small, maybe half an inch, and curved on the sides. She could easily see it as a teeny-tiny little bottle or a—

"Probably a vial," Aleks said at the same time that word popped into her head.

She looked at the glass then tilted her head to look back at him. "A vial for what?"

He stepped away from her back and circled so she could see him. "For drugs, Portia. Probably Vyne."

"Vyne?" she gasped. The delicate glass fragment in her hand suddenly transformed into a terrifying monster. She almost dropped it back onto the ground, but Aleks plucked the napkin from her hand and put the whole bundle into the bakery bag.

She shook her hand violently, appalled at how close she'd gotten to the dangerous drug. If she'd cut her hand, would there have been enough of the compound on the glass to addict her?

"You don't seem surprised," she said after her initial shock wore off.

His sigh practically echoed in the alley. "I'm not," he said finally. "Vyne use is growing in Seattle."

"I've heard a little about it, but I've been too busy dealing with the mess my father left to pay much attention to the news."

His sudden bark of laughter felt inappropriate for the situation.

"What's so funny? What am I missing?" She frowned at him, not liking the feeling that he was laughing at her.

He studied her for a long moment. "I'm not sure we should have this conversation here."

Portia looked around the alley. While it was creepy and dirty, it was also empty. She was pretty sure. "This is possibly the most private place we can talk. No meetings, no phone calls, no drones. And we certainly aren't going to get carried away doing anything else." Her skin crawled at the thought. "What aren't you telling me?"

He looked at her long and hard. She thought she saw resignation in his gaze as well as . . . was that pity? She didn't need anyone's pity.

Portia drew herself to her full height and stared back.

"All this?" Aleks gestured at the glass on the ground.

"Vyne? It's Tremaine Corporation's fault. Is that what you wanted to hear?"

The words struck like blows. Before she could ask any questions, like why was he blaming her company for this, he continued.

"You talk about cleaning up your father's messes—well, this is another one. The Tremaine Corporation created Vyne. Congratulations. Good job." He gave a mocking little clap.

Portia was going to be sick. *This* was another Tremaine-caused problem? Her stomach turned. "How do you know?" How she managed to keep her tone steady, she had no idea.

"I did my research. Followed the whispers and the rumors. Maybe if you came down from your penthouse office and paid attention to the people in 'your' city, this wouldn't be such a surprise."

Every accusation he flung at her hurt, but she still needed more information. "Why were you looking into this? Is this another method of destroying my company?"

"It's better than you being destroyed!" His impassioned answer rang out in the narrow space.

Both of them froze. Aleks winced and looked away from her.

"Is that a threat?" Portia asked carefully.

Aleks ran his free hand through his hair, leaving the blond strands mussed. "The Solveigs want you out of the picture."

"They want me dead? That seems a little extreme."

Aleks ignored her question. "I thought if I gave them another option, they might be satisfied with just destroying the company. Not you." The look he gave her pleaded with her to understand.

Understand? No way in hell. "So, you were what? Going to give them the Vyne info? Or were you going to leak it yourself?"

Ignoring the crunch of glass under her boots, she stalked toward him. "You can tell your employers that they're not getting their hands on my company. And they sure as hell aren't getting rid of me."

With that she snatched the bakery bag out of his hands and stomped toward the other end of the alley. Glass crunched with each step, amping up her anger. He called out after her and she ignored him.

Damn her father for leaving her yet another mess to clean up. And damn Aleks for trying to use it against her.

CHAPTER 22

"DID YOU KNOW?"

The office door had barely closed behind Ash and the other hacker before Portia started demanding answers.

The bomb Aleks had dropped about Vyne being a Tremaine product had sent shockwaves through her. She didn't *not* believe him. With every damn day that she spent in the CEO role—one that she'd once coveted—she learned how deep the corruption in the company ran. Her father had left a number of messes to clean up, but the thought of one being a highly addictive and deadly drug was especially egregious.

After leaving Aleks in the alley, she'd fired off messages demanding to see Ash and Mendez in her office.

"Hello, Portia, good to see you too," Ash drawled.

He sounded just the same as when he had worked for the corporation. The clothes were different—much less corporate—and he seemed happier and more relaxed. She wondered what that was like and ignored the twinge of jealousy.

Mendez shot Ash a sharp look before offering a more formal greeting. "Ms. Tremaine," he said with a nod.

She had the good grace to return it. "Mr. Mendez." Then she turned back to Ash. "Did you know about Vyne?"

The smirk slid off his face. "I know it's a highly addictive deadly drug. And a very unpleasant way to die."

His somber tone indicated that he had firsthand experience with the latter. She was curious who, but that wasn't the priority now.

"Did you know that there's a rumor that it came from my company?" Her voice rose on those last words. She grimaced, hating the outward expression of her concern.

"No. I hadn't heard that specific rumor. What do you need from me?" Ash seated himself on the small sofa, taking the same spot Dizzie had. Apparently, her relaxing corner was becoming the corner of difficult conversations.

She frowned at his disregard for formality and rules, then sighed. He'd never change and he was no longer her problem. Following him to the alcove, she took the wingback chair. Mendez trailed behind them, looking unsure of his role. "Have a seat."

"You know something." Portia held Ash's gaze, while Mendez joined him on the sofa.

"Maybe," Ash said. "I gave you several files before I left. I think one of them was about drugs."

Portia remembered the day, somewhat. Before she spoke again, she turned to the third member of their little group. "Mr. Mendez. I would like to remind you that everything said in this room is confidential and disclosing it is strictly forbidden. If I learn that you have shared this with anyone, well, you won't like what I do next." She gave him the Ice Queen stare.

He didn't blanch or otherwise freak out. "Yes, ma'am."

She studied him a moment longer. He didn't have the same insouciance that Ash did, but she sensed the same underlying energy from him. Like he was going to be trouble. She just didn't know how yet.

"I have a vague memory of you downloading files for me, but not their specifics." She'd been barely keeping her head above water at that point. Grief had still been wearing her down and she'd been putting out little—and big—fires constantly. "Do you remember which file it was?"

"Can I use your computer?" His gaze flickered from her to her desk.

Portia considered Ash's request. "Is this an official job?" Part of her deal with Taryn had been putting Ash on retainer so she could continue to access his skills after he left the company. So far, the hefty fee had been worth it.

Ash sighed. "If I was just offering as a friend?"

Portia's hands clenched in her lap. *Were* she and Ash friends? Their relationship was . . . complicated due to his role in the events leading up to Tommy's death. But before she'd learned that, she'd thought they were building to a friendship.

She couldn't do this on her own, as much as she wanted to, since there were just too many problems to solve. Drawing on her experience with Ash—and because of her growing potential friendship with the Jack—she took a leap of faith and nodded.

Mendez watched the whole interaction intently. She felt uncomfortable with him witnessing it, but she was the one who'd requested his presence.

Ash bounced up off the sofa and was seated behind her desk in the blink of an eye. "You wouldn't believe how often I wanted access to the whole system like this," he said.

"Oh, I probably would. You mentioned it almost every

day," she said, a thread of humor in her voice, then sobered. "If you plant a backdoor in my computer, I will personally sic Taryn on you."

"She wouldn't do it," he said confidently. He waggled his fingers dramatically and placed them on the keyboard. "She's a savvy businesswoman."

She was. A sinking feeling filled Portia's stomach. "Never mind," she said. "I'll look for the file myself."

Ash paused. His smile faded and his expression turned serious. "Portia, I was kidding. I swear I won't leave a backdoor in your system. I want—*we* want—to get this drug off the street as much as you do. Let me find the data."

Oh god. What should she do? She took a long breath, exhaled slowly. "Do it," she said and prayed she hadn't made the wrong decision.

Every fiber in her being wanted to get up and pace. Or stand over his shoulder and watch him work. But that would just stress them both out.

She turned to Mendez. Might as well use her time productively. "What have you found about the Solveig Consortium's cyberattacks?"

"They've gotten more frequent. Starting about a week after the, uh, news broke."

She swallowed a smile at how delicate everyone was regarding mentioning Dizzie.

"Identifying where every attack comes from isn't possible, but we've got a good system that yields pretty high probability. There was another bump two weeks ago that hasn't let up."

"Have any of the attacks gotten through?"

Mendez scoffed. "Our cybersecurity team is very good."

"That's a no?" She raised her brow. That was what reminded her of Ash.

"That's a no. There have been no successful incursions to our system since he did it." He indicated Ash with a chin lift.

Portia's lips pursed. Ash's little trick wasn't something she wanted to be reminded of. "You're sure?"

"Double and triple checked. Ash even scoured the system."

That was a relief at least. "And you're sure they won't get through?"

"There are no guarantees. But we dug into who they might be hiring as well. While they're good, they're not better than we are."

"Is everyone on the cybersecurity team as confident as you and Ash are?"

His expression sobered. "Yes. And the team has been briefed on what to watch for and to report any suspected attacks by the Solveig Consortium immediately."

That was smart. Somehow she didn't believe that it was the head of cybersecurity who had made that decision. The man in front of her was definitely someone to watch. "How did you end up here, Mr. Mendez?"

"Same as everyone else, got caught by Tremaine Security."

His words told the story she expected, but there was something off about his tone.

"I've got it!" Ash said. "Found the file. And a lot more."

Portia left the question of Mendez hanging and hurried to peer over Ash's shoulder.

CHAPTER 23

"I FOUND the original file I sent you. The short version is that it was an implant anti-rejection drug that showed promise, only to have devastating side effects."

Portia placed a hand on the back of her chair and leaned over Ash's shoulder. Staring at the screen, she quickly read the first page of the document. "And?" She waited for him to turn to the next page.

"It gets pretty grim from there. Want your chair back?"

"Yes, please." Reading over Ash's shoulder was too much like peering over her father's on the rare occasions he actually spent time with her. She didn't have time for bittersweet memories right now.

Relief swept through her after she and Ash changed places. This was where she belonged.

Her fingers danced over the keyboard—not as quickly as Ash, but she could hold her own. Tapping out a command, she turned one of the floor-to-ceiling windows opaque, transferring the file to the makeshift screen.

Ash whistled. "That's a cool trick. Why didn't you ever use it when I was here?"

"Because you didn't need to see it." Ash had access to way too many Tremaine secrets already. Not to mention, she'd had the experimental tech installed a few months ago after she'd purchased a small tech company. It saved her eyes when she was tired of staring at a small screen.

As she flipped through the file, she struggled to keep her breathing calm and her stomach steady. Ash hadn't lied when he warned that the file contained gruesome images of the failed trial subjects.

According to the file, Vyne had been created several years ago as an anti-rejection drug for augmentations. It was designed to prevent the body from rejecting some of the more intrusive mechanical modifications, as well as computer–brain interfaces. Portia shuddered. Thankfully, she didn't think that Aleks had received something like this after his surgery.

While the drug had been moderately successful at preventing rejection, the side effects had been too severe to keep it on the market.

"'Drug produces unfortunate side effects.'" Mendez approached the window-screen and read the note just before the photos. "Yikes. That's one way of putting it."

The images showed a variety of limbs, all with green, vine-like patterns marring the skin. Some were just thin threads, while others showed excessive pigmentation. Once the vines appeared, generally users had a few weeks before their veins weakened and they died.

"'Test subjects report euphoric highs,'" Ash read. "This is really fucked up, Portia."

"I know." She could barely speak. "Forty people died during the trials. That's more than the statistics from the implants themselves." Her voice was hushed.

"The file says that the program was shut down," Mendez pointed out.

Portia thought of the broken glass littering the alleys. "Obviously, someone saw the money-making potential of the drug on the black market and didn't care how many more people it killed."

"Do you think it was your father?" Ash addressed the elephant in the room.

Rubbing her temples, Portia glanced at Mendez. She hated airing her dirty laundry like this. She'd have to keep an eye on him and make sure he didn't spill any of the secrets he was learning. "Probably," she admitted. "Or maybe someone in the lab going rogue."

Her father seemed a more likely candidate, but he hadn't been seen in months. According to Aleks, there'd been a recent spike in Vyne sales. What did that mean?

She flipped through the rest of the file, hoping for more clues to what was happening with the drug now, but it was thin on details. "Can you dig up more information on the program? I need to know what lab created this and its current status. I also want to know how easy it is to get the ingredients to make the drug. And figure out where the money is going."

Ash whistled. "You don't want much, do you?"

She glared at him and he laughed. "I'm just kidding," he said. "I've already got those queries running. I've set it up so both of us will receive alerts when there are results."

"The files will come directly to me?"

"Yes, via the email encryption I set up for you."

"Okay, thank you."

Portia swiveled around in her chair and studied the two men. "Keep an eye on hacks that you think are coming from the Solveig Consortium," she directed Mendez. "And help

Ash however he needs. Just remember, whatever you find goes no further."

"Yes, ma'am," Mendez said.

Ash just rolled his eyes. "Wait for me outside," he told the other man. "I need to talk to Ms. Tremaine about something else."

They both watched as Mendez left the room.

"Can I trust him?" Portia asked.

"As much as you can anyone," Ash said.

She sagged back in her chair. "Well, that's a no then." At this rate, she wasn't entirely sure that she could trust anyone in the company. Not for the first time, she wondered what would happen if she let it all burn down.

But she couldn't. This was her inheritance, good or bad.

"He's probably more trustworthy than most," Ash said. "I've worked with him for years. He was actually a really good teammate. Which is wild, since hackers tend to be a bit on the antisocial side."

She looked at him incredulously. "You're the least antisocial person I've ever met. You talk constantly."

His smile was bright. "Well, sure, that's because I'm the best of the best." She rolled her eyes and he laughed. "Seriously, though, I think he'll keep quiet. You don't mess with him, he won't mess with you."

That made a bit more sense to Portia than someone keeping quiet out of the good of their heart. "What do you know about him?"

Ash leaned against the side of her desk. "He's been here about as long as I was. Never really got his story, but that's not unusual. Most of us don't want to reveal how we got caught."

"Is he good?" It felt like a valid question. After all, Mendez had been caught, just like Ash had.

"Yes, he's good. Almost as good as I am," he said with a wink. "He's right about the potential incursions from the Solveig Consortium. They made it in once, years ago, before either of us were here, and they were cut off quickly. Nowadays, even if they pay for help, they're unlikely to get in."

That eased some, but not all of her concerns. "What did you find on the outside?"

"Basically what the other analyst told you. The consortium sold some patents and have funneled some of that money to the cyber team. But they haven't bought the best talent."

"Okay," Portia said slowly. She hated that she didn't know enough about the cybersecurity side to do this research herself.

"So, the Solveig Consortium." Ash leaned back and crossed his arms over his chest. "That got anything to do with the guy from the bar?"

"What guy from the bar?" Her cheeks warmed and panic fluttered in her stomach. She'd been sure Taryn wouldn't say anything. She'd *trusted* the other woman. "Thank you for the update, Mr. Cutter. You should go now."

"Taryn didn't say anything, Portia."

She should reprimand him for using her first name, but she was too embarrassed at how easily he'd read her.

"I live there too, in case you've forgotten. Some of the waitstaff are chatty. They mentioned you left with a hot guy, so I found his tab and did a little poking around."

"Aw, were you worried about me?" She fell back on sarcasm because his concern—and the way it warmed a piece of her lonely heart—was disconcerting.

It was his turn to blush. "Maybe a little," he said defensively. "It was out of character for you."

If only he knew *how* out of character it had been.

"This guy from the Solveig Consortium, Aleksander Lind. They send him to deal with problems." He held her gaze. "Are you a problem to them?"

Portia sighed. How much to tell him?

Not all of it, but some.

"He's here for Dizzie," she said. "Her grandparents want to meet her."

"That can't be all they want." His tone said he wasn't buying it.

"No, they want revenge on my father. Since he's not here, they've decided the company is an acceptable substitute."

"Just the company?" Ash's voice was hard.

She leaned back in her chair. That was the kind of question Killian would have asked. The absence of his friendship had left a bigger hole in her life than she'd realized, if Ash's concern was affecting her like this. Maybe they had been on the way to becoming friends.

"Aleks told me that they want me out of the way so Dizzie can take over the company."

"Aleks?" His brow rose. "No, never mind. We'll deal with the first-name basis later. He threatened you?"

She shook her head vehemently. "No. It wasn't a threat. He was warning me that they won't stop. They physically want to hurt me, but he suggested that maybe they could just discredit me if the information about Vyne got out."

"That's seriously fucked up, Portia." He stared at her and she looked away.

"I know," she said. Oh, how she knew.

"That's why you wanted us to dig into Vyne." Ash

pushed off from the desk and crossed to the window they'd used as a screen. He peered at it closely.

"Yes. We need to uncover who's running the program and shut it down before they can use it against me." Saying it out loud made the scope of the plan seem much larger.

"Do you want us to dig up dirt on them? Mendez penetrated their system last night. The security isn't great, so it wasn't hard."

"You did what?" Portia jolted out of her chair and joined him at the window.

"Hackers gonna hack, Portia." He shrugged. "It was untraceable. You asked us to explore their capabilities. Knowing their system's weaknesses is part of that."

Her head dropped against the glass. "Leave their system alone for now." What could she do with access right now? She had no idea.

"You can't take on the Solveig Consortium alone, Portia."

She raised her head. Exhaustion washed over her. She was so damn tired of fighting alone. "Who else is there?" She gestured around the office. "Everything ends up here."

Ash patted her on the shoulder. "You're not alone," he said quietly. "Let us know when you figure that out."

He exited her office, leaving Portia staring down at the city, considering his words.

CHAPTER 24

"GOOD MORNING, PORTIA," Dizzie said when she met Portia at her office Monday morning for the meeting with her grandparents.

Portia waited until her assistant had closed the door before greeting Dizzie. "Good morning. Coffee?" She gestured toward the small seating area where they had met before.

"Yes, thank you."

Tension filled the air as they crossed to that side of the office, both of them on their best behavior. Dizzie took the same seat she had before, smoothing her pants over her thighs.

Portia studied her sis— No, that still didn't feel right. She studied the other woman, taking in the tailored black pants, blue silk shirt, and heeled boots. With her hair in a sleek twist and the discreet sparkle of diamonds in her ears, Dizzie could be any wealthy woman of the investor class. The only anomaly in her outfit was her nail polish. It was a glittery blue that shimmered in the light.

Taking her seat, Portia straightened the edges of her

dress. She'd chosen blue today as well, but a different shade. It coordinated, rather than clashed, with Dizzie's shirt, almost as if they'd planned it. Portia had completed her outfit with nude heels and a more subdued pale pink polish.

Facing down the Solveigs would never happen if they didn't work together. This tension was going to ruin everything. "I like your nails," Portia said. It was true, even if she'd never wear such a vibrant color.

Dizzie grinned and held up her nails to study them. "I love this color," she said. "Something about it makes me happy."

"I can see why." The exchange didn't fully break the tension, but eased it enough that Portia could take a deep breath. "Help yourself." She gestured to the coffee service.

After Dizzie had fixed her cup, Portia poured her own.

"You have the best coffee," Dizzie said after her first sip.

"Thank you. It's blended especially for me."

"Of course it is," Dizzie muttered into her glass.

Portia clenched her hand around her own cup. "Tommy had the blend created for me one year for my birthday."

Dizzie's eyes widened and coffee sloshed in her cup as her hand shook. "Shit, Portia. I'm sorry."

"Thank you. Drinking it reminds me of him. They're good memories." To Portia's surprise, Dizzie's comments actually broke the tension.

"Are you ready for this?" Portia asked abruptly.

Dizzie set her cup down on the table with a small clatter. Clearly, she wasn't as calm as she tried to project. She huffed out a breath. "I don't know. How are you supposed to prepare for something like this?"

"No idea." Portia shook her head. "I think this is one of those once-in-a-lifetime moments that no one can prepare you for. Like finding out you have a half-sister."

Dizzie laughed as Portia intended. "Right. There's no manual."

"Do you want me to take the lead with this meeting, or am I just here for moral support?" Portia asked.

"I've been thinking about that," Dizzie said. "Let's start with moral support. But please, intervene if things start going seriously off the rails." She picked her coffee up again, her hands steadier this time.

"That's probably a good plan. The Solveigs don't even want me at the meeting."

"What do you mean?"

"They were *not* pleased that I set up this meeting for you and made their feelings quite clear on a call with them." Portia's lips curled into a half-smile, as she remembered the call with Aleks and his employers. She'd enjoyed tweaking the older woman's nose about her lack of access to Dizzie.

"You've spoken to them?" Was that hope or dread in Dizzie's voice?

"For less than a minute. They didn't believe Aleks when he told them about the meeting."

She watched Dizzie take in the new information. When she spoke, it was not the topic that Portia expected. "Aleks is . . . ?" Dizzie's words trailed off and she watched Portia with curiosity.

"Mr. Lind is the Solveig Consortium's agent here in Seattle. He's the one that the Solveigs sent here to set up the meeting."

Dizzie raised her brow. "Is that the guy you left the bar with the other night?"

Her teasing tone made Portia bristle. "Are you spying on me?" Portia set her cup down on the table with a thud. Her outrage was over the top, she knew that. But why was everyone talking about that night?

Dizzie raised her hands in a placating gesture. "Whoa, easy. Don't get your panties in a twist. One of the waitresses at Razor Jack's mentioned it when we were there. No one knew who he was, but they said he had a sexy accent." She stopped speaking and stared at Portia. "Oh my god. It *is* him. You like him."

Portia's face heated. She pressed her lips together, refusing to confirm or deny. "Mr. Lind and I have been working together since his arrival." Hopefully Dizzie wouldn't suspect the real reason she'd left the bar with Aleks.

"Sure, Portia, whatever you say." She saluted Portia with her coffee mug.

Taking a deep breath, Portia tried to get the conversation back on track. "I wasn't sure whether to tell you this before the meeting, but I think you have the right to know. I don't know how to sugarcoat it. The Solveigs want to eliminate me and put you in charge of the company."

Dizzie's jaw dropped. Portia was weirdly relieved that her look was one of shock rather than interest.

"Wait, what?"

"In revenge for your mom, the Solveigs—your grandparents—want to give you the Tremaine Corporation. Like a birthday present or something." Part of her recognized that it might be considered a sweet gesture in some circles—mostly without the whole murder aspect.

"That's . . ."

Portia held her breath, waiting to see how she finished that sentence.

"That's crazy," Dizzie said.

She exhaled slowly. "Yeah, that was my thought, too. Plus, I don't really want to die." She'd come perilously close during the bombing and didn't want to experience that again.

"Is he your source? Aleks? I mean, Mr. Lind? Are you sure you can trust him?"

Portia shrugged but held Dizzie's gaze. "I'm not sure I can trust anyone these days."

"Look, I know you don't like me," Dizzie said. "And you have no reason to trust me. I'm not going to tell you to get over it because I can't imagine losing Killian, but I'm not your enemy. I never was. The only way that changes is if you hurt Killian. Then the gloves would be off."

Unbidden, Portia's gaze dropped to her nails in their sparkly blue glory. Portia had seen them dripping with blood, so she believed her. She hid a shudder. Dizzie had saved her life when she'd used those nails on the man trying to kill them both.

Now they faced another threat. One that only wanted to kill Portia.

"So, you don't want the company?" Portia asked.

Dizzie stared at Portia. "Are you kidding me? You've been training for this for years. I have my hands full dealing with the creche kids, finding them jobs or new homes since the organ harvest orphanage was shut down. Plus, you work all the damn time. Why would I want to work that hard when I can spend time with Killian instead?"

Unexpected bitterness hit Portia. Or maybe it was jealousy. Dizzie spent time with her boyfriend. Prioritized it, even. Had she ever done that with Tommy?

The thought made her frown. If she hadn't dragged him to that damn event, he'd still be alive.

"Take care of him," Portia blurted.

Dizzie blinked at her.

"Killian," Portia clarified. "You never know when it all could end."

"Is that a threat?" Dizzie looked about ready to launch off the sofa.

Portia shook her head. "No, not at all," she said wistfully. "It's a lesson I learned too late and wouldn't wish on anyone."

Tension seeped out of Dizzie. "Thank you," she said softly. "I know you hate that Killian and I are together. I wasn't sure if that changed how you feel about him."

Portia wasn't sure how to respond. "He's still one of—" Her throat clenched and she bit back a rush of tears. "He's still my best friend. We're just taking a break."

Dizzie nodded like she was agreeing to something. "That's good. You're still his best friend too. He's available if you want to talk or hang out or something." Her cheeks flushed. "He asked me to pass on that message."

"Thanks." Portia spoke around the tears that threatened again. She cleared her throat. "Okay, now that's out of the way, we need a game plan for facing the Solveigs. And to keep them from getting their hands on my, I mean, the company."

"Can't I just tell them that I have no interest in owning it?"

Portia shook her head. "I don't think they'll listen to you. Or care. From what I've been, ah, told, they're really looking for revenge."

Dizzie snorted. "Yeah, I remember how you were. You weren't letting anything get in the way of getting your revenge on me."

Portia flushed. Dizzie's tone was bland, but neither of them had forgotten Portia's dogged pursuit.

"It's okay," she said, when Portia remained silent. "I

forgive you. If anything happened to Killian, I'd react the same way."

Portia filed her comment about forgiveness away to think about later. Did she even want or need it? It was too much to contemplate now.

"Oh, and another thing," Portia said. "I wouldn't put it past them to try to kidnap you if you don't agree."

"Are you serious?" Dizzie squeaked.

Portia nodded. "You should probably let Killian know about that." She raised her hand to stop any questions. "I'm not 100 percent certain, but it's not zero either."

"Shit," Dizzie said. "That's fucked up."

Portia laughed. "Yeah, well, welcome to life at the corporate level."

"Then I *definitely* don't want the job. Why would you even want it?"

Portia had asked herself that many times over the last several months. "I guess because it's what I was born to do."

Dizzie stared at her. "Nope, definitely don't want your life."

If only she knew that this meeting was only one of Portia's current problems. She somehow needed to cement her claim to the company, avoid whatever bad shit the Solveigs planned to throw at her, and solve the Vyne problem.

"Let's figure out how to give them a united front."

CHAPTER 25

ALEKS HELD the door to the conference room open. Two Solveig Consortium security personnel entered first. They brushed by him in their stark black uniforms, reminders of what could have been. The jealousy wasn't as strong as it usually was. He filed away that little tidbit, then focused on his job: the meeting with Portia and Dizzie.

"Clear."

Aleks rolled his eyes. Of course, the room was clear. The hotel had been selected as neutral ground. Portia hadn't even offered a room in Tremaine headquarters, smart enough to recognize that the Solveigs wouldn't accept.

"After you, Mr. Solveig. Mrs. Solveig," he said to the couple who stood just behind him. He stepped out of the way to let his employers pass into the room. Agnarr Solveig entered first, moving stiffly with age. His gray hair almost matched his gray suit. His wife, Iduna, followed. Gray hair perfectly styled, she wore a black dress and sensible black shoes.

She stopped just inside the doorway and sniffed haughtily. "It will do, I suppose."

"Come, dear, let us take our seats," her husband said.

Aleks waited until they had cleared the doorway, before entering the room. He was followed by four more security personnel. His gut twisted. A half-dozen guards seemed like overkill to him. Surely, the Solveigs weren't concerned for their safety. His mind conjured up a dozen possibilities for that number of guards, ranging from assassination attempts to corporate espionage.

He turned to close the door and to hide his wince. If he showed any hint of weakness now, they would likely demand that he leave the meeting. And he couldn't leave Portia alone with them.

That thought pinged around his head with all the others. Ruthlessly stuffing them all down, he faced his employers.

They'd seated themselves at the head of the table on the other side of the room. Security had taken up positions around them, fanning out to the halfway point of the table.

There was an energy to the Solveigs that he'd never seen before. The CEO and her husband rarely traveled together. She preferred to remain close to headquarters, managing the company with an iron fist.

Usually subdued—the loss of her youngest daughter had haunted her for years—she was practically vibrating in her seat. When Dizzie's existence had made international news several months ago, Iduna Solveig had immediately wanted to rush to Seattle to meet her. Security had discouraged it, citing the continued chaos at the Tremaine Corporation.

Phillip Tremaine's absence and Portia's steady leadership had seemed to calm some of her security team's fears. First, they'd sent a reconnaissance team. Then Aleks had been sent ahead for further study and to make the arrangements.

Initially, he'd had no qualms about getting close to Portia. The Tremaines were responsible for the turn his life had taken when the implant had failed.

And then he'd met her. Seen the softness under her Ice Queen reputation. Never to be confused with weakness. That woman had survived some serious shit this last year.

A small stab of guilt pierced his heart. He was very afraid that he was developing real feelings for her, but his first loyalty had to be to the company. Right? They'd given him a job when all the Tremaine Corporation had done was given him a faulty implant.

"Good morning. I trust you slept well," he said, his tone formal, his manner respectful. He couldn't imagine treating the Solveigs with the same informality that had grown between him and Portia.

Mrs. Solveig waved away his greeting. "Where is she? When can we see her?"

The only other time he'd seen them so animated was right before he had left for Seattle. Aleks glanced at his watch. "We have five minutes until the official meeting time. Can I offer you something to drink in the meantime?" The hotel had offered a coffee service for the meeting, which he'd gratefully accepted.

"How dare they keep us waiting like this?"

Aleks bit his tongue. Nothing good would come of trying to reason with her. He wished that Portia and Dizzie would arrive early, but that was unlikely. Portia wouldn't be at anyone's beck and call, especially not the Solveigs. He'd even had trouble reaching her yesterday to confirm the meeting details.

Time crawled until, finally, the door opened. A

Tremaine Security guard stepped inside. His gaze swept over the room's occupants, then he stepped back and held the door open.

Dizzie entered first. Aleks immediately picked out her similarities to Portia. How could anyone not have seen them? Then again, he saw hints of the Solveigs in her features as well.

"Anna!" Mrs. Solveig gasped. She bolted up from her chair and likely would have rushed to meet her granddaughter, except Dizzie frowned and took a step backward.

Mr. Solveig tugged on his wife's arm. She resisted until he said something that Aleks couldn't hear.

Only when Mrs. Solveig was seated did Dizzie enter the room fully. She didn't say anything as she took a seat at the other end of the table. Instead of taking the seat directly at the head, she sat just to the right.

The Solveigs scowled, but Aleks was intrigued. From everything Portia had said, she and Dizzie weren't close. Yet, Dizzie was clearly aligning herself with Portia.

His breath caught when Portia entered the room. Her blue dress was all business and screamed power and control. Of course, he also admired the way it skimmed her body, highlighting the curves he knew intimately.

She entered the room with little fanfare, but she owned it. Even the Solveigs turned their attention to her. It was the first time he'd seen her fully embody the Ice Queen and it was sexy as hell. She was a woman to be reckoned with and the more time he spent with her, the more he wanted to be at her side while she kicked ass and took names.

That was the crux of his problem. He owed everything to the Solveig Consortium. How could he possibly leave them for another company? Because that's what loving Portia would mean.

But that was a problem for another day. For now, he had to survive this meeting and ensure that his employers—and Portia—did too.

Portia nodded to the Tremaine Security guard in the doorway. He stepped out of the room, closing the door behind him. She slid into the empty seat at the end of the table with a grace that Aleks admired.

The Solveig security team shifted nervously in their positions. Were they wondering how the two women dared appear here alone? Obviously, Tremaine Security was right outside, but anything could happen in the time it took them to enter the room. Nerves of steel must run in the family, because neither woman flinched under the scrutiny.

Tense silence hung in the air and no one appeared in a hurry to break it. Until Dizzie spoke.

"You said you wanted to meet me. Here I am." She held her hands out in a questioning gesture.

Aleks glanced at Portia, curious what she thought of her sister's opening salvo. Her expression gave nothing away, but he swore he saw a twinkle in her eyes. Had they planned this? It certainly put the ball in his employers' court.

They were stock still, staring at Dizzie.

Aleks took advantage of the moment to study Portia and Dizzie side by side. When Dizzie caught him looking, something flashed in her eyes and then a corner of her mouth tipped up in a smile. What did that mean?

The silence stretched too long and Aleks stepped in to fill it. "Allow me to make the formal introductions." He hesitated, realizing that to do this, he would need to snub

Portia, since etiquette required he treat his employers as the senior party.

"Mrs. and Mr. Solveig, allow me to present Portia Tremaine, CEO of the Tremaine Corporation. And her sister, Dizzie—" Oh crap, he didn't know what last name to use.

"St. John," Dizzie added smoothly.

Portia jerked to face her sister. Dizzie smiled serenely and gave a slight nod.

Holy shit. That was something he hadn't seen coming.

Apparently neither had Portia. He hoped he'd have a chance after this to talk to her about it, to see how she was taking the news.

But he couldn't deal with that right now. He had a meeting to facilitate.

"Ms. Tremaine, Mrs. St. John, I'd like to introduce you to Mrs. Iduna Solveig, CEO of the Solveig Consortium and her husband, Mr. Agnarr Solveig."

Grim-faced nods from both sides of the table.

"Now that we all know each other, shall we get down to business?"

CHAPTER 26

PORTIA LOOKED AROUND THE ROOM. She took in the security present—six Solveig guards—and smiled quietly to herself. Apparently the Solveigs thought they needed to be protected from big bad Portia Tremaine.

Of course, they could also be planning to do away with her here. Her thumb ran over the simple silver band on her index finger. It was a sleekly designed panic button. Sure, her team might not make it into the room in time, but it meant she—and Dizzie—weren't completely alone.

Dizzie, who was now married to Portia's best friend. That had been a shock. Mrs. Solveig had yet to say anything, even a generic greeting. Portia thought she'd seen a flicker of disapproval on the other woman's face but it had been gone too quickly. If she had problems with Killian, well, she could fuck right off. No one got to disparage him in her presence.

Her gaze drifted to the other people in the room. Mrs. Solveig looked more matronly than Portia would expect from a company CEO. She wasn't photographed very often, so Portia wasn't sure if it was her usual look or a ploy for sympathy. Agnarr Solveig looked like any other old, white male in the corporate world. She'd dealt with plenty of those in her career.

She lingered on Aleks for just a moment longer than was probably prudent. He looked quite handsome in his suit. It was a stormy gray and his shirt brought out the blue in his eyes. After the introductions, he'd taken a seat toward the middle of the table, slightly closer to the Solveig CEO than Dizzie. But just slightly. She filed that piece of information away.

"Well," Dizzie said. "What did you want to meet about?" Not subtle at all, but Portia understood the other woman's impatience. Being summoned tended to irritate Portia too.

Under the table, she nudged Dizzie with the tip of her shoe.

"We . . . it's just . . . we wanted so much to meet you." Mrs. Solveig's voice trembled. "You look so much like our daughter Anna."

"That was my mother's name?" Dizzie's tone was softer this time.

Mrs. Solveig gasped. "You didn't know her name?"

Dizzie shrugged as if it didn't mean much to her. "No, I didn't know anything about my parents until this year."

Portia winced. For the first time, she thought about what it must have been like to grow up in the Tremaine orphanage, not knowing anything about your parents. Portia's mom had died when Portia was young and she still missed her every damn day.

"That's your fault," Mrs. Solveig hissed at Portia. "You and your bastard of a father."

"I had nothing to do with Dizzie's parentage," Portia said coolly. "I found out after she did."

The other woman glared across the table. Her husband put a restraining hand on her forearm.

"I'm sorry you didn't know your mother, Dizzie. May I call you that?" he asked.

Dizzie nodded stiffly.

"She was the light of our life. The baby of the family. When she ran away and then," he paused and dabbed at his eyes with a handkerchief, "when she died, it left a hole in our family. If only we'd known about you."

"Why didn't you?" Dizzie asked. Her voice was tight.

Portia didn't know her well enough to gauge how this reunion was affecting her.

"Know about you?" He took a deep breath. "We received a box of ashes and a form letter. She'd been identified by her DNA and they were sending her back to us. We didn't get a body to bury, just a box." His voice broke.

"From the Tremaine medical facility! Some low-level tech had more compassion than your father!" Mrs. Solveig lashed out.

Portia withstood the onslaught of words. Her father was a cold-hearted bastard, but damn, that was a new low. "I'm sorry for your loss," she said quietly. She understood the pain and the power of grief.

"Oh, we don't want your pity. You're as bad as your father. We want our granddaughter as far from you as possible." Mrs. Solveig glared at Portia for a long moment. When she transferred her gaze to Dizzie, it softened. "We can't wait for you to come back with us."

"What? No," Dizzie said. "I'm not going back with you." She shook her head.

"Of course you are, dear. You'll have everything you need to start a new life. The life you should have had instead of being forced to live like a gutter rat."

What the hell? Portia blinked. She couldn't be serious.

Next to her, Dizzie clicked her nails together. "I have everything I need here. I'm married to the man I love. What else do I need?"

"Pfft. He doesn't love you. We can get an annulment." Mrs. Solveig smiled coldly. "I'm sure it's just a cruel trick that *she* put him up to. They've been close since childhood, you know."

The gleam in Mrs. Solveig's eye and her tone told Portia exactly what she was trying to imply. Which, no. *Ew.* She and Killian had one date before they'd even graduated high school and there was nothing romantic between them. Ever.

Portia looked at Aleks. His eyes were wide and he looked as confused as she felt.

Dizzie's clicking increased. "I've never had grandparents before," she said, "but I'm pretty sure this isn't how it's supposed to be." She stood abruptly. "You wanted to meet me. Now you have. We're done."

She stepped toward the door. One of the Solveigs' guards stepped toward her.

"I wouldn't do that," Portia said very softly and pinned him with a glare.

He flinched and stepped back.

Aleks coughed, though it sounded like he was smothering a laugh.

Portia stood. Her fingertips rested on the edge of the conference table. "Meeting adjourned."

"You can't do that." Mrs. Solveig stood as well, moving so quickly that her chair hit the wall.

"You wanted to meet my sister. As she said, you did. That's all you get."

Turning her back on the Solveig contingent, Portia followed Dizzie out of the room without a care in the world, despite the never-ending threats Mrs. Solveig continued to throw at her back.

CHAPTER 27

ALEKS GOT one last glimpse of Portia before the Tremaine Security guard closed the door behind her. Despite her departure, Mrs. Solveig continued to hurl vitriol at her.

"That woman brainwashed my granddaughter. Why would she want to stay in this horrible city with these horrible people?"

Behind her, one of the Solveig security personnel quietly set her chair upright, then stepped back to his position against the wall.

Her husband grabbed her hand. Cradling it between his palms, he patted it soothingly. She wrenched her hand free, then dropped into her chair with a wail.

Aleks hid his wince. The high-pitched sound battered his ears, but he couldn't let his discomfort show.

"You!"

He should have known that he would be her next target. "Yes, ma'am?'

"This is your fault. You were supposed to set up a meeting with our granddaughter, not that, that . . . "

She trailed off and looked to her husband for a suitable word. He shrugged.

Aleks wished he could do that. Instead, he had to sit here and take whatever abuse she hurled at him with a smile. Like always.

"Why was that woman here?"

Aleks chose his words carefully. "Ms. Tremaine was here because Mrs. St. John requested her presence."

"Her name is Solveig, not St. John."

"Why are you concerned that she's married?" He honestly didn't understand. From his meeting with Killian St. John, the other man seemed a standup guy. And the sparkle in Dizzie's eyes and the joy in her voice when she'd announced her marriage—well, that didn't seem like any kind of problem to him. In fact, that was the kind of thing he dreamed about.

What made the situation even stranger was that Aleks had always believed that the Solveigs had a loving marriage. Had it all been for show? Or had grief and the last six months broken that? Wouldn't they want that for their granddaughter?

"The marriage is obviously a way to trap her into staying in Seattle and under Tremaine control," Mrs. Solveig said. "We'll need to start the paperwork for an annulment immediately."

She shot him an icy look. Portia did it better. Was it wrong to be amused by that thought?

"Does Portia Tremaine always travel with an armed contingent of guards?" she asked.

He worded his response carefully. "I can't say." More like *wouldn't* say, but no way would he jeopardize Portia like that. "My meetings with her have been at the Tremaine Corporation headquarters or over the phone."

"Hmmm," she said, studying him closely. "And what about this rumored new man in her life?"

Aleks nearly swallowed his tongue. "Pardon?"

She sniffed. "Obviously you haven't been taking your job here very seriously. I expected you to stay on top of all the news about the company." Pulling a tablet from her purse, she swiped across a few screens, then slid it across the table. "That's what I'm talking about."

The image on the screen had obviously come from the drone he'd taken down. Fortunately, the fog and the buildings' shadows made the image nearly dark, with few clear details. Just Portia's blond hair barely visible over his shoulder.

He was so thankful that he hadn't worn that same jacket today. Likely he could never wear it again, but that was a small price to pay for keeping his relationship with Portia secret.

His brain whirred with possible reactions, most of them focused on protecting Portia from the Solveigs. He settled on, "Sorry, I must have missed that."

Would she accept it?

"Of course you did. If I didn't know your implant had failed from the beginning, I'd think that she had tweaked it somehow," she sniped. "Remind me to send someone more qualified next time. Have you found anything useful about the company that we can use against them?"

The familiar fire burned in his belly at her casual dismissal. All these years, he'd taken it because he'd been told he should be grateful. That he should be pissed at the Tremaine Corporation for the faulty implant in his head. But since he'd been in Seattle, Portia had treated him like anyone else. Warm at times, cold at others, burning hot in his arms in the best moments. But she'd never treated him as lesser. Compared to the people he'd known for years, that was huge.

"Nothing yet," he lied. He'd keep the secret of Vyne's origins for Portia. He might not be able to hide it forever, but he'd give her time to solve her problem. "I have some feelers out," he said.

"Imbecile," she muttered under her breath. "Get this situation under control. I expect results soon."

She stood again, as did her husband, who took her elbow. Aleks stood out of respect. Bracketed by guards in front and behind, the couple filed out of the conference room.

Aleks sat and dropped his head into his hands. This whole assignment was getting out of hand. His loyalty was being tested and for the first time, he honestly didn't know who he would choose.

His brain immediately contradicted that, throwing memory after memory of Portia at him.

Shit, how was he going to get out of this?

CHAPTER 28

PORTIA WAITED until her driver closed the door before turning to Dizzie. "You and Killian got married?" That announcement had thrown everyone at the meeting for a loop.

Dizzie smiled like the cat who ate the canary. "Yes."

"How the hell did you keep it secret from the newsies?" Portia would never admit it, but she'd been surprised and, more surprisingly, hurt when Dizzie had shared her news so nonchalantly.

"It wasn't easy," Dizzie said. "Killian pulled some strings." She shrugged. "It worked."

"Why didn't you tell me?" Portia pressed her lips together. That wasn't what she'd meant to say at all.

"Killian was afraid you'd try to talk him out of it. I didn't think you'd care." Dizzie's even tone gave nothing away.

Portia's mouth opened, then snapped shut. "Okay, fair point."

"Why are you so bothered by this?" Dizzie shifted on her seat and turned to face her.

"I don't know!" It was as frustrating as it was

maddening. "We've been friends forever. He was at *my* wedding. I always thought I'd be at his."

Dizzie grabbed Portia's hand. She flinched at the unexpected contact and Dizzie pulled back immediately.

"Sorry. It's not you. I'm just . . . not used to being touched." No one ever dared get that close to her. Except Aleks.

"What about Tommy?" Horror colored Dizzie's voice.

Portia laughed. "Well, obviously. But I wasn't raised in a touchy-feely family."

Dizzie didn't reply right away. "I don't know how to respond to that," she admitted. "I wasn't raised in a family at all. At least not an official one, but in the orphanage, we rough-housed just like normal siblings."

"You met my father. Our father. Can you picture him roughhousing?" The look on Dizzie's face was worth Portia's earlier awkward admission.

"Ohmygod."

"I know. I had Killian and Tommy. But it wasn't the same. There were rules for the daughter of a corporate CEO. Etiquette lessons. Meetings and extra classes."

"Sounds fun." Dizzie's tone implied the opposite.

"You're not wrong, but it was the only life I knew." She'd never complained in public—no one would have any sympathy for the poor little rich girl. Portia smiled. "Tommy tried, though. He made sure our home was always filled with love and laughter."

His name hung in the space between them.

"I'm sorry about Tommy," Dizzie said after a long pause.

Portia's heart clenched and her breath caught. She didn't want to have this conversation, but she'd been avoiding it for months.

"Thank you," she said, because she didn't know what else to say.

Dizzie started to say something but Portia held up her hand to stop her.

"Thank you," she repeated. "I'm getting better at separating you from the whole plot, but I'm not there yet. I'm glad you're willing to work with me on the Solveig visit and I'm glad we're able to talk civilly, mostly at least. I want to forgive you, but I'm not there yet. I know that his death wasn't intentional on your part." She paused. "That's probably not what you wanted to hear."

Tears rolled down Dizzie's cheeks and Portia felt a tiny pang of guilt. She thought she'd let her down easy. "Shit." The word slipped out.

Dizzie's eyes got wider, if that was even possible, then she burst out laughing.

Portia blinked. She'd broken her.

Dizzie laughed and laughed.

Portia had no idea what to do. "Do you need to go to the hospital? Should I call Killian?"

Dizzie stared at her. Tears streamed down her face. "What are you talking about, Portia?"

"This." Portia waved her hand in loose circles in Dizzie's direction. "I don't know how to deal with someone who's having a breakdown. Is it better to call Killian, or to take you to the hospital first?"

"You think I'm having a breakdown?" Dizzie laughed harder.

"I don't know," Portia said, her tone defensive. Her shoulders tensed. This was what she got for trying to be helpful and forgiving.

Dizzie made a visible effort to stop laughing or breaking or whatever it was that was happening right now. She sucked in heaving gasps of air as she fought to get her breathing under control. She wiped her eyes with her sleeve. "I'm fine," she said, then laughed again.

Portia set her jaw. "I still think you should get checked out." Dizzie's eyes were red and her face was blotchy.

"I'm fine, Portia. Really. I didn't think you'd ever even get close to forgiving me. That there's even a possibility is a gift. I'm fine. Better than fine, even." She reached over and squeezed Portia's hand.

"Oh. Well." Portia had no idea what to do with that information. In all honesty, she'd never imagined forgiving Dizzie for her involvement in Tommy's death. Time may not have healed all her wounds—and likely never would—but maybe it had given her the ability to see through her grief.

She lightly squeezed Dizzie's hand in return and then swiftly disengaged. "Oh look, we're at your home," she said brightly.

Dizzie's half-smile said she saw too much. "Thank you for the ride, Portia. And for meeting them with me."

"You're welcome," Portia said. "I can't say it was a pleasure, but I'm glad you asked."

Dizzie laughed again. "They were awful, weren't they?"

Portia nodded. Yes, she'd been less than impressed with Aleks's employers. Why did he work for such terrible people?

"Hopefully they got the message and go back to Sweden," Dizzie said.

Personally—and from what Aleks had shared—she thought that was unlikely. But she was oddly reluctant to burst Dizzie's bubble. At least right now. "That would be nice," was all she said.

Dizzie swung the door open and was mostly out of the

car before Portia added, "Congratulations to you and Killian, Dizzie. I hope you're very happy."

Dizzie's only response was a smile so full of love and happiness that Portia felt a twinge of jealousy. Then the door closed and she was gone.

CHAPTER 29

PORTIA REACHED her apartment door with a sigh of relief. She'd returned to her office after dropping Dizzie off, but had been too distracted to do much work. She either kept replaying her conversations with Dizzie or obsessively checking her email for news about the Vyne research from Ash or Mendez. Neither activity had left her any brain power for the other business of running the company. Hopefully tomorrow would be more productive.

All afternoon she'd mulled the idea of inviting Killian and Dizzie to dinner. She still didn't love the idea—she'd never pictured herself socializing with Dizzie. The only place she'd ever pictured Dizzie was a jail cell or a grave.

Had she gotten weak? That was what her father would say. For a lot of years, she'd believed him.

What her father thought didn't matter anymore.

On that happy thought, she pressed her palm to the door sensor and it unlocked with a quick snick. Closing it securely behind her, she set down her bag and kicked her heels off in the entryway.

As she padded toward the living room, she released her

bun. Her hair fell loosely around her shoulders and she breathed a sigh of relief as the pressure on her temples eased. She'd overdone it this morning, but she'd wanted to look as no-nonsense as possible for this meeting. The Solveigs had needed to understand that she was not someone to fuck with. All in all, Portia thought that message had been delivered.

"What did those fucking Swedes want?"

A scream froze in her throat and her heart beat double time. Someone was in her apartment. She stepped backward, intending to flee and call security. Her thumb was hovering over her ring's panic button when the light flicked on in the living room, illuminating her unexpected visitor.

"Dad?" This couldn't be happening. "I thought you were dead. *Everyone* thought you were dead."

Yet, there he sat. On her couch. In her living room.

"You had a meeting with the Solveigs tonight. Tell me why," he demanded.

What? That was all he had to say? No way. She had plenty of her own questions. Cautiously stepping into the living room, she turned on every light she could reach and studied him.

Graying blond hair a little longer than he usually wore it. A suit that wasn't nearly as pressed as his usual standard. Cheekbones that were just slightly more pronounced than when she last saw him. "Where the hell have you been?"

He set the glass he'd been holding onto the coffee table, next to the scotch he'd apparently helped himself to, and stood. "You don't speak to me that way, daughter. Now sit down and answer my question."

Portia held her ground and fought the conditioning of her youth. She'd always done everything her father told her to do. The need to win his approval had been overwhelming, but nothing had ever been good enough. These last several months, running the company on her own, had been so freeing.

So, she steeled her spine and overrode the ingrained need to obey. "No."

Her heart nearly pounded out of her chest as she refused his order. It took everything she had to fake nonchalance and lean against the wall, arms crossed over her chest. "No, I don't think so. It's your turn to answer my questions." Just as with the Solveigs, she layered every ounce of don't-fuck-with-me she had into her voice.

His brow furrowed and his cheeks flushed. Once again, she had to fight the deep-rooted desire to apologize and do what he said.

Until that moment, she'd never realized how fucked up her childhood was. Tommy and Killian had tried time and again to point it out, but she'd never truly understood what they were saying until this moment. "What are you doing here?" And how had he gotten in?

Turning on the charm, he asked, "A father can't visit his daughter?"

It was such an absurd question, she couldn't contain the laugh that burbled up. She laughed long enough and hard enough that his scowl deepened, the skin between his brows pinching together. She enjoyed the novelty of knocking him off balance. It was only fair, considering he'd spent years doing the same to her.

"Not when he's been missing for months. You never wrote, never called," she said mockingly.

"I had things to take care of." He grabbed his glass for another swallow.

Portia raised a brow. "Really? What could possibly be

more important than comforting your daughter in her grief? Or steering your company through a difficult time?"

He started to answer and she waved him off. "You know what? I don't care. You let everyone think you were dead and I stepped in. I stepped up. I'm the CEO of the Tremaine Corporation now. So, you can go back to wherever it was you were and enjoy your retirement."

He growled at that and took a step toward her.

Her heart rate kicked up again. Would he actually harm her? She honestly wasn't sure.

Despite her concerns, she didn't let her worry show. Just like he'd taught her. "They wanted to meet their granddaughter. You know, the one you kept locked in the basement to use as spare parts?"

He glared at her and she waited for his rebuttal. The way he would tell her that she wasn't good enough. Surprisingly, it didn't come. She didn't believe he had changed, so what was he waiting for?

They stood in silence, tension crackling between them. When it became clear he was waiting for her to break, she pasted on her Ice Queen smile. "If that's all, you should leave. I've had a long day."

"Where do you expect me to go?" She couldn't read his expression or his tone.

Portia stared at him. "I don't really care. Back to your home or wherever you been hiding." As far as she knew, his place had been sitting empty. She hadn't been willing—or ready—to make a permanent decision about it until she knew for sure what had happened to him. She'd hired a caretaker to check on it weekly. Surely her father hadn't been holed up there this entire time. She couldn't imagine him not succumbing to the bright lights of the city.

"Next time you want to talk to me, make an

appointment. Anything we need to discuss can happen in my office."

Rage flared in his gaze. "Oh, we'll be speaking further, missy."

That cold, angry tone used to make her quiver in fear. She refused to show distress this time.

His nostrils flared, the only outward sign that her defiance had angered him. Portia stepped aside as he strode past her. The door closed behind him with an angry click.

She hurried behind him and engaged the deadbolt. Then she sagged against the wall as the adrenaline rush that had kept her upright finally dissipated.

Holy shit. Her father was alive.

That was a problem she really didn't need right now.

Summoning enough strength to push off the wall, she returned to the living room. The decanter was on the coffee table where her father had left it, next to his empty glass. Clean glasses were across the room in the kitchen.

"Screw it," she muttered and picked the glass bottle up by its neck. She brought it to her lips and took a long swallow. It burned, but she didn't care. A drop slid down her chin and she wiped it away with the back of her hand.

Setting the bottle back on the table, she dropped onto the couch. Her father's return was a complication she didn't need. Not right now. He had the potential to screw up everything she'd done since his disappearance. All her improvements and fixes, erased.

She leaned back and closed her eyes. Maybe she wouldn't have to deal with him again any time soon.

Haha. Not likely.

She'd barely rested her head on the cushion before she realized that he was most likely back to reclaim the company. She wouldn't put it past him to stroll in tomorrow like he owned the place.

Screw that. The Tremaine Corporation was hers now. He'd thrown it away the moment he disappeared. Now she would do everything in her power to keep it, no matter who was trying to take it from her.

But as much as it galled her, she couldn't do it alone.

It was time to put on her big girl panties and start rebuilding some bridges.

CHAPTER 30

PORTIA STEPPED into the dimness that was Razor Jack's and momentarily felt like the weight of the world—or at least of the Tremaine Corporation—wasn't on her shoulders. Until she remembered that she was here to ask for help to save it.

Damn her father for his games and power plays.

With a sigh, she wove her way through the tables to her preferred corner. Which was occupied.

Of course it was.

She wasn't in full incognito mode tonight, but probably wasn't obviously Portia Tremaine either.

She took a risk and approached. "Excuse me. This is my table," she said politely.

The two dudes at the table glanced up at her. "We were here first," one said.

"And I'm here last," Portia countered.

"Who's going to make us move, you?" He looked at his buddy and laughed.

Portia shrugged. "I have friends in high places," she said. She glanced over at the bar. "You can move for me," she said, coating her words with Ice Queen frost, "or you can move for the Jack. Which would you prefer?"

The men glanced at each other and then scrambled to leave.

"Ah-ah-ah. Don't leave without paying your bill. And don't forget to leave a really big tip," she added as she watched them insert credit chips into the payment system.

"Good boys. Now shoo."

After a last glance between her and the bar, the two men hightailed it out of there.

With a laugh, she pulled herself onto one of the bar stools, careful not to touch the empty glasses and plates the men had left. One of the waitresses would be by to clean it up.

"I'm not sure how I feel about you running my customers off."

Portia turned toward the speaker. She was a tall woman with long dark hair and dusky skin. Tonight she wore all black and a faint smile.

"Good evening, Taryn," Portia said smoothly.

"Good evening, Portia," Taryn—known to most of the city as the Jack—parroted.

"They had my table and I needed it."

One dark brow rose. "I believe it's *my* table, given it's in *my* bar."

"Semantics." Portia waved her hand as if it didn't matter. She loved sparring with Taryn. The other woman had a shrewd mind and didn't take shit from anyone. Over the last months the two of them had danced around the idea of friendship, neither willing to take that last step. "I made sure they paid and left a hefty tip."

"Well, that makes it all okay then." Taryn laughed. "Your usual?"

Portia tilted her head and considered the question. "No. A whiskey, please," she said, remembering the drink she'd shared with Aleks the night they'd met. She needed to shake things up if she was going to save her business.

"I'll have someone bring that out."

"Thank you," Portia murmured. When Taryn turned to go, Portia added, "Wait. Please. I invited Dizzie and Killian tonight—"

"No fights in my bar, Portia," Taryn interjected.

"It's not that. I'd appreciate it if you and Ash could join us."

"Why?"

Portia swallowed and looked away for a moment. This was the hardest part. "I need some help," she said when she looked back.

Taryn held her gaze for a long moment. "Okay. We'll hear what you have to say, but no promises."

"Fair enough."

"I'll send someone over with your drink and to clean up the table." Taryn strode toward the bar, leaving Portia alone with her thoughts.

What if everyone heard her out and declined to help? She hadn't really been all that helpful herself lately. Or maybe ever.

Well, if they didn't want to help, she'd figure out how to do it on her own.

CHAPTER 31

"I NEED your help to save the Tremaine Corporation," Portia told the people gathered around her.

Dizzie had taken the other stool at the table. Killian stood protectively behind her, one hand on the back of her chair. Ash leaned against the table, one elbow propped on its surface, while Taryn stood slightly off to the side, arms crossed over her chest, her gaze on the room around them.

"Are you sure it's worth saving?" That was Ash, though honestly, she wouldn't have been surprised if the words came from Dizzie.

"I think it is," Portia said. What she didn't say was that it was all she had left. She wasn't looking for their pity.

"Is this about the Solveigs' proposals to buy Tremaine stock?" Killian asked.

Portia blew out a breath. "That's part of it," she admitted. "But only a small part."

God, she hated laying her problems out for the world. But it was the only way she could think of to get the help she needed. Time to rip the bandage off. "The Solveigs want to take over the company, yes, or else destroy it.

Whichever, they want me out of the way, preferably permanently."

She held up a hand when the questions started. "They want Dizzie to go to Sweden with them."

Killian cursed.

"Against that backdrop, I've learned the company was the original manufacturer of Vyne. And, to top it all off, my father's back from the dead."

Chaos erupted around her. Questions, statements, curses. She was bombarded with all of them. Her hand shook around her glass so she just clenched it tighter and sipped the whiskey.

The noise finally eased and everyone stared at her. "Feel better?" she asked.

Someone, maybe Taryn, laughed.

"How long have you known your, our—that man was back?" Dizzie asked.

"When I walked into my apartment tonight and found him waiting for me."

"Did you let him in?" Dizzie asked suspiciously.

"No," Portia said, not bothering to hide her shudder. "I don't know how he got in, but I changed all the security codes before I came here." Not knowing how he'd originally accessed her home, she hoped it was enough.

"I've got a few tricks if you want me to help," Ash offered.

"Yes, thank you." The thought of her father having constant access to her home made her downright uneasy.

"What does he want?" Killian asked, his voice hard. He stepped closer to Dizzie, as if his mere presence would keep her safe.

"The first words out of his mouth were about the Solveigs. He wanted to know what they wanted. But underneath it all, I think he's here to try to take back control of the company." Her tone hardened.

The mutters around the table contemplated Phillip Tremaine's return.

"I can't let him do that. It's my company now." Portia's voice was hard. Determined.

"What do you expect us to do about it? It sounds like a family problem," Taryn commented.

The others nodded in agreement.

"My father cannot be allowed to run the Tremaine Corporation again. It's not good for the company and it's not good for the city. I can't fight a war on multiple fronts by myself," she admitted. "I need help."

For a long moment, the only sound around them was the clink and glasses and murmurs of the other patrons.

Would they agree to help her?

"Vyne is part of this?" Taryn asked, her voice hard and cold.

Portia swallowed hard. "Yes. I only learned that a couple of days ago. Ash has been looking into it for me."

Taryn and Ash shared a look. "You'll shut it down?"

Portia nodded. "As soon as I find out exactly where it's coming from."

"I'll have that data for you soon," Ash said. "Just making sure I'm not missing anything."

"Thank you." Portia meant it. She'd shut down that business if it was the last thing she did. Which wasn't out of the realm of possibility.

"That leaves the Solveigs and your father," Killian said.

A shadow fell over the table. "Your father? What does he have to do with this?" Aleks asked incredulously.

"What are you doing here?" Portia asked at the same time Dizzie said, "Everything, apparently," her tone dark.

CHAPTER 32

THE NEED for a drink had brought Aleks to Razor Jack's. The chance of running into his employers at the hotel bar was too high and the thought of drinking in his room had been too damn depressing. So, he'd come to the one bar in the city he knew.

Who was he kidding? He'd come here hoping against hope to see Portia. He'd automatically headed for her corner and there she was. Like he'd conjured her from a dream.

What he hadn't expected was the cluster of people at her table. He studied the faces around her. Killian St. John he recognized and nodded in greeting. He smiled at Dizzie. "Nice to see you again."

She smiled back. Her gaze bounced from him to Portia and back. Something like humor lingered in her gaze.

Aleks didn't recognize the wiry man who stood next to the table. He'd straightened from a lean when Aleks had spoken. He didn't look like a fighter, though Aleks had met enough wiry guys to know they could be scrappy.

The woman standing next to him, though. She was a

survivor. He recognized the look in her eyes and the way she held herself. She uncrossed her arms and let them drop loosely to her sides. A simple but effective way to show him her wicked-looking cyberarm.

Yep, she was the threat. But like Dizzie, she studied him with interest and curiosity.

"Your father's back?" Aleks repeated when no one answered his question. "Where has he been? How long? What does he want?"

"Who the hell are you?" the wiry guy asked. "This doesn't concern you."

"It's okay, Ash," Portia said before the tension ratcheted up any higher. "Aleksander Lind, meet Ash Cutter. Ash, meet Aleksander Lind, employee of the Solveig Consortium."

"Gotcha," Ash said, looking between Aleks and Portia. He didn't offer his hand or apologize or make any of the social niceties. That was fine with Aleks.

"The woman next to Ash is the Jack."

"I like your place," Aleks said.

"Thanks," she said simply. "I do too."

"What are you doing here, Aleks, I mean, Mr. Lind?"

Aleks wanted to laugh at the correction, but the fact that she was trying to whitewash their relationship hurt. Which was absolutely ridiculous, because he'd done the exact same thing at the meeting.

"You think he's back to take over the company," he said, focusing on the more immediate issue.

She nodded, lips pressed tight together.

"Isn't that his right?"

Portia pursed her lips. "No. Possession is nine-tenths of the law."

He raised a brow. "That's probably stretching it a bit."

"I don't care," Portia said mulishly. "He's not taking my company. He abandoned it and now it belongs to me."

Aleks was aware of the others paying close attention to their conversation. He'd prefer to get her alone. To hold her and tell her it would be all right because he wouldn't let anyone hurt her, but that wasn't his job. His job was to learn as much as he could and report back.

That job description no longer felt right.

"Should we table this discussion until later?" Ash asked.

Portia studied Aleks for a long moment. He implored her with his gaze to let him stay. Finally, she gave him a slight nod. "No. It's okay."

"Are you sure you can trust this guy?" Ash again.

If he didn't stop trying to undermine Aleks, they were going to have words.

"As much as I trust anyone," Portia said, her tone cool.

"That's good," Ash said, "because I don't think we have a lot of time to deal with your father."

"Why do you say that?" Portia asked with a tilt of her head.

"He's obviously back for a reason. Maybe it's because of them," Ash pointed at Aleks, "or maybe it's because you've made the connection with the Tremaine Corporation and Vyne. Whatever it was, it was obviously important enough to bring him out of hiding."

"And?"

"And what would be more important than getting his former glory back?"

His question was met with murmurs of agreement.

"Your dad wants back in and he's used to getting his way. I don't know where he's been, but until the bombing, he ran the company for what, twenty, twenty-five years on his own?"

"My grandfather died when I was three. So yes, twenty-five is about right."

"Not only isn't he going to let go of the company easily," Ash said, "he's probably got at least one backdoor into the system, if not more."

Portia paled. "Sonofabitch." She rubbed her brow. "My father isn't a hacker. How would he do that?"

Ash shrugged. "Probably found a hacker to do it. Paid them off or maybe—" He stopped speaking and mimicked a blade over the throat.

She frowned. "Did you do that for him?"

He shook his head. "No. It's just a guess, Portia, and it probably happened years ago."

She spun her glass around on the table, watching the liquid slosh up the sides. Aleks remembered her doing that the night they met too. "Did you find backdoors or workarounds while you were sneaking around my systems?" she asked without looking up.

"A few," Ash admitted. "Though I don't know who used them or who put them there. We can try to cut him off at the pass. Make some educated guesses like overriding his building access and access to your office."

"Can you cut him out of the whole system?" Aleks asked.

Ash took a few seconds to think about that. "I can try, but it could take days or weeks to find any and all access points."

"We definitely don't have that kind of time," Portia agreed.

"What about people loyal to him? He ran the company for years. Does he have people in place he can use as proxies?" It was an obvious question to Aleks. Computers and technology may run everything, but it was the people-to-people connections that made and broke companies.

Portia rubbed the bridge of her nose. "Fewer than there were, but probably more than I know about."

"You think he still has loyalists in the company?" Killian asked. "Why didn't you say anything?"

"When?" Portia asked. "It's not like we've been on speaking terms most of the year."

He ran his hand through his hair. "Right. But you could have told me."

She sighed. "I've barely been keeping my head above water, Killian, fixing all the problems my father's absence created. Every time I turn around, there's a new problem from one of his old programs. I've eliminated some of his old cronies, but I have no idea who's on his side. How would I?"

"I think a lot of people are loyal to the company, not a specific person," Dizzie said.

Everyone looked at her. "What do you mean?" Portia asked.

"People like me were so far down the corporate ladder, you and your father were really just names. It never felt like you had a direct impact on our lives."

"You were loyal to the company when you were a courier?" Portia's tone said she didn't believe her.

Dizzie shrugged. "I didn't think in terms of loyalty. At least not to the company. I was loyal to my friends. Mostly, I did my job and dreamed of paying off my contract. I wasn't disloyal. I just didn't think about it at all."

"Well, that's helpful," Portia snapped.

"I wasn't alone, Portia. The company may have raised us, but it also kept us on a financial leash. Most of the people on the lower rungs just want to live their lives with as little interference from above as possible."

Portia dropped her head to the table with a thunk. The action took everyone at the table by surprise.

Aleks circled around the Jack and Ash and placed a hand on Portia's shoulder. "Are you okay?" He ached to pull her into his arms and comfort her.

Portia raised her head. "No, not really. Everything I've worked for is falling apart, my father's back, and my company is a shithole." She took a deep breath.

"Maybe Dizzie's right. Maybe with all the shady shit that my father did, the company isn't worth saving. Maybe I should just abandon it to the Solveigs and walk away."

"Anyone got a direct line to the newsies?" the Jack asked.

Everyone's heads swiveled toward her. Portia sat up and glared at the other woman. "What the hell? I thought I could trust you with this."

The Jack sneered. "Oh, you think I'd be calling them about your business problems?" She snorted. "Nah, I just want to let them know to change your nickname. You're not the Ice Queen. You're a fucking drama queen."

Against the shocked silence around the table, Portia's gasp was loud. Loud, angry, and horrified all at once. Aleks choked back a laugh.

"How dare you?"

"Aw, is the poor little rich girl getting mad? About damn time!"

Aleks turned away because he did not want to piss off Portia by laughing. Dizzie didn't seem to have that concern, because her laugh rang out around the table.

"She's right, Portia," Killian said. "You've faced worse than this. If anyone can do this, it's you. But you've got to commit, because we're all risking something by helping you."

Portia glared at the Jack. "Fine. I get what you're saying, but you didn't have to be such a bitch about it."

"Right," the Jack said. "Because you were just going to pull out of that spiral on your own."

"You have my support whatever you decide to do, Portia. Whatever you need, I'm here," Killian said. "As long as it doesn't harm Dizzie," he added.

"Mine, too," Dizzie added. "But I'm not going with the Solveigs. That I refuse to do." She glared at Aleks when she said it.

"Can you keep the investors calm, Killian? Make sure none of them sell to the Solveig Consortium?" Portia asked.

"I'm on it," he said.

Ash and the Jack weren't as quick to align themselves with her.

"I prefer to keep my business separate from the corporations. I don't need the scrutiny or trouble that comes with the multinationals," the Jack said.

Portia nodded." I understand."

"That said, we're already intertwined and there haven't been any serious repercussions. Yet. I'll provide what assistance I can when possible. For a price."

Ash elbowed her and she sighed. "Fine, I'll give you the friends and family discount, but that's as low as I can go."

Portia looked surprised. "Thank you."

"Locating the Vyne lab will be our priority," Ash said. "I'll close the backdoors we talked about as soon as we're done here. If you want others identified, you'll need to find somebody else. Want me to put Mendez on it?"

Portia's sigh was long-suffering. "If you think he's up to it, then yes."

"We don't have a lot of options, you know."

"Fine, do it." She rolled her eyes.

"What about me?" Everyone's gaze laser-focused on Aleks.

"Just don't tell your employers." Portia looked up at him, her eyes pleading.

"I won't." The words felt like a vow.

CHAPTER 33

"THANKS FOR ESCORTING ME HOME," Portia said as she and Aleks walked to her front door. She'd tried to get him to leave her at the building's lobby, but he'd insisted on door-to-door service after they'd left Razor Jack's. She hadn't argued too hard—honestly, the thought of coming home late to find her father in her apartment again was too much.

"You're welcome." He studied the hallway. "How did he get access?"

Portia followed his gaze. There were only a few doors: her apartment and the one across the hall, the doors to the stairwells at the ends, and the dedicated elevator. "I don't know." That had been worrying her all night.

"Do you want me to come in and check your place?"

She hesitated. The apartment had been hers and Tommy's. She'd never expected to bring another man here —even if that wasn't why Aleks was here at the moment. But her home had felt so empty lately. And Aleks was so . . . comfortable.

"Yes, please," she said quickly, before she could change her mind.

She entered her code and scanned her palm. When the door unlocked, Aleks gently pushed her behind him and entered. She'd left the lights on when she left, concerned about coming home to an intruder and a dark apartment.

"Stay here," Aleks said.

On a good day, she would have argued, but tonight staying by the door, by the escape route, felt right.

Aleks moved silently through the apartment. To keep her worries at bay, she wondered what he thought about the place. There were remnants of her life with Tommy all through the apartment, but every day, her life without him encroached on those memories more and more.

He returned looking slightly more relaxed than when they'd arrived. "It's clear," he said. "Make sure to lock the deadbolt when I leave."

She nodded. All of the sudden the thought of spending the night here, alone in her home, overwhelmed her. "Stay. Please."

Shock widened Aleks's eyes, followed quickly by heat.

Was that what she was asking? She wasn't sure. "To keep me company. I've got coffee. Or juice. Or water. There's scotch." She was babbling. She never babbled.

A slow smile spread across his face. "I'll stay, Portia. Whatever you need. You don't need to bribe me with coffee or juice or water. Or even scotch. Your company is enough."

Her cheeks warmed and she slapped her hands over them. "Thank you. I just . . . I don't want to be alone here right now."

"Are you afraid of your father? Do you think he'll hurt you?" he growled.

She started and dropped her hands. "No! I mean, I don't think so . . ." she trailed off helplessly.

"It's okay," he said gently. He reached past her and locked the door.

The warmth of his body hovered over hers and she wanted so badly to grab onto his shirt and haul him against her. But that wasn't what she needed. At the moment, she needed to feel safe and not so alone.

She ducked under his arm and he swiveled to face her. "Make yourself at home," she said, gesturing toward the living room. "I'll be right back."

Keeping her pace to something that didn't look like she was running away was hard, but she made it to her bedroom in a semi-dignified manner. Closing the door behind her, she sagged against it. "What are you doing, Portia?"

Only silence met her whispered question. Her eyes drifted over the bed, where the covers were only rumpled on one side. Tears welled in her eyes. She missed having someone to come home to every night. That was something she should have appreciated more with Tommy. She'd know better next time.

But it was too soon—wasn't it?—for next time. She was thankful for Aleks's presence, nonetheless.

Stripping out of her bar clothes, Portia pulled on well-worn leggings and an oversize sweater. She released her hair from the bun and gathered it into a loose ponytail at the back of her neck.

She didn't want Aleks to think that she'd asked him here to stay over. She hadn't, had she?

Padding barefoot back to the living room, she paused at the entrance. Aleks was sitting on the couch, his back ramrod straight. He looked so uncomfortable.

"I'm sorry," she said as she stepped into the room. "I shouldn't have forced you to stay."

He turned toward her with a frown. "You didn't force me to do anything, Portia."

"You look so tense." She stepped closer. His gaze tracked her every move.

"It's not you," he said. "It's the start of a headache. I'm trying to keep it from getting worse."

She frowned. "Oh, I'm sorry. Can I get you any painkillers?"

He shook his head slowly. "No, I took the ones I have." He patted his pocket and something inside rattled.

Hands clasped in front of her, she studied him. Now that she was looking for them, the little tension lines around his eyes and mouth were obvious. "Can I get you anything?"

"If you could turn down the lights, that would help a lot."

"Oh, of course." Grateful to have something to do, Portia made the rounds of her apartment, turning off the lights until the only lights left were in the living room. She opened the drapes about a foot, letting the city gently provide illumination before she turned off the last lamps. "Is that better?"

"Much," he said. He leaned back against the couch and closed his eyes.

"Are the city lights too much?" She looked from him to the window and back. She'd close the curtains if he asked, but she didn't want to. The nighttime sparkle brought her peace.

"No, they're fine. Perfect, even." She heard the smile in his voice.

"Good. Ever since the bombing, I haven't liked full dark." Her hand slapped over her mouth. She hadn't meant to share that. She hadn't intended to share that with anyone, ever.

"I understand." He patted the couch. "Will you come sit with me?"

Portia hurried over to the sofa. She eyed the cushion next to him and the one at the other end. She should be professional and sit at the end, but she was tired of always doing what she should. She took a seat gingerly next to him, not wanting to be too needy, too demanding.

He opened his arm along the top of the couch. "It's your choice," he said, his voice a soft rumble.

Letting herself succumb to the gravity of him, she leaned into his side and his arm wrapped around her shoulders. Portia scarcely breathed as she settled into Aleks's side. Into his warmth. This was what she missed, especially in the dark of night. Cuddling.

CHAPTER 34

ALEKS'S FINGERS rested gently on her shoulder when all he wanted to do was pull her closer. Her cheek pressed against his chest and he thought this might be as close to heaven as he'd ever been.

"Is this okay?" he whispered. He didn't want to do anything that made her uncomfortable.

"Yes," she whispered back.

He rested his cheek on the top of her head and let his eyes close again. He hadn't been lying about the headache. Hopefully the painkillers and the dim lights would make it go away. His head had been spinning from the moment he'd heard her father was back. That he'd broken into Portia's home.

Aleks's jaw clenched and he very deliberately loosened those muscles. All that tension would only exacerbate the headache.

Focused on the sound of Portia's breath, he sank into the moment, clearing his head of everything except the here and now.

"I miss this," Portia said, minutes or seconds or hours later. "Being held."

What did he say to that? "I'm sorry. That must be hard for you."

He held his breath, waiting for her response.

"Sometimes it's the hardest thing ever. Waking up in the middle of the night, forgetting he's not with me until I reach for his side of the bed and it's cold." Her soft voice was one of the most heartbreaking sounds he'd ever heard. "Other days, the hardest thing ever is cleaning up the messes my father left behind. That night . . . it changed everything."

Aleks knew how one moment could change the trajectory of your life forever, but his surgery hadn't been nearly on the level of Portia's loss. "Tell me about him."

Portia's body went rigid. "Tommy?"

He kept his hand loosely draped over her shoulder. Not holding her in place—she was free to move anytime—simply letting her know she wasn't alone.

"No one likes it when I talk about him," she said quietly.

He tilted his head to look at her in the dim light. She was staring at a wedding picture he'd noticed when he'd cleared her apartment. "Really?" That sounded ridiculous to him, but her experience was her experience.

"Well, obviously, they don't come right out and *say* it. But I can tell. They say 'um' a lot and their eyes dart away from mine as they look for rescue." Her voice held a touch of humor when she added, "You froze and pulled away so fast."

"Hey! To be fair, we weren't talking about your husband. You called me by his name. I think most men would pull away."

"Fine," she huffed. "I'll give you that." Her tension lessened and she leaned into him again. "You really want to hear about him?"

"I really do." It was the truth. Portia had been lucky enough to love and be loved and he wouldn't denigrate that. "He was your husband. I'd be more upset to learn that you didn't love him. That your whole relationship was a business deal."

"Not even close," she said with a laugh. "My father thought he was useless, but we'd known each other forever." As they sat there in the dark, she spun the story of three friends. Their adventures and misadventures. Bad dates and the best dates ever. Sadness tinged her voice at times, but throughout their conversation, the love and happiness she'd felt with Tommy never wavered.

She burrowed into his side. Aleks picked her up and settled her on his lap. "Is this okay?"

With a nod, she snuggled closer.

"I think I'm jealous," Aleks said.

"Jealous? Of what?" She twisted around so she could look at him.

He hadn't meant to say that out loud, but it was the truth. "That he met you first."

"Oh, Aleks." Her hand brushed against his cheek in the briefest caress. When she pulled her hand away, he still felt the heat of her touch against his skin.

Realizing he was perilously close to admitting feelings that he'd hidden even from himself, he shifted the topic. "What would Tommy tell you to do about all this? Vyne, your dad, my bosses?"

"That's easy," she said with a sigh. "He'd tell me to quit. He hated my job, hated all the time I spent at the office. The time I spent trying to get my father's attention."

"Why didn't you?" The woman in his arms was strong, but he didn't think anyone, including Portia, realized how strong.

"I didn't want to quit. I still don't." She shifted until she straddled his thighs. This close he could see her scowl. Her voice was strong and sure. "I'm good at my job. I'll be a great CEO."

"So do that. Be the leader the company needs right now."

"What does that even mean? I *am* the CEO." She growled at him. It might have been scary if she was wearing her Ice Queen armor rather than soft, oversize clothes. Instead, it was so hot it sent a frisson of excitement to his groin.

He met her gaze. "Are you just filling in for your father or are you Portia Tremaine, CEO? You have the ability to mold the company into your vision of it," he told her. "That vision needs to come from here," he tapped her temple, "and here." He placed his palm over her heart and felt its rapid beat.

"You make it sound so easy." She dropped her head to his shoulder. "It's so damn hard."

"That's why you need to surround yourself with people you trust. You made a good start tonight."

She heaved a deep sigh. Her breath warmed his neck. "I'm never sure if I can trust them all the way."

Aleks's laugh echoed around them. "Portia, they all tried to protect you from me."

"That's because you work for the Solveig Consortium."

"Exactly. They put themselves between you and the enemy."

"Hmm," she said into his neck. "You don't feel like the enemy," she murmured.

Every cell in his body flared to life with her sleepy words. Each neuron raced to imagine all the possible futures with Portia, all at once. His headache flared to life, a white-hot burst of pain before everything went black.

CHAPTER 35

PORTIA'S EYES fluttered closed and she had to blink twice to open them. She couldn't fall asleep, not yet. She had to stay awake until she was sure Aleks was going to be okay.

Her heart had nearly stopped when his eyes had rolled back into his head and he'd passed out. He was lucky he was sitting on the couch, because otherwise she was sure he would have crumpled to the floor.

She'd tried to rouse him by calling his name and when that didn't work, she'd slapped his cheeks. Just a little. The only things that kept her from utter panic were his strong pulse and regular breathing. Those were also the things that kept her from calling Tremaine Medical Services. She had no idea how either of them would explain his presence in her apartment.

Pushing and dragging, she'd managed to lay him full-length on the couch and then had sat on the couch with his head on her lap. That had been hours ago. Long hours spent hoping he would wake up. How much longer should she give it?

"Stay awake, Portia," she said when her eyelids drooped

again. She was so tired. "C'mon, Aleks, please wake up." Checking his pulse with one hand, she smoothed back his hair with the other. Her leg had fallen asleep hours ago, but she didn't want to leave him alone in an unfamiliar place. And she couldn't move him on her own.

"Please wake up," she whispered again. It had become a mantra of sorts as she sat here in the dark with him.

"I'm . . . awake," he croaked suddenly.

"Oh my god, finally!" Her hands patted his cheeks, his forehead, his chest. "Do you know where you are? Do you know who you are?"

"I'm Aleks. You're Portia. And I'm . . ." His eyes blinked open slowly. "I'm staring at your ceiling?"

"You're all right!" Tears welled in her eyes. "I was so scared. You collapsed so suddenly. I was terrified."

"It was a headache." He reached for her hand where it rested on his chest and curled his fingers around hers. "It's my glitch."

"Your glitch?"

"That's what I call it," he said. "When my brain gets overloaded, sometimes it jumps from headache to off switch."

"But you're okay now?"

"Yeah, I should be." He dropped her hand and placed one of his on the back of the couch and other on the cushion by his side. Using that leverage, he pulled himself up to a sitting position.

She kept one hand on his back between his shoulder blades in case he needed a little help. He didn't.

"Still okay?" she asked as he shifted until he was seated by her side. Pins and needles rushed into her newly freed leg and she gasped.

"What's the matter?"

She gave him a weak smile. "My leg was asleep. It's waking up now."

"That's kind of how my brain feels," he said with a laugh.

"Really?" She couldn't imagine that tingling sensation in her brain.

"No, not really. But I'm usually a bit slower right at the start."

Portia tucked her hands between her thighs. "Do you need anything? Is your headache gone?"

"I'm fine, Portia." He bumped his shoulder against hers. "How long was I out?"

"A few hours." She gestured to the curtain she'd opened last night. "It's not nearly as dark anymore."

They contemplated the early morning in silence.

"I've never understood the appeal of augmentations," Portia admitted. She kept her gaze focused straight ahead, not quite comfortable sharing something that deeply personal. She'd thought about it—the same way people contemplated tattoos or piercings—but there had never been anything that she thought would make her better than she already was.

That part she kept to herself.

"What if you were injured?"

Portia sucked in a surprised breath. Tears blurred her vision and she wiped them away violently.

"I'm sorry, Portia. I shouldn't have asked."

"No, I'm the one who brought it up." She pulled her knees up to her chest and wrapped her arms around her shins. "If it could have saved Tommy, of course I would have done it. At the hospital after the bombing, I begged. I pleaded. I would have done anything to save him. But there was nothing they could do."

His arm wrapped around her shoulders and he pulled her close. Getting comforted by this man could become addictive. "For me? I guess, maybe? I'm not against it." She couldn't put it into words, so she shrugged.

"Why did you want it?" she asked. *Wait, was that rude?* "Sorry. That's a super personal question. You don't need to answer it."

His sigh filled the air around them. "I wanted to belong. The super-soldier program seemed like the perfect opportunity. A tight-knit group of people who knew exactly what you were going through. That dream ended when the chip malfunctioned."

Resting her head on his shoulder, she said, "Can I ask—why didn't they take it out?"

His laugh carried an edge of bitterness. "The implant surgery was dangerous enough. According to the implant team, the risks of removing it were too great."

That right there seemed like a good argument for not getting one, but she wasn't going to insult his choices by saying so. Instead, she said, "I hope you sued the company that designed the implant. You should at least get some money for your troubles."

Aleks dropped his arm. Portia twisted to look at him. He was staring at her with the strangest look on his face. "Really? You think I should have sued?"

"Of course! Companies shouldn't be able to sell harmful products." That was one of the many, many reasons she was so pissed about finding out Vyne came from her company.

He smiled sadly and shook his head. "No, no lawsuit."

Portia growled, she was so offended on his behalf. "That makes me so mad! Who was it? Maybe it's not too late."

There was no humor in his laugh this time. "It was a Tremaine product, Portia. Your company caused my glitch."

His words hit like a punch. She couldn't speak. Could barely catch her breath. She tried to process what he said, but the words just didn't make any sense.

"No." She shook her head, denial the first emotion she was able to access. "No, that can't be right. Our products help people. They don't do that."

She waited for him to take it back. To admit that it was a joke, one made in very bad taste.

That didn't happen. He looked at her with a mix of pity and disappointment.

"You're lying." She didn't mean it. But to believe him meant . . . Well, it meant another giant problem for her to deal with. She pushed up off the couch and started to pace.

"I'm not. It was Tremaine model SSB-2103-12." His voice was quiet, almost gentle as her world blew to smithereens. Again.

"We don't sell defective products. It's a fluke. Maybe even a knockoff. Did they buy it on the black market?" This couldn't be happening.

His expression shuttered. "Your company isn't infallible, Portia. Look at this mess with Vyne."

Portia stopped mid-pace. She opened her mouth to argue . . . but he was right. Thanks to her father—and potentially every family member before him—the Tremaine Corporation had skeletons in a lot of closets.

"I'm sorry," she said. "I'm so sorry."

Aleks pushed off the couch and stepped in front of her. "I was mad for a long time. Mad at the Solveigs. Mad at the implant. Mad at the Tremaine Corporation. Mad at life in general." He sighed. "But signing up for the program was my decision and I've accepted that. So, it's not your fault.

Yes, it's a Tremaine product," he said when she started to argue, "but you aren't personally responsible for it."

She started to protest again and he laid a gentle finger against her lips. "Did you design the product?"

She shook her head. Her lips brushed against his fingers.

"Did you build it with your own two hands?"

Holding his gaze, she shook her head again.

"Would you have sold it if you had known there was an issue?"

She shook her head vehemently. Grabbing his wrist, she pulled his hand away from her mouth. "No, never."

"Then it's not your fault."

Although she couldn't shake the feeling of guilt—her family had caused him harm!—she slowly nodded. She wanted to rush back to the office and discover more about it, but she also didn't want to leave him when he'd made himself so vulnerable.

Using the wrist she'd captured as leverage, she pulled him back to the couch. She sat on one end and tugged him down with her. "What did your family think when you signed up for the program?"

He jerked back. That obviously wasn't what he'd been expecting her to ask.

"All my life I'd intended to go into the Solveig Consortium's security service," he finally said. "My father was a military man. My grandfather, too, back when they were national forces, not corporate."

Portia nodded. She knew all about familial expectations. "Did you want the implant?" She wanted to understand why he'd accepted it.

Shoulders stiff, he shrugged. "It was supposed to make me

stronger. Increase my reflexes. Make me a better soldier." Aleks tugged his hand free. He was withdrawing into himself and she couldn't do anything to stop it. "Why wouldn't I want that?"

"It was assigned to 30 percent of the new recruits, all tested for compatibility when we signed up. There shouldn't have been any problems." His voice caught on *shouldn't*. "The implant sent me into seizures just hours after the surgery."

"Oh, Aleks, that must have been terrifying." Her heart ached at the thought of him hurt because of her family.

"At first, the doctors thought the seizures were a fluke, but they happened a few more times over the next several days. Then, suddenly, they stopped."

"And you've never had them again?" What would she have done if he'd had a seizure last night?

"Headaches are the only side effects now. The only physical side effects," he corrected. "According to the implant's documentation, the increased reflexes should have been obvious after a week. The doctors and my command had designed tests to put our new skills through their paces. I failed every single one. Man, I got my ass kicked." He laughed.

Portia didn't understand how he could find humor in something like that. "Did the increased reflexes ever develop?" She'd seen him in action taking down the drone. Surely, they must have.

"Not to the level promised," he said after a long moment.

"So, you're just . . . normal?" She couldn't think of a better way to phrase it.

"Normal? Even if I knew what the fuck that was, I wouldn't say that." He stared at her. "Whatever the implant did to my brain, it's definitely not normal. It rewired it somehow. I make connections faster."

Portia laughed. "So, you're what, like a genius now?"

"Does that matter?" He sounded genuinely curious.

"Not at all. I don't like you for your brain." Her cheeks flamed as she realized how that sounded. "Or not just for your brain." Ohmygod, Portia, could you sound more idiotic? "I like you, as you are. The whole package." Dammit!

His smile was the first genuine one she'd seen since he admitted to his headache last night. "No, it didn't make me smarter. I put things together faster, make connections easier. I don't know any other way to describe it."

Portia studied him. If the Tremaine Corporation had caused his implant problem, could they fix it?

"Deciding if I'm a freak?" There was an unpleasant undercurrent in his question. One she wasn't sure if it was directed at her or at himself.

"No. Just admiring how strong and how resilient you are." It wasn't a lie. She reached out and ran a hand over his biceps. Then, using the element of surprise, she pushed him backward and crawled into his lap.

Her lips caught his surprised "oof" and his arms wrapped around her waist.

CHAPTER 36

"YOU'RE OUT EARLY this morning, Ms. Tremaine," the doorman said as Portia exited the building.

"Getting an early start today, Sam." She and Aleks had gotten a couple of hours of sleep curled together on the couch, but then he'd needed to leave to get back to his hotel with no one being the wiser. After she'd ushered him down the back stairs and waited for his all-clear, she'd taken a long, leisurely shower.

"Do you need your car, Ms. Tremaine?"

She flashed him a bright smile. "No, it's nice enough out that I think I'll walk."

"It's a good day for it—no newsies," he said with a nod and a smile.

Any day without newsies was a good one and lately they'd left her alone. She'd worried that would change with the drone photo, but thankfully it had been too blurry to gain much traction.

"They're covering a running gun battle down by the docks," he added.

"Oh," she said. The docks existed as sort of a no man's

land between the corporations like the Tremaine Company and the gangs who had carved out their criminal empires on the edges of the city. "Thank you for the heads-up."

"You're welcome, Ms. Tremaine. You have a nice day."

"You too, Sam."

The sun was up, but the morning still had a chill. It would likely burn off, so Portia had dressed in layers. She finished her outfit with her black leather jacket and chunky black leather boots. She looked good and she *felt* good. Confident. Like a bad ass.

Quite the difference from the last time she'd woken in Aleks's arms.

Taking off at a brisk pace, she glanced up, checking for drones, just in case they weren't *all* tracking the shootout.

With the skies above her clear of spies, she pulled out her phone and selected a number from her contact list. When it rang several times and kicked her to voicemail, she dialed again.

"Someone better be fucking dead," Ash growled on the other end after several more rings.

"Good morning to you too, Ash," she said cheerily.

"Portia? What's wrong? Why the fuck are you calling me at . . . whatever time it is?"

"Nothing's wrong. I need you to look into something for me. Shouldn't you be up and working by now anyway?"

"I live in a bar, Portia. We've just barely gone to bed."

Oops. She should probably feel bad about waking him up, but nothing was going to bring down her mood today.

"I need your help. Just write this down and then you can go back to sleep."

"Does it have to do with Vyne?" Ash asked.

Portia looked around again. She didn't need anyone to overhear *that* word in connection with her company. "No.

It's potentially another problem project my father had his hands in."

"Can't help you then. We're focusing on Vyne. Send it to Mendez. Or give it to your new frie-eend," he singsonged.

Portia sighed. "I can't. It's . . . Never mind. It's a long story."

"Send it to Mendez. And Portia, you might want to think about moving him out of cybersecurity. He's almost as good as me." With that he hung up.

Moments later, her phone buzzed with Mendez's contact info.

She bit her lip. This wasn't really something she wanted to put in writing. She'd call him to her office when she got there.

———

When Portia entered the Tremaine Corporation lobby, she sensed the difference immediately. A tension hung in the air, one that was noticeable because it had been gone for months. Her father had been here and had somehow done this. The question was, how much damage had he managed to do in the few hours head start he had?

Though her happy mood deflated like a balloon, she kept a smile on her face. No need to preemptively comply with any changes he'd made. She was the CEO of the company, she had control, and she'd stay that way, come hell or high water.

As she crossed the lobby, she studied the employees. Very few dared to meet her gaze, but in the few that did, she found a range of emotions. Respect. Fear. Pity.

The last one pissed her off. It told her that some

employees thought she would be—could be—so easily removed.

Sonofabitch.

Channeling calm, projecting vibes that said she had no problems, she crossed to the executive elevator.

"Good morning, Ms. Tremaine," the guard said.

"Good morning." Portia smiled and studied him. His gaze was respectful. Turning Dizzie's words over in her head, she wondered if he was one of the people who just wanted to do their job and live their life.

She pressed her palm against the scanner, silently praying that her access hadn't been revoked between late last night and this morning.

It flashed green and the elevator doors opened.

Relieved, she released the breath she'd been holding. One obstacle down. Who knew how many more before this whole father problem was resolved.

Although she and the others had roughed out a plan last night, she still wasn't sure it would work. No matter how many changes Ash made to the system, how many access points he blocked, her father had friends in both high and low places. More than she'd ever realized.

That was one lesson he'd neglected to pass on.

Although she was alone in the elevator, there was no way to tell who might be watching her, so she didn't dare do anything but smile and check her phone. She pulled up a local news site, careful not to expose anything important or damning to the cameras.

Last night they'd discussed a number of ideas on how to deal with her father, but no matter how good any of them sounded, Portia only saw a few ways this situation could end.

The easy way—she let her father return to his role as CEO and everything continued on the way it always had.

The hard way—where she battled her father and somehow won. She laughed softly. She had no idea how to make that happen.

Or the nuclear way—she destroyed the entire company before he could get his hands on it again.

In the dark of the night, as she'd sat on the couch and stroked Aleks's hair, she'd wondered if that last idea was the best one. She was coming to understand how much this company had taken from her and from so many other people.

If only she could start over, build something true. Something that didn't carry the taint of her father and his corruption.

The elevator dinged her arrival and she shoved her phone into her jacket pocket. There was no need to decide just yet, but the day was coming. She could feel it.

CHAPTER 37

THE ELEVATOR OPENED and Portia stepped into the lobby on her floor. Her assistant barely looked up, her attention split between Portia and her computer. She could tell by the faraway look in her eyes that the other woman was jacked directly into the system.

"Any messages?" Portia asked.

"Um. No." Melanie flicked her gaze up to Portia's briefly. Then she added, "But Mr. Tremaine is waiting in your office."

Portia blinked as she tried to process that. She stared at Melanie, a deep anger building inside. "He's waiting in *my* office," she repeated, frost edging her words.

"Well, yeah. He didn't have an appointment and I tried to stop him. Then he said he was your father and you wouldn't mind." Melanie shrugged and Portia's blood boiled.

Forcing herself to breathe—because the other option would be much messier—Portia asked, "When have I ever allowed someone to wait in my office?"

"Um, never?"

Portia glared at her. "Exactly."

"But he's your father," Melanie whined. "What was I supposed to do?"

Portia leaned close and made sure their eyes met. "I don't care if it's my dead husband come back to life, don't ever let someone into my office without my permission again."

Eyes wide, Melanie nodded.

Satisfied that the other woman looked sufficiently intimidated, Portia straightened and stepped back. Invoking Tommy like that made her feel queasy. He, on the other hand, would have thought it was hilarious.

"How long has he been in there?"

"Twenty minutes?"

Portia gritted her teeth when Melanie phrased it as a question. As soon as she had time, she was finding a new assistant.

When Melanie reached for the button that opened Portia's office door remotely, Portia stopped her with a look. "Don't," she ground out. She wanted her father to have as little warning as possible, to have the best chance of catching him doing something stupid.

Keeping her steps light, she approached her office door with a gut-churning mix of rage, fear, and dread. She took a deep breath, pushed the door open and strode through.

Unfortunately, she wasn't in time to see her father in a panicked attempt to back away from her computer or struggling to close a desk drawer. Instead, he stood at the windows, staring down at the city.

Oh well, it had been a long shot. Phillip Tremaine had held power for years and, given all the secrets that had come out, he'd known how to not get caught.

Tamping down nerves and the unwelcome feeling that

she was stepping into the past, into her father's office, Portia let the doors close behind her and entered the room with confidence. She had to take control of their encounter from the beginning.

"Good morning, Father. I heard you were waiting for me." She made a show of removing her jacket and hanging it up.

Angled just enough to watch her father from the corner of her eye, she studied her computer. It was awake, so he'd probably tried to access it. No matter. Ash had locked it down so it would only work for her.

She took her seat and logged on, for all intents and purposes ignoring her father, though she could watch his reflection in the other windows.

Of course, he probably knew that trick as well.

"Good morning." Hands in his pockets, trying so hard to look casual, he circled the room until he stood in front of her. Was he pretending to be relaxed or pretending to be frail?

It didn't matter. She wouldn't be taken in by his games and manipulations. "What can I do for you?"

He took the seat she hadn't offered. "We need to continue our discussion from last night."

Portia tilted her head and studied him for a long moment. "No."

His sharp inhale was music to her ears. She'd never told him no before. Always expected to say "Yes, Father," she found her newfound freedom intoxicating.

"How dare you?" he countered and she barely managed to not roll her eyes.

"Oh, I know this game. The next line is 'Do you know who I am?'" She spoke in a mocking tone, not intending to mimic him accurately.

His cheeks reddened and his hands clenched.

Oh, she *liked* this. Before he could respond, she spoke again. "You're Phillip Tremaine and you've been missing, presumed dead, for months. So, I think before we have any conversations *you* want to have, you need to answer *my* questions. Where have you been?"

She hadn't spent much time looking for him. She'd barely been keeping her head above water as she swam through her grief. The newsies had looked for him, publishing new speculations each week for a few months before interest had dried up. Killian had tasked Tremaine Security personnel with the search, but no one had ever discovered what had happened or where the blood in his office had come from. Portia, like everyone else, had assumed that someone, probably his murderous assistant, had killed him.

"It doesn't matter where I've been. All that matters is that I've returned and that I'll be taking my company back." He stared at her silently, waiting for her reaction.

Portia laughed, cold and cruel, just as he'd taught her. "No. You won't. The Tremaine Corporation is mine. All legal and everything." Her lawyers had ensured that.

"Silly child," he said with a mocking laugh. "I was never really sure you should inherit the company, Portia. Your attitude proves me right."

"My attitude? You're the one waltzing back in here like nothing has changed. Why don't you go back to whatever hole you crawled out of?" Cold anger burned through her.

He wasn't taking her company. The Solveigs weren't taking her company. Aleks had been right. She was the head of the corporation and she needed to step up.

"Who the hell do you think you are?" His voice

practically vibrated with fury. "My name is on the building."

"So is mine." Portia gave him her shark smile. The one she'd learned from spending years at his side.

The look he shot her was so full of disdain that she was transported back to childhood. Those times when she got an A-minus, and he berated her for not getting an A. "You don't understand what's going on here, do you?" Condescension dripped from his voice.

"I do, actually. I'm running my company. Making decisions for my business." She stared into blue eyes just like hers. "There's nothing for you here."

His laugh would make a super villain proud. "I have friends," he warned.

"So do I," Portia snapped.

His brows rose in interest.

Crap. She shouldn't have said that. She didn't need him poking into her business. "I think it's best that you go back to wherever you were," she told her father, feeling incredibly sick as she spoke but fighting to hide it as she faced him down. The man had encouraged and belittled her in equal measures. Her feelings for him were complicated in the extreme, but nothing good would come of him running the Tremaine Corporation again. She knew that in her soul.

"This isn't over, Portia. You'll regret this little rebellion of yours." He stalked across the office and through the doors without a backward glance.

She clenched her hands into fists, trying to stop the shaking. She'd stood up to her father in the past, but only ever about small things. It had never gone well.

Exhaling in a slow steady stream, she tried to control her racing pulse. She'd let him get under her skin.

The warning about his friends concerned her. It wasn't a surprise—she'd been trying to uncover his cronies since the day she took over, but the stakes were even higher now.

She'd known fighting her father would be a huge undertaking, but it almost felt more daunting than just taking over the damn company in the first place.

Looking around her office, she was struck by a wave of paranoia. Had her father bugged it?

She opened her phone and messaged Ash.

How would I sweep my office for bugs?

Staring at the phone, she willed him to respond. Would he ignore her because of her earlier call?

Why do you ask?

My assistant let my father wait in my office. Alone.

Shit.

Yeah, that summed it up. She typed again. *I don't know that he did anything, but I don't know that he didn't either.*

I have the information on Vyne. I'll be by in a couple of hours and can sweep for you.

A couple of hours? She hated the thought of waiting that long, but she didn't know who else she could trust with it right now.

Okay.

CHAPTER 38

AFTER ASH HAD SWEPT her office for bugs—there hadn't been any, thankfully—he'd laid out his research for Portia. This particular lab worked on anti-rejection drugs, which was not damning in and of itself. There were always a few labs with those types of projects. Ash had also uncovered a slow financial drain in this particular lab, as well as inconsistencies with certain supply orders. The types of supplies that you might need to make an illegal drug.

In addition to identifying the primary lab on one of the lower levels of Tremaine headquarters, he and the Jack had gone a step further and located the single Vyne cookery in the city. Portia's blood buzzed with anticipation. If everything went as planned, they would soon be shutting down the Vyne pipeline before it got too big to stop.

The moment Portia entered the main lab, three things would happen. The lab would be coded for her entry only. The external lab would lock everyone in and communication with the outside world would be blocked. And Tremaine Security would be summoned to both the lab and the cookery.

Portia had no idea how Ash was going to manage the second. The man's hacking skills terrified her and she was glad that he was mostly on her side now.

She pressed her hand against the scanner outside the lab. There was a slow whir as the computer registered her palm print. The scanner turned green and the lock hissed open.

Showtime.

Pulling the door open, Portia stepped into a near-blinding white room. She hadn't realized the lab was this big. Lab tables sat in the center of the room, topped with a mix of modern technology and classic glassware. Desks with monitors and computer terminals lined the periphery.

It was quieter than she'd expected, given the number of scientists and technicians working in the space. Most were so focused on their work that they didn't notice her entry.

She stood near the door, hands on her hips, and watched them work. She'd always tried to understand the details of each project she'd been assigned to as she worked her way up in the company. Science fascinated her, but her brain was wired for business. Portia would never be the one curing cancer or discovering the secrets of the universe, but maybe she'd be the one funding it.

It took several minutes for her presence to be noted. She sighed. These people might be geniuses, but observant they were not.

"Mm-m-Ms. Tremaine, what are you doing here?" The first technician brave enough to speak looked so alarmed she worried he was going to pass out.

The fear intrigued her. Was it because of her reputation? Or because he was doing something wrong, like making Vyne?

"I thought I'd pop by for a visit," she said. They'd know

her reasons soon enough, but she was curious about what they were working on right now.

The room went quiet, but it was a different quiet. Not the studious, highly energized one of before. No, this silence was scared.

"Which teams work on anti-rejection medications?" Those were big sellers for Tremaine Corporation. The corporation was always striving to make better products, especially ones that worked together. Creating drugs specially formulated for Tremaine implants would not only help the bottom line, but also benefit patients.

Portia honestly believed that. Her father apparently hadn't.

Murmurs filled the room before a dozen scientists tentatively raised their hands. They looked at each other, unease clearly visible on their faces.

Portia asked a handful of questions about the process and the drugs. She generally understood their answers and by the time she moved on to the next group, most of the scientists and techs had stopped cowering.

"Who's working on experimental drugs?" About half raised their hands. She asked about their projects before repeating the process with the scientists who had reached the active testing stage.

Once she'd set them at ease discussing their projects, she turned to the matter at hand. "How many of you worked on Vyne?"

Most of them looked at each other in confusion, although she could tell by their expressions that at least some of them had heard of the street drug. "Oh, come on. I know you've heard of it."

Whispers traveled through the group quickly. They

were too low for Portia to hear, but she'd gotten them talking. "What about compound 60648?" That was the project number, according to the documentation Ash had provided.

The murmurs increased in volume, with most of the scientists looking confused. She studied the group more closely.

There. In the back. A couple of scientists looked nervous and seemed to be edging toward the rear exit.

"You two, in the back of the room." Everyone turned to look at them. They froze. Unfortunately for them, the lab was locked down and the only way in—or out—was through the door behind her.

Portia gestured for them to come to the front.

Both squared their shoulders and stood straighter, trying to look important as they approached. She scoffed. She'd faced down bigger assholes in her life.

"Dr. Vance and Dr. Johnson." Both looked much sweatier and redder than their official employee photos. "Anything you want to share with the group?"

They shook their heads.

"No? You don't want to tell everyone how you turned a failed Tremaine project into a deadly street drug?"

The rest of the lab employees gasped.

The scientists spoke over each other as they tried to deny the charges.

"I'm sure the rest of you have questions," she said, interrupting them. "While I don't owe you any explanations, I will explain what is going on."

The room got very quiet and Portia used that to her advantage. "It was brought to my attention that the street drug known as Vyne was originally created by Tremaine Corporation scientists. The intentions were good—to create a new anti-rejection drug. Unfortunately, the drug didn't work as expected and failed its trials."

She paused and swept her gaze over the employees in front of her. "The project was shelved until some enterprising soul decided they could make a profit off it. I don't know if it was sanctioned by my father or not." She hardened her voice. "I don't care."

The room got very quiet.

"Vyne has proven to be 100 percent fatal to those who become addicted to it and nearly everyone who tries it becomes addicted. If the information about its origins gets out, it will become 100 percent fatal to this company. Especially now, when our competitors are looking for ways to bring the Tremaine Corporation down."

Whispers filled the room. Portia raised her hand and they silenced. "I don't care if other companies do it. I don't care if it has been company policy under other CEOs here." That was an understatement. "It stops now."

She stopped speaking and let the silence lengthen until her captive audience shifted uncomfortably. "Questions?"

More murmurs, then one brave soul raised her hand. "What will happen to Dr. Vance and Dr. Johnson?"

"They'll be taken to holding while the matter is investigated."

She heard a muttered "Yeah, right" from someone in the crowd.

"You have doubts, I understand that. The last few months have been tricky for all of us. The Tremaine Corporation is a proud company, a strong one. It has always had a reputation for excellence and I intend to keep it that way." She chose her words carefully, knowing that there was a high chance that they would end up in public, no matter how many requests for confidentiality she made.

The only way through was by trusting her employees and herself. And hoping Dizzie was correct that most of the workers just wanted to do their jobs with as little drama as possible.

"Is anyone else working on a project that I should be concerned about?" She really hoped not. She didn't want to gut the R&D department. There would be nothing left.

Could she trust that these people were loyal? She studied their faces as they looked around the room. Most of them looked nervous. None of them looked like the mastermind of another black-market drug scheme.

One man raised his hand. "We've, uh, we've got another drug that isn't showing any usefulness as a pain reliever, but it does offer some euphoric side effects."

"Thank you for letting me know." Just what she didn't want. She kept her tone even when she responded, not wanting to spook anyone else who might come forward with potential problems. "I'd like you and your team to schedule a meeting with me. Bring your research. We can discuss your concerns and if you think the project can be tweaked and remain viable or if there are other areas for your team to explore."

The man swallowed audibly. "Thank you, Ms. Tremaine." He stepped back behind a few of his colleagues.

Portia understood. Being in the limelight was not for the fainthearted. Good or bad, she had years of practice.

"Anyone else want to talk about their projects?" A handful more scientists stepped forward and she smiled.

Her phone vibrated. Excusing herself, Portia pulled it out of her pocket. The front screen showed a message from Ash.

Done.

Relief washed over her. Maybe they really could shut

down the whole operation. She composed a message to her assistant.

Join me at the lab. Need you to schedule meetings for me. Then she slid her phone back into her pocket.

"Thank you all for your candor." She gave them a sincere smile, because this could have gone very differently. "This is what's going to happen now. Those of you who just came forward, please be patient, because I want to hear from you. Right now, though, I'm going to open that door and Tremaine Security is going to take these two into custody."

More gasps and a moan from Dr. Vance.

"My assistant will be joining us to schedule meetings for everyone." Another wave of panicked murmurs started. "There's no reason to panic. I want—and need—to learn more about the projects you all are working on. I should have done that sooner. That's on me. I would like to speak to everyone, although you can decide if you'd like a one-on-one appointment or to come in with your team."

The tone of the room started to shift to a less fearful one. "In the meantime, this lab will be shut down for the rest of the week. You'll all receive your pay as if you'd worked. Your project deadlines will be adjusted to reflect the timing."

"Any last questions?"

She studied the gathered scientists as they shook their heads and murmured no.

Satisfied she'd handled the situation for now, she opened the door and let security in.

THE NEXT MORNING, Portia's first stop wasn't her office. Instead of going up to the executive levels, she went down to the holding cells. The closer she got to them, the harder it was to breathe. The very thought of returning to them filled her with dread. She hadn't been back since the day Leopold, her father's assistant, shot her.

Her steps slowed as she got off the elevator. She rubbed her left hand over her right shoulder. There was barely a scar thanks to Tremaine Corporation technology, but down here near the cells, her shoulder throbbed with phantom pain.

Memories assaulted her and Portia paused, overwhelmed. She'd been sure she was going to die down here with the madman who had killed her husband. Instead, Dizzie had rescued her when she could have used the time to escape.

Portia still found that hard to believe. Wracked with grief, Portia had been perfectly willing to end Dizzie's life in revenge for Tommy's. With a strength of character Portia admired, Dizzie had taken down their tormentor and dragged Portia to safety.

She owed Dizzie her life. That was a damn hard pill to swallow. But holding a grudge was wearing her down. With the clarity of time, Portia was beginning to see that maybe, just maybe, they could forge a relationship of a sort.

That was a matter for later. Right now, Portia still needed to kill the Vyne program, deal with her father, and get the Solveigs out of her city.

Her shoulders drooped for a moment. It was too much for one person to deal with. So, she would deal with it in chunks. The Vyne scientists and the drug cookers were the first chunk.

She passed a number of empty cells. Everyone in the company had heard whispers and rumors about this floor, but most of them, including Portia, didn't know how often it was used. Honestly, she didn't want to know what had been done down here in the past. She was only using the holding cells now because she didn't know what else to do with the scientists. They were a flight risk and she couldn't risk them setting up shop in a different city. No one deserved the scourge that was Vyne.

She kept her gaze forward and her steps quick as she passed the cell that had held Dizzie. In such close proximity, it was too easy to relive the terror of those moments. Did her blood still stain the floor? She didn't want to know.

Breathing easier once she was past that cell, she approached the guards she'd stationed outside the two cells. One held the two scientists. The other held the two cookers that Ash and the Jack had rounded up yesterday. They'd offered to keep them, but Portia had asked that they be transferred here. They were all part of the same problem. One she had yet to uncover a solution to.

"Have they said anything?" Portia asked. The guards had been here overnight because she hadn't wanted to risk a shift change. The fewer people who knew what was happening, the better. But she was treading a very fine line. The longer she held the scientists down here, the more shift changes she would need and the more chances that people would find out what was going on.

"Nah. Not really, ma'am. Those two," one of the guards said, pointing to the scientists, "kept begging to be let out. The other two spent the night making threats."

Portia raised a brow. The scientists' behavior didn't surprise her. Neither of the men looked like they'd ever faced true hardship. The threats from the cookers were interesting, though. "What kind of threats?"

"'Do we know who they are. We're gonna pay. We can't keep them here.'"

"Oh, those kinds." She was relieved that there was no indication of a higher leadership level to the external Vyne business.

Portia studied the cell holding the scientists. Like most of the cells, this one had a cot and a chair. Throwing them in a single cell had been a calculated risk. She wanted them tired and afraid.

One was seated on the chair, the other on the cot. Both stared out the glass walls of the cell. The men looked wrinkled and disheveled. One still wore his lab coat, while the other was down to shirt sleeves. Neither looked like they'd had a good night's sleep. Good.

"I'm going to have a little chat with the scientists," she told the guards. "I'd like you to wait outside the door in case there's trouble." She didn't expect any, but after the last time, she didn't want to take unnecessary chances.

The guard frowned. "I think one of us should be in there with you, Ms. Tremaine."

Portia wanted to agree, but she recognized the need to project an image of strength, especially with the street cookers looking on. "I'll be fine." She patted his arm reassuringly.

With a nod, the guard opened the cell.

She took a deep breath and walked into the room alone. The moment the glass door closed behind her, her heart rate picked up and her hands started sweating. Propping her hands on her hips, she used the movement to wipe her sweaty palms on her slacks.

Both men awkwardly rose to their feet. "Ms. Tremaine," one started, but she cut him off with a glare.

"Sit." She pointed to the cot.

They looked at each other and then sat at opposite ends of the cot. The scientists wore electronic bracelets that would snap their wrists together if either made a sudden move. As long as they behaved, they had free movement. The moment they didn't . . . Well, life would become much more difficult for them.

She dragged the now empty chair towards her and turned it to face the men. Slipping into her Ice Queen armor, she carefully sat, crossing one leg over the other. She tamped down her dislike of being in this enclosed space and channeled icy calm.

"You both know why you're here, yes?"

She held Vance's gaze, before moving to Johnson.

Vance opened his mouth and she was sure he was going to argue. "We created an anti-rejection drug as we were directed to do by management."

So that's how they wanted to play it. She could work with that.

"I believe what you meant to say was you created an anti-rejection drug that proved to be ineffective and was shut down. You kept making it anyway."

"That's what we were told to do," Vance insisted.

Her pulse thrummed. Finally, she was getting somewhere. "Really? I don't recall seeing that order in the project files," she drawled. "Who ordered you to keep making it?" She'd spent the previous evening reviewing every document Ash had provided. As far as the official files were concerned, the project had been shut down as demanded and the scientists assigned to new ones.

The men paused and shared a look. Would they spill or clam up?

"The head of the R&D department," Johnson finally said.

Dammit. That wasn't as high level as she'd wanted. "What were your instructions, exactly?"

"To take the drugs to a club and sell them. Then see what happened. Will I get immunity?" Johnson looked at her.

Did they think they were in court? This was an internal company matter. Portia didn't know what would happen to them yet, but she wasn't feeling very inclined to give them immunity.

"I'll need to hear the whole story before I make that decision." It was as uncommitted a statement as she could make.

Apparently, that was enough for them. Johnson and Vance practically tripped over each other to speak. According to them, they were told to keep an eye on the people who took Vyne and see if they became repeat users.

They each were given a burner phone for communication. The initial supply sold out in a matter of weeks and nearly all of the buyers came back for another hit.

Through it all, Portia kept an uninterested expression on her face. It was a struggle—their story made her sick to her stomach.

"And the money?"

They got quiet then. Squirrely. At ease in the silence, she merely watched them. The longer the silence lasted, the more she let the Ice Queen seep into her gaze. Finally, Johnson broke.

"We each got a 10 percent cut of whatever we sold."

"And the rest?"

"We used the burner phones to transfer it into an unregistered account."

Portia bit back a curse. Unregistered accounts weren't impossible to trace, but they were hard enough that it usually wasn't worth the effort. "Where are these burner phones now?"

"Mine is in my desk," Johnson admitted. Vance said that it had been in his pocket when they'd been rounded up. She made a note to retrieve both after she completed the interview.

"That was your cut for the initial experiment, right? What's your current cut?" Ice coated her voice.

"F–forty," Johnson stammered.

That was a lot of money. "Where did you get the supplies?" Ash's research had uncovered that the company had paid for them, but she wanted to see what they said.

"We ordered them through the lab."

Portia closed her eyes. When she opened them, only the Ice Queen remained.

She was merciless as she continued to question them.

She pressed them for another thirty minutes, getting more details on the process and how the external lab was related. As far as they knew, the formula hadn't been sold and distribution was—probably—only through Seattle.

Portia knew deep in her soul that her father was behind the Vyne scheme. The unregistered bank account likely belonged to him. Unfortunately, the only other person the scientists had named was the head of R&D, a Phillip Tremaine loyalist who'd committed suicide after she'd let him go. Now she had to wonder, had his death really been self-inflicted?

"Thank you . . . doctors." It sickened her to use the title that they'd abused, but she needed to keep their cooperation.

"What about immunity?" Vance asked.

Portia stood. "I'll get back to you on that. I still need to question them as well." She pointed to the other holding cell where the street cookers were staring at her.

With that she turned on her heel and exited the cell. Conscious of the clear walls, she paused to catch her breath before she stepped into the second cell.

CHAPTER 40

THE MAÎTRE D' smiled in recognition when Portia entered the restaurant. "Ms. Tremaine, how wonderful to see you. Please, follow me. Your party is already here." As he led her past the other diners toward a more secluded table, her misgivings grew. Clutching her purse under her arm, she willed away her nerves.

This was so stupid. She shouldn't be this nervous. Killian had called right after her mostly useless interviews with the street cookers. They hadn't offered up much additional information, just the same story about burner phones and solid cuts of the profits. The lab building and equipment had been provided as well. Once again, her gut pointed to her father, but she had no proof. The only positive to come out of that interrogation was that the cookers didn't appear to have connections to the organized gangs that ran some of the city's drug rings.

Killian had caught her in a weak moment. She'd been so happy that he reached out, so thrilled to talk to a friendly face, that she'd immediately said yes. It wasn't until after she'd hung up that the doubts had begun.

Was she ready to have dinner with Killian and his new wife—her sister!—in public? She could only imagine the headlines if the newsies found out.

"Your table, madam." He gestured toward a table partially hidden by a cascade of plants. Killian and Dizzie smiled at her approach.

"Thank you," she said quietly, her voice betraying none of her inner turmoil.

The maître d' faded away and Portia was left facing her dinner companions.

"It's good to see you, Portia." Killian stood and placed his hand on the empty chair to pull it out for her.

An overwhelming sense of wrongness washed over her. She and Killian had frequently dined here, but Tommy had been their third. To see Dizzie in his place . . .

Her lungs froze. Suddenly she couldn't get enough air. She couldn't do this. "I'm sorry . . ." she blurted, before she turned and raced to the restrooms.

On autopilot, Portia smiled and nodded hello when people greeted her, but nothing stopped her until she reached the doors to the ladies' lounge.

She flew through the doors—ignoring the startle gasps of the women in the lounge—and ran right into a sleek wooden stall. In her haste, the stall door banged closed behind her. She flinched, then locked it with shaking hands.

Portia hung her purse on the hook and watched it swing erratically back and forth while she tried to catch her breath. Her heart was pounding hard enough to burst out of her chest.

"Are you okay?" someone asked quietly from outside.

Portia sucked in enough oxygen to be able to answer. "Yes," she said, forcing false cheer into her voice. "Just, uh, in a hurry."

The woman laughed sympathetically. "We've all been there."

Portia clamped a hand over her mouth to keep a hysterical laugh from escaping.

She couldn't do this.

How was she supposed to do this for the rest of her life?

How was she supposed to look across the table—a table without Tommy—and see Dizzie?

But it wasn't just that. When she, Tommy, and Killian had dined together, Killian had been the third wheel. Now she occupied that role and to be honest, she hadn't expected it to hurt this badly.

Dabbing her eyes with a wad of toilet paper, Portia stared at the wooden door. How was she supposed to go out and face them after running away like that? All she wanted to do was disappear into the floor.

Just when it had felt like she had things under control, the universe had knocked her back down. Her laugh turned into a sob.

Portia didn't know how long she stayed in there. Voices came and went until, finally, she didn't hear anyone else.

Then the outer door to the ladies' room opened again.

"Portia?"

The last voice in the world she expected.

"Aleks?"

It couldn't be.

She peered through the crack between the door and the wall. And there he was, dressed in a well-cut suit, looking like he'd walked out a high-end menswear catalog. In the ladies' room. Her mouth dropped open and her brain fogged, just a bit.

Portia opened the door just enough to glare at him.

"What are you doing in here?" she hissed. "This is the women's restroom!"

"You looked upset. I wanted to make sure you were okay." Concern coated his words.

Her heart melted a little bit. She ignored it. "Are you following me?"

Aleks sighed and rolled his eyes. "I'm not following you. My employers decided to have dinner here tonight."

Portia dropped her head against the door with a thunk. Of all the restaurants in the city . . . The universe must really hate her. "Did they see me?"

Please let him say no.

"I don't think so. Mrs. Solveig might have seen Dizzie, though."

"Ugh. That's . . . almost worse." "Almost" because Dizzie would have to deal with them, not Portia.

Aleks shrugged. "That's not my problem. At least, not yet." He stepped closer. "What's the matter?"

"I . . ." She trailed off. No matter what he said, she couldn't keep dumping Tommy on Aleks. It wasn't fair to whatever was happening between them. She stepped out of the safety of the small cubicle. "Grief. It was grief."

He grasped her shoulders and pulled her close.

She went willingly, melting into his chest. Aleks wrapped his arms around her. His woodsy cologne tickled her nose, bringing to mind cold nights in front of a fire. She snuggled closer and wrapped her arms around his waist.

"What if someone comes in?" she worried half-heartedly. Her day was already ending spectacularly badly. What would be worse—the newsies, Dizzie, or Mrs. Solveig walking in on them? Right now, in the comfort of Aleks's arms, Portia wasn't sure she cared.

"The door's locked," he whispered against her cheek. "We have a couple minutes. Probably."

Wrapped up in each other, they swayed slightly in the quiet room. Portia focused on his steady heartbeat as it thump-thump-thumped under her ear.

"How was your day?" she asked. The question felt completely natural. Was it too soon to feel that? It had to be too soon.

"Boring," he told her. "Mrs. Solveig didn't want to do anything but wait in their suite. She's sure that Dizzie will change her mind and want to join them, so she spent the entire day waiting for her call."

Portia shivered. She understood dwelling in grief, but Killian and Dizzie seemed truly happy. "That's a lost cause," Portia said.

"I know," he said. "I've tried to get them to see it, but they insist that my implant is making me stupid."

A growl rose from her throat. "You can't let them get away with that." She raised her head to look at him. "If they don't recognize your potential, they don't deserve you."

"There she is," Aleks crooned. "The most badass woman in the city." He smoothed his hand over her hip. "Feeling better?"

She stared up at him. "Did you do that on purpose?"

"Do what?"

"Get me riled up at the Solveigs so I forgot that I was sad?" It was kind of genius.

He shrugged, but a tiny smile played around his lips. "I don't know what you're talking about."

She rose onto her tiptoes and pressed a kiss against his cheek. "Thank you."

"You're welcome." His eyes dropped to her lips. "I'd kiss you for real, but it might mess up your makeup. Then people would start questioning the Ice Queen and we can't have that."

"No, can't have that." She trailed her fingers over his lapels. "Thank you for cheering me up."

He put his knuckle under her chin and brushed the softest kiss over her lips. "You've got this."

"I've got this." She exhaled shakily.

Someone pounded on the door. "Hey! Why is this locked?" The outer knob twisted violently.

"It's time," Aleks said with a laugh. "Ready?"

Portia nodded. She wasn't, really, but she didn't have a choice.

"Go back into your stall. I'll leave. Wait a little bit before you do."

She nodded. "Thank you again." She grabbed his lapel and kissed him again, a little harder. "Thanks for getting me out of this."

Aleks held the stall door for her and Portia stepped back in. She moved as far back into the corner as she could, hoping they wouldn't notice that one stall was already occupied.

Several women entered the restroom. Portia waited through a couple rounds of people coming and going before she flushed then slipped out of her stall.

Washing her hands, she stared at her reflection. She was still pale, so she splashed a little water on her cheeks, gave them a little slap. Aleks was right. She could do this. She could do hard things. With a deep breath, she opened the door . . . and stepped into chaos.

ALEKS SMILED at the women waiting outside the restroom door. "Sorry," he said. "There was a line." He winked and tilted his head toward the men's room.

They laughed in response as he passed them to return to the dining room.

Aleks hadn't been thrilled when Mr. Solveig had insisted they go out for dinner. In Aleks's opinion, they should head home. He agreed with Portia that Mrs. Solveig was waiting for a call that would never come.

But now he took back all his complaints about this dinner, since it had allowed him time with Portia, no matter how brief.

When he'd seen her hurrying across the room, he'd immediately known something was wrong. He'd waited until Mr. and Mrs. Solveig were deep in conversation before excusing himself.

But five stolen minutes with her weren't enough. When she was in his arms, his world felt right. His brain quieted when she was around. No matter how quickly this had all come about, he believed that she felt that way too. The pull between them had been there from the start.

Now he just had to figure out what to do about it.

The moment he stepped back into the dining room, Aleks had to put that problem aside.

The attention of nearly everyone—diners and kitchen staff alike—was turned toward the back corner of the dining room. The corner where Dizzie, Killian St. John, and Portia had been seated.

Fuck.

Quickening his pace, he glanced toward the Solveigs' table. It was mostly empty, confirming his worst fears. The lone Solveig employee left at the table looked like he wanted to be anywhere else. Aleks knew how he felt.

Already running through possible scenarios—most of which were the worst possible case—Aleks wove through the onlookers so he could approach the table from the side.

He was nearly halfway there when he heard the raised voices.

"Take your filthy hands off my granddaughter!" Mrs. Solveig's strident voice was made worse by the rage powering her words.

Perhaps her husband would be able to talk her down, but Aleks didn't place much faith in the man. While his grief was as deep as his wife's, he lacked the backbone to support her in a way that didn't also enable her.

He couldn't hear a response from St. John or Dizzie, but whatever they said made Mrs. Solveig change her tack. "Please, Dizzie, come home with us. You'll have everything you ever wanted. A chance for a new life."

Aleks shouldered his way past the last of the onlookers and studied the tableau before him. His stomach sank. It was worse than he had imagined.

The waitstaff and maître d' had obviously tried to stop the confrontation and protect them from prying eyes, but there were too few of them to do much good. They formed a loose semi-circle between the rest of the diners and the Solveigs and the St. Johns. It was a valiant attempt, but in vain.

Mrs. Solveig had one hand on the dinner table and was leaning as far over it as she could. Her other hand was stretched out beseechingly toward Dizzie. Mr. Solveig stood at her side, his hand resting on her shoulder.

Aleks had no idea if he was urging her on or trying to talk her down.

Talk about useless.

At the table, wine slowly seeped out of an overturned wine glass, turning the white cloth red. Place settings were jumbled up and the centerpiece was askew. What the hell had happened?

Dizzie stood defiantly on the other side of the table. Hands on her hips, she looked ready to lunge over the table at any movement. "No. I don't know you. Why would I want to come with you? This is my home."

St. John stood behind Dizzie, one hand resting possessively on her lower back, letting her fight her own battles. His expression was strained and Aleks was sure that it was taking all his control to not step in. Would he snap? And what would that mean for Aleks's employers?

A few members of the Solveigs' security team had joined them for dinner. Mrs. Solveig had insisted, citing potential harm from Tremaine-backed plots. But right now, their security was the only threat Aleks saw.

Fucking perfect.

He stepped closer to the standoff, ready to intervene when it made sense. There was nothing he could do until the situation worsened. Any sooner and the Solveigs would not thank him for his assistance.

"What the hell are you doing?"

Oh no. Nonononono.

Of all the worst possible times for Portia to return to the table.

Phones and cameras turned in Portia's direction. Her lips pressed together for a moment, the only outward sign of her discomfort.

Mrs. Solveig whirled away from Dizzie. "You! This is all your fault!"

Hands on her hips, Portia glared at the other woman. "Are you okay?" She looked past Mrs. Solveig, obviously speaking to St. John and Dizzie.

"Fine," Dizzie said through clenched teeth. "It would be nice if she would go away, though, so we can get back to our dinner."

Mrs. Solveig spun around again. "Her? You're having dinner with her, but you won't have dinner with me? Your grandmother? Your own flesh and blood?"

"Iduna, please. People are watching." Mr. Solveig finally spoke. To Aleks's mind, it was too little and far too late.

Mrs. Solveig had doubled down and the crowd was clearly invested as well. There was no possible way this was going to end well.

St. John, his arm now wrapped protectively around Dizzie's shoulders, spoke for the first time. "She isn't going to change her mind. Dizzie's stubborn. She takes after her sister that way."

Oh fuck. However much St. John had intended to help, he'd chosen the wrong way.

"You did this! You're the reason I don't have my

granddaughter! This is all your fault!" Hand upraised, Mrs. Solveig lunged for Portia.

Moving without thought, Aleks stepped between Portia and the other woman. He caught Mrs. Solveig's hand before it made contact.

"How dare you?" She turned her ire on him.

"There are cameras," he hissed. "It's highly likely someone is posting this live right now."

Mr. Solveig stepped up behind her. Brow furrowed, his eyes somber, he nodded and Aleks released her arm. Mr. Solveig laced his fingers with hers and tugged her back a few steps.

Aleks didn't move. He wouldn't move until the threat to Portia had left the room.

"You idiot! I knew I should've sent someone else to take care of the Tremaine problem."

Dizzie gasped, as did several of the onlookers. That appeared to be what snapped Mrs. Solveig out of her rant.

Slightly subdued, she allowed her husband to usher her away from Dizzie's table. But not without one more withering glare at Portia. She extended it to Aleks when she saw he hadn't moved.

Portia stepped up behind him and put her hand on his arm. "Thank you," she whispered over his shoulder. "Is that going to be a problem for you?"

Probably. Not wanting to worry her, he just shrugged. "No."

"Come by tonight?" Her words were barely a whisper.

His breath caught. Had she really just asked that? He nodded.

She squeezed his forearm. "You can go," she said. "I've got this."

He was reluctant to leave her. Honestly, what he really wanted was to join her for dinner with the St. Johns.

She stepped away and he felt the loss immediately. He pivoted slightly, tracking her movements in his periphery.

She drew the maître d' to the side and whispered in his ear. His expression cleared and some of the tension dropped from his shoulders.

He grasped her hands in his, vigorously shaking them as he smiled and responded. She smiled in return.

The maître d' dropped her hands, then clapped to get the attention of servers and patrons alike. "Ladies and gentlemen. If you would, please return to your seats. Your meals will be out shortly. And I'm pleased to inform you that Ms. Tremaine will be covering all your dinners this evening. Please accept our apologies for the disturbance and enjoy the rest of your evening."

Very nicely done, Portia. She'd come late to the fight, but she was smoothing it over the best way she could. Which made sense. This was her city and the goodwill would go a long way to building her reputation beyond the Ice Queen.

Aleks rubbed the crease of his brow. If only Mrs. Solveig understood that.

"Mr. Lind." He turned toward Dizzie when she said his name. "On behalf of myself and my sister, thank you for stepping in."

"I didn't do anything," he insisted.

"Yes, you did," she said with a gentle smile. "Would you like to join us? We can easily add another place." She smiled at the waiters who were replacing the soiled tablecloth and place settings.

His heart leapt. She was offering him everything he'd ever wanted. His gaze flickered to Portia, who watched the interplay closely.

"Thank you so much for the offer. Unfortunately, I'm needed elsewhere." With a sigh, he looked in the direction of the Solveigs' table. He couldn't see them at all from his current position.

"Duty calls?" Dizzie asked. Her gaze flicked from Aleks to Portia and back again.

"Something like that."

He wanted to let her know that Portia was in a delicate space, but that wasn't his place. Not tonight and maybe not ever.

"Enjoy your dinner," he said.

"Thank you." Speculation lingered in her gaze.

St. John nodded.

With a last glance at Portia, he turned away to face the music.

CHAPTER 42

"WELL, THAT WAS EXCITING," Dizzie said when the crowds around the table had dispersed.

Portia waited for her to comment on Portia's abrupt exit, but the other woman seemed more focused on Mrs. Solveig and her very public outburst.

"How long was she bothering you?" Portia asked.

"Not long," Killian said. At the same time Dizzie said, "It felt like forever."

"Do you want to meet with them again?" Portia was curious if anything had changed.

Dizzie shrugged. "I might have considered it, but she won't take no for an answer. It's like my feelings don't matter. I'm not willing to accept that." She sipped the glass of wine that had been replaced. "If they started with a quiet lunch, maybe. Coming at me with double barrels both times? No, thank you."

Portia considered Dizzie's words as she took a sip of water. Her nerves were too shot tonight for anything stronger. When she'd reached the table and seen the Solveig disaster unfolding, the first thought in her head was that she was glad Aleks was here to help. "It's unfortunate that they chose this restaurant for dinner tonight."

"But it was pretty heroic the way Mr. Lind stepped in to protect you," Dizzie said slyly.

Portia thought so too, but she wasn't about to admit it. "He knew an incident like that would be bad for business." When he'd prevented Mrs. Solveig's slap attack, Portia's heart had done that funny little hiccup it did when he was around.

"Yep, I'm sure business was the only thing on his mind," Dizzie teased.

"Mmhmm." Portia studied the menu in front of her. It hadn't changed at all since the last time she'd been here, but she needed a distraction from Dizzie's probing.

"The Solveigs are going to continue to be a problem, Portia. What are you going to do about them?" Killian asked.

Like she had any idea. But since he was pushing . . . She gave him a bland smile. "I'm going to hand Dizzie over. That should get them out of my hair long enough to solve the other problems." She flashed him a toothy grin.

"Haha. Real funny," Dizzie said. Then she got a faraway look in her eyes. "Actually, that's not a bad idea."

Killian tugged on one of her braids. "No. You are not handing yourself over to them."

"Aw, it's so sweet when you think you can tell me what to do." Her tone was teasing and her hand came up to rest gently on his cheek. Her pink nails sparkled against his skin.

Jealousy was an unwelcome lump in Portia's stomach.

"But I wasn't talking about myself," Dizzie continued.

"I'm not giving myself up either," Portia protested. Her gaze swung to Killian.

He frowned. "They certainly don't want me."

Dizzie rolled her eyes. "You're both so dense," she said with a laugh. "Who do they really, really hate?" She didn't give them a chance to respond. "Our father. We give them what they want."

Portia's menu fell from lifeless fingers. It was so simple . . . and so diabolical. She wasn't sure whether to be impressed or fearful of the woman across the table.

"That's . . . that's . . ." She didn't even know what to say.

"Genius!" Killian planted a loud kiss on Dizzie's lips. "Pure genius. It solves two problems with one move."

"Do you think they'll hurt him?" Portia asked in a small voice. Phillip Tremaine was a right bastard, but he was still her father and the only parent she had left. Could she live with herself if her actions led to his death?

"Oh, Portia." Killian reached across the table and grabbed her hand. "We'll figure something out."

She laced her fingers with his and gave him a tremulous smile. "Thanks," she whispered. "I thought he was dead all this time and now that he's alive . . . I don't know what to do with that. He wants to take everything back. How can I let him do that when so much of it was bad? But then . . . he's my father and he's alive and that's a good thing, right?"

Neither Killian nor Dizzie answered. Which was fair. They both had their own issues with the man.

She gave Killian's fingers one last squeeze and released him.

Forcing a smile for Dizzie, she said, "It's a good idea. Really. And if it were anyone else, I'd be all in without a second thought."

"We'll figure out a way to make it work, Portia," Dizzie said. "One that doesn't get your heart broken again."

That was more kindness than she could have expected

from the other woman, especially after the way Portia had treated her. "Dizzie, I—"

"Are you ready to order?" A waiter appeared at their table.

Portia snapped her mouth shut. That was enough sharing for one night.

CHAPTER 43

PORTIA WAVED AWAY a dessert menu and sipped her after-dinner coffee. She lingered to be polite, when all she wanted to do was race home and wait for Aleks. Their stolen moments in the women's room hadn't been nearly enough. Plus, she wanted to make sure that the Solveigs hadn't punished him too badly. Mrs. Solveig had looked pissed when he'd caught her arm.

Across the table, Killian and Dizzie argued over which dessert to order. Portia sighed. The sooner they decided, the sooner she could leave.

Killian ended the discussion by ordering two.

Dizzie playfully nudged him with her shoulder. "You didn't have to do that." She smiled up at him. Even from her vantage point, Portia saw the cartoon hearts in her eyes.

"Of course, I did." Killian leaned forward and pressed a kiss to the tip of her nose. Then he sat up. "Portia's paying for it."

Portia laughed like she was supposed to.

Dizzie slapped Killian's hand. "No. She is not paying for our dinner. We invited her, so we pay."

Killian frowned and cradled his hand. "But the maître d' said she was paying for everyone's dinners. We're everyone."

"Ohmygod. We are not 'everyone.'" She formed air quotes around the last word. "We're not even remotely close."

Portia couldn't help but stare at Dizzie's nails. She would never be able to forget what the other woman was capable of doing with those nails.

"I'm so sorry, Portia. I apparently can't take him anywhere."

"It's okay." Portia gave her a soft smile. "Tommy was the same way. There's a reason they were friends."

Startled silence fell over the table. Portia wasn't sure who was more surprised at her unsolicited mention of Tommy, her or her dinner companions. But Aleks was right. She couldn't be afraid to talk about him. He'd been an important part of her life. Killian's life too. She couldn't—wouldn't—pretend that he hadn't lived. That he hadn't loved and been loved in return.

Killian offered her a sad smile. When Dizzie started to say something—probably another apology—Portia caught her eye and shook her head. She hadn't brought Tommy up to make Dizzie feel bad.

"So, how are things going at the company, Portia?" Killian asked. "Have you managed to sort out the other problem you uncovered?" He tapped his wrist, mimicking an injection.

"Killian!" Dizzie gasped.

"It's fine, Dizzie," Portia said. "We closed down the lab yesterday. Now I need to figure out what to do with the people who know the recipe."

At Killian's look of curiosity, she continued. "There are

two scientists and a couple of um, civilian entrepreneurs who know how to make it. I can't let them go with that knowledge, but I don't want to keep them locked up indefinitely."

"In those cells?" Dizzie shuddered. "Zero stars, do not recommend."

Portia laughed without humor. "Exactly. My father's answer would be to eliminate them or use them. Since neither are viable options, I need another way."

When they started to question her, she shrugged. "No, I don't know exactly what, but I have an idea."

Changing the subject slightly, she gave them a quick rundown of what happened when she visited the lab. "Once all the meetings were set up, I asked Melanie about the numbers. Now, among all the other issues, I have nearly a dozen meetings with scientists to discuss their projects."

"No rest for the wicked," Killian said with a smile.

She smiled in return. "But that wasn't all."

"What else did they want?" Dizzie asked. "Money?"

Portia laughed. "That's probably what at least half the meetings will be about. No, the craziest thing is that she said there were two requests for coffee meetings and three requests for dates." Portia still found that last bit shocking, as well as hilarious and the tiniest bit flattering.

"Dates?" Dizzie giggled. "Those are some brave scientists."

"Yeah, that part surprised me. Obviously, I'm not accepting any of them."

Dizzie gave her a knowing smile. "Of course not. You've got Mr. Lind. You don't need anyone else."

"Aleks has nothing to do with it," Portia protested. "I'm their boss! I can't date an employee. The power differential —it's too much."

"*Aleks* isn't your employee, so it works out perfectly." Dizzie smirked at her.

"Dizzie!" Portia ground her teeth and practically sat on her hands to keep from strangling her. If this was what she had missed for all those years—teasing from an obnoxious sibling—well, that was fine with her.

"Just admit it, Portia. You like him. And he likes you too. I saw the way he looked at you."

"Fine, maybe I do like him. But he works for the Solveig Consortium and they're gunning for us. It couldn't possibly work." Though wouldn't it be nice to have more than stolen moments?

"But—"

"Dizzie," Killian broke in. "I think Portia's had enough of this conversation."

"Yes, it's getting late," Portia said. "Thank you for the invitation. I didn't expect dinner and a show."

With a soft smile, she excused herself for the evening and left to settle the bills.

CHAPTER 44

ALEKS APPROACHED the doorman at Portia's apartment carefully. He'd walked from the hotel, taking a circuitous route in case the Solveigs had sent anyone after him. He hadn't noticed any tails—or drones—but there was no way to be 100 percent sure. Especially since Mrs. Solveig had been livid at him.

If she somehow learned he'd come here . . . Well, he wasn't actually sure what the Solveigs would do. Somedays, he thought his life would be so much easier if they fired him. Or if he quit.

But it was hard to leave years of service and loyalty behind with the snap of a finger.

The doorman caught sight of Aleks and looked him up and down. Aleks tried not to squirm under the scrutiny. "Mr. Lind?" the doorman asked.

Aleks blinked, surprised to hear his name. "Yes," he said slowly.

"Ms. Tremaine has asked me to escort you to her elevator. Please follow me."

"Thank you . . ." He leaned close enough to read the man's name tag. "Thank you, Sam."

The doorman accepted his thanks with a perfunctory nod. Aleks felt like he was being judged, but he had no idea why.

He followed the older man through the lobby. There were two banks of elevators on either side of the room. A small seating area sat between them and a desk—for visitors, he assumed—stood near the doors.

They stopped in front of one set of elevators and Sam pressed his badge against the reader. "Will there be anything else, sir?"

"No, thank you." Aleks placed one foot into the elevator then stopped. "Actually, Sam, Ms. Tremaine had an unwelcome visitor the other day. Do you know how that happened?"

The man's lips pinched. "Her father, yes. She told me about it. I have no idea how he gained entrance, but if I see him again, well, it will be the last time."

It amused Aleks to imagine the older man confronting Phillip Tremaine, but Aleks didn't want to insult him by laughing. "You didn't help him?"

Sam drew himself up to his full height. "No, sir, I did not. I wouldn't do a thing to hurt that sweet girl."

Hearing Portia called a *sweet girl* brought a smile to Aleks's face. "Thank you, Sam. I'm sure she appreciates it."

The door was nearly closed when it stopped again. Aleks looked down. Sam's foot blocked the doors. "Don't you dare hurt her, Mr. Lind. That girl has been through enough. Losing Mr. Gilmore wounded her deeply. She doesn't need you coming along and breaking her heart too."

Aleks wanted to argue that he would never hurt her, but

that wasn't a sentiment that he'd ever share with a perfect stranger. "Thank you for worrying about her, Sam."

This time, the elevator doors closed like they were supposed to. While the elevator whisked him up to Portia's penthouse, he considered the interaction.

The dossier he'd been provided at the start of his trip hadn't mentioned the incredible loyalty she commanded from the people she worked closely with. He shook his head. Solveig Security had really fallen down on the job there.

While he didn't remember the file verbatim, Aleks was sure there had been no mention of the staff here in the building. True loyalty like that developed over time. Surely a woman called the Ice Queen wouldn't inspire such loyalty if she were truly as cold, as heartless, as the name indicated. What else had they missed?

The elevator arrived at the top floor smoothly and soundlessly. He still couldn't believe that Portia had invited him over, but he was glad she had. He wanted to make sure she was okay.

Her door opened and she stepped out with a smile. "Hi." Her voice was low, throaty. Like the night before, she wore comfortable clothes. Tonight's outfit consisted of body-hugging black leggings and an oversized shirt that hung off one shoulder. Smooth skin and her bare collarbone were visible in the gap.

Her hair flowed loosely over her shoulders. It was the first time he'd seen it all the way down since their first night together. It had been so soft against his fingers. Against his skin.

His blood heated.

"C'mon in." She held the door open for him then closed it behind him.

He turned to face her. "I'm glad you invited me." He brushed a wayward strand of hair behind her ear.

Yep, it was as soft as he remembered.

He gazed into her eyes. "How are you doing?"

"I'm fine. Really." She placed her hand on his forearm and leaned closer. Her gaze never left his. "Glad you're here, though. Tonight was . . . a lot." She shook her head. "That show your boss put on? I'll give her one thing, she really knows how to make a scene."

He huffed out a laugh. "That's one way of putting it."

Portia led him into the living room. "Have a seat." She released his hand and gestured to the couch. "Can I get you anything?" She bit her lower lip as she studied him.

"Not a thing." He sat at one end of the couch. "Join me?"

After a slight hesitation, she perched daintily on the edge of the couch. He could reach out and touch her, but he really wanted her to come to him.

Had he misread her invitation? Had he glitched again? His thoughts had been fully focused on her—maybe he was seeing what he wanted to, not what was actually going on.

His hands clenched in frustration. With his stupid, malfunctioning implant, it could go either way. He hated it.

He stood abruptly. "I should go."

Portia stood with him. "Oh, why? Is it another headache? You can lie down in the other room if that will help." She reached up to touch his temple.

He flinched from her touch when all he wanted to do was lean into it.

She drew her hand back with a jerk. "Oh, I'm sorry. I just wanted to help." The lost expression on her face tore at his heart.

What if he was misreading his misreading?

"Portia, why did you invite me here?"

She looked away.

He forced himself to ask for clarification. The vulnerability made his stomach crawl into his throat, but he soldiered on. Either he ripped his heart open for her or her pain would do it for him. "I thought you wanted to . . . spend time with me. But now I'm not sure. Did I read the situation wrong?"

"Oh," she said. Then stopped.

What did that mean?

"Yes. I wanted to spend time with you. I wanted to see how you were doing because they're so awful to you." She looked down, then up again. "But . . . it's hard, you know? It seems so fast. And we're on different sides. Like Romeo and Juliet."

The dead teenagers? No, they had nothing in common with those two. "The only side I'm on is yours."

She stared up at him, her blue eyes wide. "What?"

Yeah, Aleks. What? You were just thinking about your long-term loyalty to the Solveigs and boom, now you've given it to Portia Tremaine?

"Yours is the only side I'm on," he repeated. Saying the words a second time wasn't nearly as scary because they were true. He hadn't even accepted it himself and yet, there it was. All his cards on the table.

"I . . . But what does that mean? What about your job? The Solveigs?"

He held out his hand, relieved beyond measure when she placed her hand in his. "I have no idea." It was the truth. "I don't know how we make it work when our companies are on opposite sides. I have to see this assignment through.

And then . . ." he paused. Took a deep breath. Took a leap. "And then we see what the future holds."

Portia squeezed his hand. "That sounds absolutely terrifying, but I'm in."

CHAPTER 45

PORTIA STARED at their joined hands with shock. Had they just agreed to a . . . a relationship?

What would that even look like?

"Are we crazy?" she whispered.

Aleks released her hand and grasped her waist. "Probably," he whispered back. "But I've felt this way from the moment we met."

She sagged against him, resting her head on his shoulder. "I was so surprised that I just left Razor Jack's with you," she admitted. "That wasn't like me at all. I guess it was fate."

Her cheeks burned and she buried her nose in his neck. "Which sounds idiotic when I say it out loud."

"I like it," Aleks said. He swooped her up in his arms and carried her back to the couch. "Okay?"

"Very okay."

He lowered them to the couch, keeping her cradled in his arms. She ended up in his lap, her back resting against one arm of the sofa, with her feet dangling over his knees.

She lifted her hand to his temple again, slowly. "No headache?"

"No headache," he confirmed.

"Would you ever let one of the Tremaine scientists look at the implant?"

"Portia." Her name was a cross between a growl and a laugh. "You really know how to kill a mood."

"What? Ohmygod." She slapped her hands on her cheeks and closed her eyes. "I didn't mean to. I just thought about you hurting and I didn't want you to and that kind of led to doctors. I'm sorry."

"It's okay. That's how my brain frequently works." He laughed. The deep rumble caused her to squirm.

When he slid his hand under her shirt, the warmth of his skin against hers made her shiver.

"But would you?" The words just popped out. She had all those meetings with the scientists scheduled for next week. Maybe one of them could study the implant to determine what caused the malfunction. And maybe she could get someone to study pain mitigation. She hated to see him suffer because of her family.

"Portia!" He dropped his forehead to her shoulder and laughed. He didn't remove his hand from her back, but the soft circles he'd been rubbing stopped. She had only herself to blame.

"What?"

"You aren't going to let this go, are you?"

She threaded her fingers through his hair and gently tilted his head back so they were face to face. "No." She'd be honest with him. "I hate that you're hurting and my family is the cause. I want to make it right if I can." Too many people she loved had been hurt because of the Tremaines. That ended here.

He was already shaking his head before she finished speaking. "For months after the surgery, they studied me. Scan after scan, theory after theory. Nothing helped. Nothing magically made the problem go away. I'm tired of people poking around in my brain. It's my problem and I've learned to live with it."

"So, you're just going to 'live with it' for the rest of your life?" Her heart ached for him.

"Yeah. I am. Is that a dealbreaker?" His gaze was serious. Intent.

Whatever it was between them had sprung up so quickly, it would be so easy to doubt. But it felt real. Did she want to lose that? Could she live with his decision?

She sighed. "It's not a dealbreaker. But can we find a compromise?"

"Like what?" That wasn't a no, but it wasn't a yes either.

"New discoveries are always being made. What if one day they find a way to block the signals? Or to remove it safely altogether? Would you at least be willing to revisit your decision?"

He was quiet so long that she thought she'd lost him. "I'll consider it," he said finally.

"Yay!" She did a victory wiggle on his lap. His erection hardened beneath her, so she did it again.

"Portia?"

She loved the way he growled her name. "Yes?"

"You're going to put Tremaine resources behind this, aren't you?"

Why lie when he'd figured it out? "Yes."

He tilted his head up to the ceiling. "What am I going to do with you?"

"Oh, I've got a few ideas." She wiggled her brows suggestively.

He laughed and pulled her closer for a kiss.

CHAPTER 46

SHE GRIPPED his upper arms as he lowered her back to the couch cushions. Her fingers curled around his rock-hard biceps.

"Are you sure?"

Not trusting her voice, she nodded. "Yes," she said when he didn't move.

No sooner had the words left her mouth than he smiled then dipped his head. His lips brushed over hers. It should have been a chaste kiss, but his restrained passion was evident.

He lifted his head and stared at her with that fire in his eyes.

Using his arms as leverage, she raised up and pressed her lips against his. Wherever they touched, her body felt like an inferno was raging through it. She liked it.

No, she *loved* it. She loved *him*?

That thought was swept away as he tugged her even closer. Her breasts pressed against his chest and she hated the barrier between them, even if it was only a few thin layers of fabric.

"Hi," she said when she pulled back to catch her breath. She suddenly felt shy, though she didn't drop her gaze.

"Hi." He lowered his head again to scatter kisses on her lips. Her forehead. The tip of her nose. When his breath tickled her eyelashes, she laughed.

"I like hearing you laugh," he admitted, his words a murmur in her ear.

Her cheeks turned pink and she didn't know how to respond.

But she didn't need to.

Aleks's lips were butterfly soft as they pressed against hers. "I've been wanting to do that since I saw you tonight."

In a move too quick for her to register, he shifted their positions. Suddenly, she was pressed full-length between the back of the couch and his body. Her cheek rested on one of his arms, while his fingers played with her hair. His other arm was securely wrapped around her waist, pressing them together.

She splayed one of her hands over his chest, fiddling with the buttons of his shirt with the other. She hitched one leg over his hip, anchoring them together, pelvis to pelvis. She rocked slowly, experimentally, and they both groaned.

Her other arm snaked around his neck and she used that leverage to guide his mouth to hers.

Their earlier kisses had been soft. Playful. This one wasn't.

He'd offered himself to her and she was claiming him.

After the briefest moment of surprise, he kissed her back. His mouth was relentless over hers. She stopped knowing—stopped caring—where she ended and he began.

He pulled away, sucked in a deep breath and asked, "Are you sure?"

"Yes." Her consent was breathless.

His hand gripped the bottom of her shirt and slid it slowly, so slowly, up her back. His knuckles skimmed over her bare skin. His touch was a brand and she arched into it, practically purring.

By some miracle of acrobatics, they managed to free her from her shirt without losing contact.

"Your turn," she whispered, then nipped his neck.

Her fingers loosened their grip on his belt and dipped below his waistband, scrabbling to free his shirt.

After a little fumbling, she found his shirttail and tugged it from his pants. He growled against her mouth when her fingers slipped under the smooth material and met the bare skin of his back.

He was like a living flame, his body radiating heat. If she got too close, she might burn.

And god, did she want to burn!

Her hand slid up his back, enjoying the play of muscles, as they tasted and touched each other.

Pressed together as they were, she couldn't manage the buttons on his shirt. She wanted skin to skin.

Wanted full body contact.

Breaking their kiss nearly killed her. She only lifted her lips enough to demand, "Off. Now."

His laugh was a rumble against her body.

She helped—tried to help?—by shoving the material up the side. But that only freed a painfully small portion of his torso.

He flicked open the buttons, then performed a magical combination of shimmy and pull to remove it. He tossed the shirt over the back of the couch and pulled her close. "Better?"

"Yesss." She sighed.

She reveled in his heat. In his touch.

Her breasts pressed against his chest, her nipples diamond-hard points. He felt so good, but it wasn't enough.

As if he had read her mind, his hand skimmed up her side, leaving devastating shivers in its wake. When she thought her skin couldn't get any more sensitive, her breath couldn't come any faster, he slid his hand between their bodies and cupped her breast.

"Ohmygod." Heat pooled between her legs and she shifted restlessly against him.

There were still too many clothes in the way. She wanted skin. Lots and lots of skin.

All the skin.

"Bed, please!" she gasped.

His smile nearly killed her. "Whatever you say."

The words were barely out of her mouth before they were moving. He lifted her easily and Portia hooked her ankles together, getting a good grip on his waist. One of his hands palmed her ass, pressing her center closer against him. The friction as he carried her toward the bedroom was delicious.

She had a moment of trepidation as he carried her across the threshold of the bedroom.

He sensed her hesitation and stopped instantly. "Still okay?"

Although lust still fizzed in her veins, she took a moment to seriously consider his question. "There's never been anyone in here but me and Tommy."

His gaze never left hers. "We can stop."

She nibbled on her lip. His eyes followed her actions and heat flared in them. "No. It's okay. I promise."

He took her at her word.

She thought that he was going to lay her down on the bed, but she was wrong. He settled on the mattress, with her straddling his legs. He lay back, leaving her on top. His arms slid from her waist, his palms smoothing down the outside of her thighs then slipping around to caress the curve of her butt.

She knelt over him as he lay on the bed. No longer kissing—not for the moment, at least—but still exploring. Her palms spread over his chest, kneading the muscles, while his fingertips dipped beneath the waistband of her leggings. They were both still wearing too many clothes.

"You're making me do all the work here," she teased.

His devilish grin set fire to her blood. "Oh, I can fix that." His hands gripped her hips and he feinted like he was about to flip them.

"Don't you dare," she threatened. "I'm enjoying it up here." Every wiggle increased the delicious hard length between her thighs.

She scooted farther up his body. Reaching behind her back, she grabbed his hands. Lacing their fingers together, she pulled them forward and then above his head. "Stay," she commanded.

That wicked smile again.

With a smile just as wicked, she braced her hands on either side of his torso and dropped her mouth to one of his nipples. He arced off the bed with a groan. "You don't play fair."

She knew it wasn't a complaint. Nipping, teasing, exploring. She did all that and more. She was working his way up to his mouth when his phone rang.

She froze, her lips hovering over his. That ring tone . . . She knew it by heart now. Mr. and Mrs. Fucking Solveig.

With a groan, she rolled to the side and dropped onto the mattress.

"I suppose you have to get that," she said as he sat up

and pulled his phone from his pocket. How the hell could they make a relationship work if he was always at their beck and call?

"Nope." He silenced the call and dropped the phone onto the floor. "I'm all yours, remember?"

"Really?" Was that hope that she felt fluttering in her chest?

"Really." He grinned down at her. "Now where were we? Right about here," he said as he knelt over her and reached for the waistband of her leggings. He slid them down her legs while Portia moaned and giggled.

CHAPTER 47

ALEKS WOKE to the clack of a keyboard.

What the hell?

He turned his head toward the sound and suddenly the night came rushing back. He was in bed with Portia. In her home. And she wasn't freaking out.

"Good morning." Even the gritty note of sleep couldn't hide the smile in his voice.

Portia looked up from her screen. "Good morning." Her voice was welcoming and a bit shy. "Did you sleep okay?"

"I slept great." He'd fallen asleep with her in his arms and it had been perfect. Hauling himself up into a sitting position, he studied her.

Her hair was pulled into a loose braid that draped over one shoulder. She wore his shirt, haphazardly buttoned, slipping off one shoulder.

She had the sheet pulled over her lap and her computer sitting on her crossed legs.

"What are you doing?"

"Hmm?" Already engrossed in her work, she blinked and looked over at him again. "What?"

He laughed. If the city could only see the Ice Queen adorably lost in her work. No one would believe him if he told them. "What are you doing?" he asked again.

"Oh, I woke up with an idea about what to do with the Vyne scientists. I know I saw a program referenced in the system, so I went looking for it."

"What do you mean what to do with the scientists? You found them?"

"Oh, yeah. We shut down the labs a couple of days ago. Sorry. It's been a wild few days." The smile she aimed at him kicked his heart rate up several notches. "They're currently in the holding cells at Tremaine headquarters."

"What's wrong with that?"

"I don't want to keep them prisoners indefinitely. That's the kind of thing my father would do and I refuse to be like him." She sighed. "I can't let them loose, though, either. They'll be cranking out Vyne in another location within days. Same with the street cookers."

"Who?" He'd obviously missed a lot, but when would she have told him? Not in front of the Solveigs. And last night, well, they'd been otherwise occupied.

"Ash and the Jack located another lab downtown. They helped me shut it down at the same time we closed the internal one. So, now I have four people who know the formula."

She was right, there were no good options when it came to a dangerous drug like this. "What's your idea?"

"There's a procedure that can erase those memories." Portia beamed at him and spun the computer screen around.

"What?" He couldn't have heard her correctly.

"It's a simple procedure, from what I understand of the documentation," she said. "It removes memories with surgical precision. Once it's done, they'll no longer remember the formula for Vyne or how to make it. I haven't decided whether they'll get their jobs back, but either way, they'll no longer be a threat."

His pulse a nearly overwhelming throb in his ears, Aleks's brain struggled to parse her words. "You're kidding, right?"

"What? It's the perfect solution. We shut down the Vyne pipeline and they get to continue with their lives. Win-win."

"Win-win?" He was going to be sick. "You're messing with their brains."

"Barely," she said. "The doctors say it's safe. It's been used by therapists for years."

"You really don't get it?" He'd told her everything. He'd bared his *soul* and she didn't understand why he thought this was so wrong?

His fists clenched at his sides. "You're talking to a guy who had his brain fucked up by a Tremaine product about removing memories from other people's brains with another Tremaine product. And you don't see the problem." His voice was cold and controlled.

She flinched from his tone, but didn't back down. "What happened to you was a terrible accident. If this goes forward, it will be their choice."

"The implant was my choice too." He emphasized *choice*. "The side effects weren't. What are you going to do when they have side effects too?"

"I can't control everything, Aleks. I can only make the best decision I can with the information I have." She slammed the laptop shut and put it next to her on the bed. "I'm not the bad guy here. The bad guys are the ones who have been making and selling Vyne."

She sucked in a breath. "My father would have killed them. Except I'm pretty sure the whole setup was his idea. Is that what you want me to do, Aleks? Kill them?"

His face paled. "That's not—"

She shoved the bedsheet off her lap. "I refuse to discuss this here. Let me know when you want to have a rational discussion."

He glimpsed long bare legs as she leaped out of bed and left the room, taking the computer with her.

HOW COULD the morning after a perfect night have ended in such a mess?

Aleks shoved the sheet aside and swung his legs over the side of the bed. He grabbed his boxers and slid them up his legs. His pants were a few paces away. He donned those then bent to grab his phone.

Missed call notifications filled the screen, every single one of them from Mrs. Solveig. "Fuck!"

He stuffed his phone in his pocket and shoved his feet into his shoes.

When he entered the living room, Portia was seated in a highbacked chair, her legs curled under her, the computer on her lap.

"I've got to go," he said abruptly. He had to leave before he said something that he'd regret. Maybe when they were both cooled off, he could get her to see his side of it.

"Okay, bye," she said, not looking up from the screen.

"Portia." Her name was a plea, though he wasn't sure for what.

She looked up then. "Oh, are you waiting for your

shirt?" She stood and in one smooth move pulled it over her head and dropped it to the floor.

Aleks nearly swallowed his tongue.

Dressed in wispy panties—pink instead of the black ones he'd peeled off her last night—and nothing else, she stared at him defiantly. Shoulders back, head proudly raised, she asked, "Is there anything else you need?"

Damn, she was magnificent. The light filtering in through the shades lit her like a goddess and illuminated the love bites he'd left on her breast and collarbone.

"Portia, please." He'd said those same words in a very different context last night.

"Aleks," she mocked. "You're the one who said you needed to leave. So, go. No one is stopping you."

Was that a waver he heard in her voice?

"We can talk about this later," he said, as he stopped to pick up his shirt. He curled his fist around the fabric to keep from caressing her smooth skin.

"There's no point," she said. "I'll be meeting with the scientists and the street cookers this morning. If everything aligns, they'll get the surgery later today."

She met his gaze then. He read turmoil and determination in her eyes.

"It's the best option for the company," she said. "And it will save countless lives by getting Vyne off the street."

He saw her point, of course he did. But brains were delicate instruments. Why couldn't she understand that?

"This isn't over," he said. "*We're* not over." They couldn't be, not when he'd just found her.

"We'll see," was her only response.

She didn't move when he shrugged into his shirt. Or when he said goodbye.

"Lock up behind me." Though every instinct was telling

him to stay, Aleks forced himself to leave. He paused in the small hallway leading to the front door and turned back toward the living room. It was empty. Her laptop sat on the chair, but Portia was nowhere to be seen.

Heart heavy, he took the final few steps to the front door. This wasn't the end. It couldn't be.

He was just reaching for handle when the door started to vibrate.

Pound, pound, pound.

"What the hell?"

"Open this goddamn door, Portia!"

Aleks whipped open the door and came face-to-face with Phillip Tremaine. Sure, the man looked a bit rougher than he did in the Solveig dossier, but Aleks would recognize him anywhere.

"What do you think you were doing having dinner with the Solveigs last night? Why are the newsies reporting that you're involved with one of their . . ." Tremaine's words trailed off as he finally realized that it wasn't Portia at the door.

"You're the Solveig bastard in that video. What the hell are you doing here? Is it true? Are you fucking her?" The vileness spewing out of the man's mouth was unending.

Aleks didn't even remember making the decision. One minute he was listening to Portia's father disrespect her and the next, his fist was in Phillip Tremaine's face and the other man was dropping to the ground.

"Whoops."

Behind him, Portia gasped.

He whirled around, careful to keep his body between her and the open door. He was relieved that she was dressed in clothes similar to last night's. Less thrilled when she looked between him and her father in shock.

"He's still alive. I just knocked him out."

That startled a laugh out of her.

"What do you want me to do with him?" Aleks asked. Nothing had prepared him for a situation like this.

"Bring him inside," she said. "We'll need something to tie him up with. And probably a gag."

Hand on Tremaine's collar, he paused and looked up at her. "What are you planning to do with him, Portia?"

She gnawed on her lip. "Funny you should ask."

She stepped out of the way and he dragged her father through the front door. Portia closed it behind him, then turned and walked back to the living room.

With no choice but to follow, he dragged the other man into the living room.

"I need to make some calls," Portia said. She paused and got a faraway look in her eyes.

Was she counting on her fingers?

"Can you set up a meeting with your employers for two days from now?"

"Yes," he said slowly. "Why?"

"I think I have the answer to our problems, but I need a little time to set it up."

"What?" He was so confused.

She'd disappeared into the bedroom, then reappeared with a handful of ties. "You're in charge of securing him."

CHAPTER 49

"PORTIA, I can't just hack into any computer system. Not with a snap of my fingers. Or your fingers," Ash said darkly on the other end of the call.

"Of course, you can, Ash. You told me that you're the best. Was it all a lie?" She gasped dramatically.

"Portia." He dragged her name out. Her heart twinged. Aleks had said her name just like that several times last night. And again this morning, when they'd had their first fight. She understood his point, but she still believed that the memory removal procedure was the best option for everyone. Why couldn't he see that?

"Portia. Are you still there?" Ash's tone turned concerned.

"Yes, sorry. Got distracted."

"By Mr. Tall, Hot, and Blond? At least that's what the newsies are calling him."

Portia stifled a sigh. She couldn't be too upset about the newsies' reports. After all, they'd brought her father right to her door, setting in motion the plan to turn him over to the Solveigs. Ash's teasing, on the other hand . . .

She ignored his question and returned to the matter at hand. "You said you and Mendez had already hacked into the Solveig Consortium's system. So a repeat performance should be no problem. Right?"

Ash's sigh came through the phone like he was standing right next to her. "Yes, but why?"

"Did Taryn tell you about the favor I requested?"

"The one that starts with your father locked in one of her cells downstairs?"

Portia pinched the bridge of her nose. "Yes. That one."

"Hmm." His tone turned speculative. "What systems do you need to access?"

"Security cameras, surveillance, that kind of thing. Air traffic control access would probably be useful."

"What?" That one had surprised him.

She held the phone away from her ear. "I said 'useful.' Not that I was definitely going to use it."

"When do you need it?"

Portia stopped in front of Tremaine headquarters. She'd walked again today, needing the distraction from her fight with Aleks. She didn't want to have this conversation in the lobby. Or really, anywhere inside headquarters.

"Two days from now."

"You realize this could be a total shitshow."

"Yep." She was going to do her damnedest to prevent that.

"I love shitshows! Count me in! I'll let you know when I'm into their system."

"Thanks, Ash," she said, but she was talking to a dead connection.

The pieces were all coming together. Dizzie and Killian would arrange for the plane and coordinate the timing with the Jack. Ash would get them into the system. And Aleks would set the meeting with Solveigs.

Fingers crossed they could make this work.

CHAPTER 50

PORTIA'S next order of business was dealing with the scientists and their memories. She held back a shudder as she walked past the holding cell where she'd been shot. She couldn't wait until she didn't have to come down here anymore.

She smiled at the guards and reassured them that she would be fine. Then she stepped into the scientists' cell. They were looking more rumpled than the day before and tension was riding high in the room. Were they turning on each other? That would be useful.

"Sleep well, gentlemen?" She didn't bother sitting this time. She wouldn't be here that long.

They peered at her with bleary eyes. "Not really," Vance said.

Good.

She didn't say that, of course. "Guilty conscience?"

"We didn't do anything wrong," Johnson whined.

"I beg to differ," Portia said. "You took proprietary Tremaine Corporation research and used it for your own gain." She ignored the whole "drugs are bad" argument with these two. She had to describe the extent of their crimes in terms they would understand. "That's intellectual property theft, and it's just the start of your problems."

"Pfft. Your dad is the one who approved the project."

Portia studied them and smiled sweetly. "Do you have proof of that?" She doubted it. Surely one of them would have tried to leverage it for a deal if they could prove her father had been involved.

They both blinked and looked away. "No," Vance muttered.

"That's what I thought." She hardened her voice. "Now I need to decide what to do with you. You both know the formula for Vyne and that's a problem for me. So, I've decided that the only way to keep my proprietary research, well, proprietary is to keep you down here. Indefinitely."

"You can't do that," they screeched in near harmony. In the cell next door, the street cookers looked startled.

"Can't I?" Portia said. "I think you forget who you're talking to." Her smile was cold and cruel.

"I have a family," Vance argued.

"Perhaps you should have thought about them before."

"What will you tell them happened to us?" he pleaded.

"Nothing." Portia shook her head. "You'll just disappear." She made a poof motion with her hands.

"We won't do it again," Johnson said. "I promise."

"Here's the thing with your promises," Portia said. "I can't trust them."

She paused, studied the occupants of the next cell. "Well, there is one other option. Two, really, but I don't want to kill you."

"What's the other one? The not-killing-us option? Please, we'll do anything," Vance wheedled.

She didn't enjoy seeing grown men beg, but they had to

accept the consequences of their actions. They knew what they had been doing and had accepted the ill-gotten gains from their work. Now they had to make a choice. She was just nudging them along a little.

"There's a procedure to remove memories."

"You want to turn us into zombies?" Vance asked.

"No. I want to remove your memory of the formula." And there it was.

"That's it?"

Portia shrugged. "It's brain surgery, so it's not without its risks, but I don't want to completely wipe your brains. I just want to remove what you stole."

The two men stared at each other.

"Okay," Johnson said tentatively. "How do they know which memories?"

"Brain scans." Portia had read the whole file twice this morning and poured over the testing and safety notes. "I can't guarantee that it will only take those memories. There might be some bleed-through to other memories, but it's the only option I can offer you that allows you to walk out of here alive."

"When do we have to decide?"

She smiled like the Ice Queen again. "Before I leave this cell."

"You can't expect us to make a life-changing decision like that so quickly!"

"There you go again, telling me what I can and can't do. You forget who I am." Portia stepped toward the door. "Tick-tock, gentlemen. Tick-tock."

"I'll do it," Vance cried. He looked pained, but at least he realized what was at stake. He shook his colleague's arm. "Bob, you've got to do it. Or else you'll be down here forever. Or worse."

Johnson stared at her with fear in his eyes. She had no plans to execute anyone, but she wasn't going to tell them that. If Bob thought there was a more permanent solution to their problem, perhaps he'd take the memory removal.

She let the silence grow for a long moment. She'd made her case and, unfortunately for them, she was the judge and the jury.

"Fine. I'll do it."

She nodded. "Good choice. Ideally, the procedure will be done by end of day tomorrow."

Two down, two to go.

"That soon?" Vance asked.

What was it with these guys questioning her authority? "You're welcome to stay here longer if you like. I thought returning to your families might be of interest."

Johnson nodded. "Yes. Thank you, Ms. Tremaine, thank you!" Then he tamped down his enthusiasm and asked, "Will we still have jobs after this?"

"I haven't decided." With that, she left their cell to make the same offer to the street cookers.

CHAPTER 51

ALEKS WAS NOT surprised when he opened his hotel suite door and found Mrs. and Mr. Solveig waiting for him. Pissed, but not surprised. He'd had over twenty missed call notifications between last night and this morning.

"Where have you been?" Mrs. Solveig demanded.

He stared at the woman who'd once commanded his respect and his loyalty, despite how poorly she treated him. All the digs and disparagement. He'd given his whole adult life to the Solveigs, and for what? They'd never made him feel half as good about himself as Portia had.

"How did you get in here?" he countered.

She held up a keycard, grinning triumphantly. "The front desk let us in. We told them about your brain injury and how we were so worried about you and they were more than happy to help."

How had he been so blind to her blatant disregard for others? To think that he'd felt bad for her when Dizzie had refused to meet her.

He closed the door to his suite and leaned against it,

hands in his pockets. Did they even realize that he'd cut off their exit? Or didn't they see him as a threat at all?

The silence grew, as did the tension. Aleks didn't care. As he'd told Portia, he'd finish this assignment and then he was done. Even if their fight this morning had broken their relationship, as fragile and new as it was, he was done with the Solveigs, done with the Solveig Consortium.

"Where were you?" she demanded again.

"What do you want?" His tone carried all his frustration.

She lurched from the couch. "How dare you speak to me that way!"

Aleks just blinked at her.

Mrs. Solveig paced back and forth. Aleks smiled inwardly. Not responding was making her lose her cool. She stopped directly in front of him and tried another tack.

"It was you, wasn't it, in the drone picture?" When Aleks didn't respond, she continued anyway. "I understand, she's a pretty girl. Not as pretty as my Dizzie, but I can see the appeal. The kind of girl you *knulla*. Not one you ruin your life over." She looked at him with that sweet grandmotherly smile. "She's poison, that one."

He'd been raised to respect women and his elders. That was the only reason he didn't respond when she said Portia was just the kind of girl you fucked. That didn't mean he had to put up with her rudeness. "Get. Out."

"Now, now. Let's all be friends." Mr. Solveig inserted himself into the conversation. He pulled his wife a few feet away from Aleks. "All she meant is that we understand why a young man like yourself would have a vacation—what's the word—fling. We just want to protect you."

Aleks counted to ten before responding. He would not screw up Portia and Dizzie's plan for their father. He'd play his role and then leave the Solveigs and their contempt behind him. "Mrs. St. John has requested a meeting two days from now. She has designated me as the point of contact with the Solveig Consortium. I will provide further details as I receive them."

Mrs. Solveig clasped her hands in front of her. "She wants to see us?" She turned to her husband. "She wants to see us! I told you we were getting through to her."

"Why didn't you tell us this immediately?" Mr. Solveig asked. "This is more important than you or that Tremaine girl."

Aleks didn't respond.

With a pinched look on her face, Mrs. Solveig asked, "Will her husband be there?"

Aleks nodded. "Yes."

"Hmmph. That gives us two days to start the annulment paperwork. Come, Agnarr, we have much to do."

The look she gave Aleks dripped with contempt, but at least she kept her tone civil. "Make sure you give us the details as soon as you have them, Mr. Lind. Now please, quit blocking the doorway."

Aleks stepped out of the way, but he never turned his back to them. Never again.

"Goodbye," he said, but neither bothered to reply.

CHAPTER 52

"ARE YOU READY?" Taryn's voice was gentle.

Ready? Portia was about to say goodbye to her father, probably forever. How was she supposed to be ready for that?

"I am," Dizzie said. "Portia?"

Portia blinked and looked at the two women with her. Both of them were studying her like she was fragile. Like she was going to break. Portia Tremaine didn't break. Well, except for that once.

She blew out a long breath. "I'm ready."

Taryn led them down the poorly lit hallway. "I never knew you had cells down here," Dizzie said. She'd been keeping up a commentary from the moment Taryn had led them into the back halls of Razor Jack's. Portia could have lived without knowing some of Taryn's secrets, but she couldn't avoid this meeting. Dizzie, on the other hand, found everything interesting. Yet another difference between them.

Finally, Taryn stopped in front of the farthest door. "We've kept him as comfortable as possible. Except for letting him go," she said with a laugh. "I've never been offered such riches before."

Portia tilted her head and looked at the other woman. "Why didn't you take his offer?"

"Are you fucking kidding me, Portia?" Taryn asked.

"What? I was just curious." Why was the other woman so offended?

"Why didn't you take the money, Taryn?" Taryn mimicked Portia in a high, obnoxious voice.

Dizzie snickered and looked away.

"Why didn't I? Let me count all the ways. Because your father is a fucking piece of shit who deserves to pay for his crimes." She ticked off a finger. "Because I'm not a piece of shit." She ticked another finger. "Oh yeah, and because I thought we were friends, Portia." Taryn glared at her.

"Oh," Portia said, her mind reeling.

"'Oh?' That's all you've got?" Taryn threw up her hands in disgust.

"I'm sorry," Portia said. "I'm . . . not very good with friends. Killian and Tommy were my only ones. But I'm trying to get better."

Dizzie sniffled.

Taryn exhaled in exasperation. "Sure, play the poor little lonely rich girl card, why don't you." She poked Portia in the chest with her cyberarm. Hard. "Don't question our friendship again."

Portia rubbed her throbbing sternum. "Got it," she said.

Dizzie clasped her hands together. "Aw, our little Portia is growing up."

Portia turned to her and glared. "I swear, life as an only child was so much better."

"Naw. I'm growing on you. Admit it."

"Like fungus," Portia responded.

"I'll take it," Dizzie said with a laugh.

Taryn rolled her eyes. "If you two are done acting like children?" When they both nodded, she continued. "He's been fed. Bathed. He did *not* like that," she added as an aside. "We haven't told him anything. Now, are you ready?"

"Ready," Portia and Dizzie said in unison.

Taryn unlocked the door, then stepped back. She kept a watchful eye out, while Portia gripped the door handle and opened it.

What she saw took her by surprise.

"It's nicer than the holding cells in the Tremaine basement," Dizzie whispered over her shoulder.

It was. There was a bed, a chair, a small table, and even a wall-mounted tablet. A half-eaten lunch sat on the table. Pretty fancy for a cell, but her father surely hated it. Only the best was good enough for Phillip Tremaine.

"Well, well, look who finally decided to show up," he said, when she stepped into the room. His lips curled up in distaste when Dizzie followed her in. "What's she doing here?"

"We're here to say goodbye." The words were difficult but Portia forced them out.

"Goodbye? Have you finally come to your senses and decided to leave the company to me? Are you going to Sweden to be the Solveig lackey's whore?"

This was just like her childhood when she hadn't done what he wanted. He really had been a crappy father. Dizzie must have sensed her distress because she took Portia's hand and gave it a squeeze. "No, Father. I'm not going anywhere. You are."

"Is this some kind of joke?" he demanded.

"No," Dizzie said. "No joke. It's time you paid for your crimes."

"I wasn't talking to you, little girl. You're not part of this family."

Dizzie's sucked-in breath held a wealth of pain. Portia squeezed her hand.

"You're going to Sweden. The Solveigs will finally have the chance to get justice for what you did to their daughter and their granddaughter."

He threw back his head and howled in laughter. "That's a good one, Portia. You almost had me."

When she didn't respond, he stopped laughing. Watching his face, she saw the exact moment he realized she was serious. That was when the berating and begging started in earnest.

She felt physically ill. She couldn't do this, couldn't stand here and take this abuse. This wasn't what she wanted her last memory of her father to be. But then, after her mom died, he'd never been the father she needed.

"Goodbye, Father," she whispered. Releasing Dizzie's hand, Portia stepped backward until she stood in the threshold.

Fists clenched at her sides, she watched Dizzie study their father.

"Goodbye," Dizzie said simply. Then she turned her back on him and walked out of the room.

Taryn locked it behind them.

Focusing on logistics was the only way she would get through this without crying. "How will you get him on the plane?" Portia asked. The flight was scheduled to leave in the evening, so he would be arriving in Sweden around the time they had their meeting with Mr. and Mrs. Solveig.

"We'll drug him," Taryn said matter-of-factly.

Portia gaped at her. "What?"

"We'll give him a sedative. Enough to knock him out for the flight."

"Perfect," Dizzie said.

Portia smiled weakly. "Perfect," she echoed.

"I'm starving. Anyone want to get lunch?" Dizzie followed Taryn up the stairs.

Portia lingered for a moment, staring at the closed door. Then she turned and followed her friends up the stairs.

CHAPTER 53

"ARE YOU SURE EVERYTHING IS READY?" Portia asked. Again.

"Ease up, Portia." Ash was getting annoyed, but Portia wanted—needed—this meeting to go well. If it did, the Solveigs would be out of their lives for hopefully ever.

"We control the video feeds. We have access to air traffic control if we need it."

"And the flight's on time?" She was never this micromanage-y, but this had to go right. It had to.

"Yes, the flight is about an hour away. It will be landing right about the time of your meeting."

Portia paced across her office. "You and Mendez will be standing by for any technical help?"

"Yes, Portia. We've got this."

He didn't understand. Nobody did. No one knew how much she had riding on this transfer. Sure, she retained control of the Tremaine Corporation if the Solveig Consortium disappeared into the sunset. But that wasn't all. Aleks would be free to come back to her.

Ash followed her movements with his gaze. "Sit down.

You're making me dizzy." He laughed at his little joke. Portia rolled her eyes.

"I'm worried we missed something." Anxiety churned in her stomach.

"Then we'll handle it."

Did she believe him? Sure, mostly. But there were so many little factors that you could never fully control for.

Her office door opened and Mendez strode in, followed by her assistant. "I'm sorry, Ms. Tremaine. He said you needed to see something, said it was urgent, but he wouldn't wait for me to announce him."

"That's fine, Melanie. Thank you." She waited until the door shut before turning to Mendez. "What's so important that it couldn't wait?"

He looked between Portia and Ash. "I was digging into that project you gave me."

"What project?" There was so much going on, she was surprised she remembered her own name.

"Model SSB-2103-12. It's a brain implant."

"Oh!" Aleks's implant. "What did you find?" Mendez had her full attention now.

"Well, first of all, it isn't a Tremaine product. Not exactly." He handed her his tablet. "See, the files start right there."

Portia took his tablet to her desk. She flipped through the files Mendez had uncovered. When she reached the end, she looked up. "You're sure about this?"

He nodded. "Yes. I checked it multiple times. Checked it again when we infiltrated the Solveig system this morning."

"Thank you, Mendez. This is . . . well, this is amazing. You've sent me those files?" There was no way she would risk losing them.

Mendez nodded. "Yes, ma'am. They should be in your email now."

"Wonderful work. Add them to the presentation, please." She checked the time. "I've got to go. Let me escort you out."

"I can stay," Ash said. "Run the project from here."

"Nice try, but no. I need you at the other location, keeping an eye on the incursion."

"Fine," Ash grumbled. "But it seems like all the excitement is happening here."

"All the excitement," Portia said, "will be at the meeting. Speaking of that, I've got to go."

She grabbed her bag and ushered the men out of her office first.

CHAPTER 54

PORTIA STEPPED into the conference room, the same one that they'd used for the Solveigs' first meeting with Dizzie. She wanted the Solveigs to feel as comfortable as possible as she and Dizzie dismantled their claim on the Tremaine Corporation.

Her gaze swept the room. Killian and Dizzie were already there, as were Mr. and Mrs. Solveig and their security. Once again, Portia had opted not to bring security with her. She wasn't afraid of them.

Aleks stood near one of the walls. Her gaze flicked over him, though she wanted it to linger. Who was she kidding? She wanted to cross the room and claim him in front of all these people. She'd get her chance soon enough.

"What are you doing in here?" Mrs. Solveig asked. "You weren't invited."

"Well, yes I was," Portia said. "I set up this meeting."

"Liar. My granddaughter did."

"Okay, you caught me," Portia said with a chuckle. "We both did."

"What?" Mrs. Solveig looked at Dizzie, shock in her eyes.

Dizzie nodded.

"This is outrageous. We were brought here under false pretenses. How dare you?"

Portia was so damn tired of that woman's voice. "Please sit down. We have business to discuss." She took a seat next to her sister.

"We have nothing to discuss with you," Mrs. Solveig hissed.

"Blah, blah, never do business with a Tremaine, blah, blah, blah." Portia rolled her eyes. "Well, guess what. Today you're going to do business with me and then you will get your ass out of my city."

Aleks cracked a smile. One that was quickly hidden by his placid expression.

"How dare you?" Mrs. Solveig screeched.

Portia would not miss that sound at all. She sighed. Loudly. "While I recognize that is your catchphrase, it's getting tiresome. Now please sit down."

"No." Mrs. Solveig crossed her arms like a petulant child and stood at the foot of the table, trembling with rage.

"Fine." Portia smiled her shark smile. "First order of business, your revenge ploy. Dealing with you has become tedious. But, surprisingly enough, I actually do think you deserve closure. So, to that end, I will be turning my father over to you. In fact, he's on a jet, on his way to your headquarters as we speak. He's the one you want for what happened to your daughter. I think that's fair."

The Solveigs gasped. "You would turn over your own father? What kind of daughter are you?"

"I'm the type of daughter he raised. The Tremaine

Corporation is mine and I intend to keep it. This way we both get what we want. It's just business."

But if it was just business, why did part of her still hate this plan?

"It's not enough," Mrs. Solveig countered. "We want our granddaughter."

"It's all you're going to get. As for your granddaughter, she's a person, not a trinket to be bartered." Who would have guessed, a week ago, that Portia would be protecting Dizzie.

"That's not fair." Mr. Solveig spoke for the first time. "Yes, we'll get to punish Phillip Tremaine, but that doesn't balance the years he cost us."

Portia's stomach turned at the mention of punishment, but it was too late now. Her father was on his way to their home turf and there was nothing she could do about it.

"What do you mean by 'punish'?" Dizzie was looking at her grandparents as if they were bugs under a microscope.

"Execute him, of course." How Mrs. Solveig thought she was better than Phillip Tremaine was beyond Portia. She was as much a monster as he was.

"No," Dizzie said.

Everyone turned to look at her.

"What do you mean, 'no'?" Mrs. Solveig asked her, an appalled look on her face.

"No, you are not going to kill my father, no matter how much of a bastard he is. That would make you just like him."

When the Solveigs opened their mouths to bluster at her, she silenced them with a look.

Portia was so proud!

"It's my turn to talk now," Dizzie said. "Here is my

bargain. For every month you keep him alive, that you show proof of life, I will grant you a visit."

Lips pressed together, Mrs. Solveig didn't look like she appreciated Dizzie's offer.

Portia suppressed a smile. She held her breath, waiting to see what Dizzie did.

"One week in Sweden every month."

Dizzie tilted her head and stared at the other woman. "You seem to think that you get a say in this negotiation. You don't. One visit, here in Seattle, for every month that Portia and I receive proof of life. Maybe, just maybe, if you clean up your act and stop treating me like an object and start treating me like a person, you'll get that visit in Sweden. But I'm not making any promises."

When Mr. and Mrs. Solveig turned away to discuss Dizzie's offer, Portia looked at her sister. "Are you sure? You don't have to do this."

"I know," Dizzie said. "But what kind of sister would I be if I let you bear this burden alone. I had the power to save him, so I did."

"He won't thank you," Portia felt compelled to remind her.

Dizzie was sanguine. "He won't, but you will, right?"

"Yes. Thank you. Really." This was more than she'd ever expected.

The Solveigs turned back to them. "Very well. We accept. You'll need to prove that you're delivering Phillip Tremaine to us."

"Of course," Portia said. "Ash, if you please."

CHAPTER 55

THE ROOM dimmed and the video screen sprang to life. It was controlled offsite by Ash. She and Ash had coordinated this move.

The time stamp was current and showed a plane landing. The video zoomed in, revealing closeups of the Solveig Consortium headquarters in the background.

On the other side of the table, the Solveigs gasped.

The plane door opened and two Tremaine Security personnel stepped out. They were joined by a third man. He looked worse for wear—his hair was disheveled and his face looked haggard. His hands were clasped in front of him, a jacket draped over them.

Beneath the jacket, his hands were shackled together. Portia, Dizzie, and Taryn had agreed that they couldn't take any chances. Phillip Tremaine was a slippery bastard.

One of the guards pulled out a phone. Seconds later, her phone rang.

She answered, then put it on speaker. "This is Portia Tremaine."

"Ms. Tremaine? This is Landry. We've just landed at

the airport with Mr. Tremaine, but there's no one here to meet us."

"I'm working on the transfer as we speak. I'm putting you on hold."

"Yes, ma'am."

She pressed the mute button, restricting the conversation to those in the room. "Would you please send someone to pick him up?"

Both Solveigs stared wide-eyed at Portia and Dizzie. Finally, Mr. Solveig picked up his phone. He spoke quickly and angrily in Swedish to whomever answered.

Portia caught the word *Tremaine*, but that was all she could understand. "Translation, now." She wasn't going to let a little thing like a language barrier tank this agreement. Her gaze caught Aleks's across the room.

Aleks circled the table to stand behind Portia and Dizzie. "He's demanding that a car with a security team get to the tarmac now. He wants them to prove that it really is Tremaine on the plane." His fingers brushed her shoulder and she shivered.

"How does he plan to prove it?" she asked.

"Fingerprints, I think. I expect they won't try DNA until he's back at headquarters."

"They have his DNA?"

She felt Aleks's gaze on her neck.

"Right. Stupid question. He's their mortal enemy."

"Exactly."

Mr. Solveig rattled off more instructions in Swedish. Aleks continued to translate them until the phone call ended.

Then he discreetly stepped back to where he'd been standing.

They continued to watch the screen in silence until a sleek black vehicle raced over the tarmac.

Portia unmuted the line. "Landry, you're about to have company."

"I see them, ma'am. Any instructions?" His voice was calm.

"Turn the prisoner over to them. They may demand proof of identity. Please allow them to confirm that it's my father if they wish. Non-invasive means only."

"Yes, ma'am."

"Then please have them sign for delivery." Why yes, she had prepared for this.

Across the table, one of the Solveigs let out a croak.

She ignored them.

There was a pause on the end of the line, then Landry turned away like he was seeking privacy.

"Are you sure about this, ma'am?" he asked quietly.

"Sure about what, Landry?"

He searched for words. "He's your father, ma'am. He used to run the company."

Aw, how sweet. She fought to keep a smile out of her voice. "Thank you for your concern. Unfortunately, when he ran the corporation, he made some choices that he needs to answer for now."

There was a long deep pause. "Yes, ma'am. I understand."

This time it was Landry who muted the line. Time crawled as the Solveig security team approached the plane and placed her father's hand on a scanner.

Another phone rang. Mr. Solveig answered.

"ID confirmed," Aleks translated.

The security guy who held the scanner nodded, then

hung up. He grabbed Phillip Tremaine by the elbow and led him off the stairs.

Her father turned toward the camera and glared.

She waited for remorse to hit. It did, but just a twinge. Were the Solveigs right? Was she a horrible daughter?

Dizzie squeezed her hand.

No. She wasn't. Her father had made his choices and now he needed to pay for them.

"It's done, ma'am." Landry's voice came through the speaker again.

"Thank you, Landry. Get some food and some rest. You and your team can return on the plane when you're ready."

"Yes, ma'am."

The audio clicked off followed by the video.

She picked up her phone. "Satisfied?"

The Solveigs glared at her, but nodded.

"Good. We'll get the paperwork drawn up."

Mrs. Solveig sniffed. "Send it to the hotel. We'll sign it and leave it there for you."

"Actually, my team is drafting it while we speak. There's one more item while we wait."

"I can't see what is possibly left," Mrs. Solveig huffed.

"Oh, you'll see."

The video screen sprang to life again and a chart appeared. There were a number of dates along the bottom, stretching back almost two decades.

"What's this?" Mrs. Solveig asked.

"I'm so glad you asked." Portia's tone was pure Ice Queen. What she was about to show them had pissed her off and she wasn't above letting the Solveigs know.

"What you see on the screen are the dates of attempted hacks of the Tremaine Corporation by the Solveig Consortium. The green ones indicate hacks we know your company made and the blue are ones we're sure of, but don't have proof."

"What does the red mean?" Mr. Solveig asked.

In the sea of green and blue dots, there were only a few red ones. Fewer than ten.

"The red dots indicate corporate espionage by your company."

They both opened their mouths to speak. To protest? Portia really didn't care.

"Yes, yes. That's an accepted way of doing business. Unless you get caught." She smirked at them. "Surprise. I caught you."

"You're bluffing."

"Really? You look at that chart and the first thing that comes to mind is that I'm bluffing?" She laughed. "I'm impressed that you think I'm so diabolical." She leaned forward. "Except here's the thing. I have proof."

Gasps from around the room.

She felt Aleks's gaze on her, but she didn't look at him. Couldn't look at him. Not yet.

"We dug into your system and uncovered some very interesting information."

"Everyone does it," Mrs. Solveig trilled. "And look at those dates. There hasn't been a successful attempt in more than ten years."

"You're right," Portia said. "No attempts in more than ten years. What happened ten years ago?" She tapped her finger on her lip. "Oh, that's right. You experimented on your own soldiers."

"Portia, what does this mean?" Aleks's question. He was the only one who she would answer.

"I'm getting there, I promise," she said gently. She hated to hurt him, but she had to make everyone in this room understand the lengths she would go to, to protect what was hers. And that included protecting Aleks.

"Ten years ago, your company hacked into the Tremaine Corporation. And, surprisingly, made it past all the security and into the gooey center. The perfect opportunity for a little light corporate espionage, right? Your team started pulling files randomly."

Nobody said a word.

"When you reviewed the files, you found the specs for a super-soldier brain implant." She wished she was holding Aleks's hand for this next part. "Except you didn't get the whole file. So, your R&D team experimented. And who did they experiment on? Your own soldiers."

Dead silence met her announcement. Aleks's brain had to be whirling at what this revelation meant. His own people had experimented on him without his permission. She'd seen the paperwork that he and the other recruits had signed. There was nothing that indicated that they'd been told the technology was experimental.

After far too long, Mrs. Solveig said, "No one will care."

"I care!" Aleks's hands were balled into fists and his jaw was clenched. He vibrated with anger. "You're a monster!"

"You didn't help him out of the goodness of your heart, did you?" Portia was twisting the knife, but when this was finished, she'd only be begging forgiveness from Aleks.

Aleks's helpless gaze flickered in her direction. His brow creased and she worried that one of his headaches was coming on.

"We gave him a job," Mrs. Solveig hissed.

"All while keeping the truth from him." Portia's temper was climbing.

"You can pretend to be lily white, but the Tremaine Corporation doesn't have the cleanest rep in the world."

"No, we don't," Portia admitted. "I'm going to change that. You've already seen proof of the lengths that I'll go to."

Neither of the Solveigs spoke for several minutes. She hoped they were sufficiently cowed.

"What do you want?" Mrs. Solveig asked finally. "How much to keep this quiet?"

Portia laughed harshly. "I've already exposed you to the only person I care about." She lifted her gaze to Aleks.

He nodded and her heart felt lighter. Whatever they faced going forward, they would face it together.

Mrs. Solveig stood abruptly. "Send the papers to the hotel. We'll sign them there. Aleks, make the arrangements." She led the procession of Solveig Consortium personnel out of the room until only Aleks remained.

"We'll wait for you outside," Dizzie whispered.

Portia nodded, but she only had eyes for Aleks. She rose from her chair as he approached. "I'm sorry," she said. "I found out right before the meeting. I wish you didn't have to learn about it like that."

"It's true, then?" The grief in his eyes broke her heart.

"It is." She wrapped her arms around him and held on tight.

His arms came around her and he buried his face in her hair.

They stood that way in silence for several long minutes. When Aleks started to untangle, she resisted. "Where are you going?"

"I have to make arrangements for their return."

Portia's jaw dropped and she stepped back. "After all that, you're going back with them?" She couldn't keep the horror out of her voice.

His hand cupped her cheek. "I told you that I had to see this through. I meant it."

"But . . . but they lied to you."

His gaze was solemn. "I know. And I need some space to deal with that too."

That sounded ominous. "What does that mean?"

"Portia, it's okay. I promise. We're okay. It just means that I need to finish this assignment and pack up my belongings."

"To move here?" She hated how needy she sounded.

"If you'll have me."

"Yes, definitely."

"Good." He kissed her gently, then stepped back. "I love you."

Portia's heart clenched, those three little words sealing the crack that had been in her heart for too long. "I love you too." She threw her arms around his neck and kissed him with everything she had in her.

"I'll be back, I promise," Aleks said when they finally separated.

"You better," she said. Her eyes welled with tears as she watched him walk out of the room, taking her heart with him.

She didn't know how long she stood there staring at the graph before Dizzie came to get her. "You okay?"

"Yes. No. Maybe?" Portia exhaled. "Today's been a lot."

"No kidding. Why don't you come back to our place? That way you won't have to be alone."

Portia started to protest. So many excuses lingered right on the tip of her tongue. She didn't want to intrude. There was so much to do. But really, she didn't want to be alone. "Thank you." She let Dizzie guide her out of the conference room.

CHAPTER 56

"HOW'S THE new assistant working out?" Dizzie asked as they sat at Portia's favorite table in the corner of Razor Jack's.

"Fine, I guess," Portia said. "She hasn't had any giant screwups yet, like letting my father into my office unattended. Then again, she's only been on the job a week."

Portia had let Melanie go on Monday morning. Ash had uncovered communications between her and Phillip Tremaine that had started a few weeks after Melanie had been assigned to Portia.

Pissed that she hadn't listened to her gut and gotten a new assistant sooner, Portia had insisted that Ash do a deep dive on the next candidates HR had sent up. Two of the three had turned up with clean backgrounds, so Portia had chosen the one who hadn't flinched during the interview. She'd directed her new assistant to reschedule all the scientist meetings for the following week and then Portia had taken the rest of the week off.

Though she and Aleks found time to talk each day

despite the time difference, his absence was weighing on her. And it had only been a week.

"You're brooding again."

"I am not." Portia sighed and then immediately regretted it when Dizzie shot her an I-told-you-so look.

"You could call him." Her sister's blue eyes sparkled.

"I'm pretty sure I didn't ask for your advice."

Dizzie covered Portia's hand with her own. "You don't have to ask. That's what sisters are for."

Portia glared at her and Dizzie laughed.

"Killian, come get your wife!"

Killian approached with a smile. He stroked Dizzie's braid, then pulled an empty stool up to their table. "You bellowed, your majesty?"

Portia stuck her tongue out at him, just like she had in elementary school. She'd missed this. The teasing. The friendship. It had been missing from her life for far too long.

"Your wife is being obnoxious," she told him.

He looked at Dizzie, then back at Portia. With a smirk he said, "You must be mistaken. My wife is perfect."

Portia mimed vomiting. She and Killian hadn't been this relaxed with each other since the night of the bombing. It was almost like old times. Except now he was married and she wasn't.

"Fine, whatever. At least tell her to back off Aleks." She sent Dizzie a glare.

"Have you called him yet?" Killian asked.

"What is it with the two of you?" When he didn't answer, just stared at her, Portia relented. "Yes, I talked to him this morning. Satisfied?"

"Always." He grabbed Dizzie's hand and kissed her knuckles.

"Get a room."

"Who needs a room?" Ash asked, as he, Taryn, and surprisingly, Mendez, gathered around the table. Ash had muttered something about owing Mendez a drink when Portia had raised her brow at his presence.

"Them!" She pointed at Killian and Dizzie.

"I can rent you a room," Taryn said.

"But it'll cost you," the three of them said in unison.

Portia dropped her head to the table. "I miss my quiet corner."

"No, you don't," Ash said. "You were sad and lonely in your quiet corner. Now you have all of us. We're like the mafia, because once you're in, you never get out."

Mendez took a step back, easing away from the group, and heading toward the bar.

"I think that's the roach motel," Dizzie said.

"Enh, who cares," Ash said. He raised his glass. "To friends new and old."

"Hear, hear."

Portia clinked glasses with all of them, then sipped her beer.

As Dizzie brought her glass to her mouth, her eyes widened. She downed her whole drink in one gulp. She coughed a little and nudged Killian's arm. "Drink up, we gotta go."

While Killian quickly drained his beer, Ash did the same.

"What's going on?" Portia asked. Why was everyone suddenly acting so squirrely?

"I just remembered I've got to go check on my sister," Ash said. "Thanks for the drink."

Ash and Taryn slipped back to the bar after exchanging a brief nod with Killian.

Killian stood and Dizzie sprang off her chair. "It was great seeing you, Portia. We should do this again sometime."

For the people who had just said she couldn't have her quiet corner back, they were all suddenly in a rush to leave her alone.

"I thought they'd never leave."

The hair on the back of her neck stood on end. She froze, afraid to turn around. What if she was imagining him?

Screw it.

She shifted in her seat and there he was. "You're here. You're really here!"

"I'm really here." Aleks's smile heated her from the inside.

Portia reached out and grabbed a handful of his shirt. "Why didn't you tell me you were coming back today?" She hauled him close.

"I wasn't sure the timing would work and I didn't want to get your hopes up." He stared at her like a starving man, his eyes devouring her.

"I missed you." She reached up and he leaned down and their lips met. She jumped into his arms and wrapped her legs around his waist.

"Get a room!" Ash shouted from the bar.

"Great idea," Aleks whispered into her ear. "Wanna get out of here?"

"Definitely," she said. Then she kissed him again.

ENJOY THIS BOOK?

Reviews and ratings encourage other readers to try out a book and I'd love your help spreading the word!

If you could take a quick moment to rate or leave a review for this book on Goodreads or your favorite book site, I'd be forever grateful!

ABOUT THE AUTHOR

Once she stopped being stubborn and learned to read, Heather always had a book in her hand. Or in her bag. Or under the pillow.

Anne McCaffrey, Nora Roberts, Agatha Christie, and Tamora Pierce. Heather devoured anything and everything, from sci-fi and fantasy novels to historical romance and Harlequins. Her favorites, though, were the stories that combined swoony romance with fantastic adventures. Now she creates her own worlds and plays "what if...?"

Heather lives in Seattle with her husband and two cats. When she's not writing (or working at her day job), she can be found reading, traveling, or enjoying a quiet cup of tea– sometimes all at once!

Find her online at heathergreye.com or on social media

instagram.com/heathergreye

x.com/heathergreye

goodreads.com/HeatherGreye

bookbub.com/authors/heather-greye

The last eighteen months – since I decided to publish Midnight's Pawn – have been an adventure. And it wasn't one I took alone. There are so many people to thank for their support and I'm surely going to forget someone. Thank you and apologies in advance!

Thom, for never once laughing at this crazy idea and always cheering me on

My mom, always willing to read a manuscript and always asking when the next book will be out

Alexis, for being excited about my books and naming her car after Dizzie!

Stephanie, my MIL, for her support and for buying so many copies for family members

Christine and Shelli, for the group chat and years of friendship and support

Christine (again!), my amazing critique partner who's always willing to share her knowledge of this crazy business

Michelle, for your support and proofreading and hanging out

Sarra Cannon, your Publish and Thrive course taught me how to actually publish my stories

Eilis, whose editing skills and story questions made these books better

Irene of Simply Gilded and all the other stationery shop owners who put out beautiful products that I can buy to reward myself for writing or editing or doing all manner of book-related things

And for all the friends, family, and strangers who took a chance on me, Dizzie, Taryn, and Portia!

Thank you all!

www.ingramcontent.com/pod-product-compliance
Lightning Source LLC
Chambersburg PA
CBHW061114310726

48974CB00002B/530